Whispers on the Ocean

Tracee M. Andrews

TO TERESA,

MAY THIS BOOK TOUCH YOU

IN A MEANINGFUL WAY.

BEST,

Tracee A.

Warning:

It is not advisable for a residential school survivor to read this book. Doing so could trigger traumatic memories. If, as a survivor, you find yourself needing emotional support, please call:

Indian Residential Schools Crisis Line - 1-866-925-4419 or your local crisis center.

Epigraph

For time does not tell its tales as it should, and only those who have lived history shall be its truest sages.

Acknowledgments

To those survivors who disclosed their darkest experiences to me, thank you for the privilege and honor of bearing witness. I am awed by your resilience and forever in your debt. Through your courage, you shocked, enlightened and changed me forever. Bless you.

To my husband Roger, thank you for your absolute and unwavering encouragement, support, and belief in this book and in me. I promise you can now make as much noise in the house as you like.

To Iain, thanks for being the best partner I could have had, for being the talented, dedicated paramedic you are, and for having my back all those years. You can retire with a smile my friend, knowing you made a difference.

Preface

The genesis of this book is quite straightforward. I was a paramedic, and I was ignorant. Let me explain.

I spent eleven of my fifteen-year career as a paramedic working in Vancouver's Downtown Eastside, Canada's poorest postal code. The neighborhood is rife with drug and alcohol abuse, mental health issues, homelessness and extreme poverty. Most people only see this shallow facade, but what lies beyond is the heartbeat of the most compassionate community I have ever had the privilege of serving. Acts of kindness rivaling Mother Theresa's were daily occurrences, performed by those whom Mother may well have tended to. From them, I learned those who have nothing, give everything. That is why I wanted to work there. And I did, but I was ignorant.

I wasn't any different from the majority of Canadians when it came to knowing anything about Indian Residential Schools. Understand that the population I served while in the Downtown Eastside were, by far, First Nations people, and as I came to appreciate well after the fact, a highly traumatized group.

I first learned about Indian Residential Schools while taking First Nations Studies at university, after an injury ended my paramedic career. One of my professors lectured on the issue and from what they conveyed I was shocked and outraged. I was outraged at having missed a great opportunity–almost twelve years and fifteen-thousand calls worth of opportunity–to help heal those wounds inflicted by that oppressive, genocidal system. Had I had a context in which to put all those people's suffering, it would have made my job easier and my approach more sensitive. And I would have made apologies. It's even possible those apologies may have made a difference, especially coming from someone in a uniform. I know my words wouldn't have cured their traumas or changed their daily struggles, but at least it would have been an acknowlegment of the wrongs they had endured.

From there, I began asking everyone I knew if they had ever heard about Indian Residential Schools. All I got in return were blank faces. Not a single person I asked knew what I was talking about. Not one. This ubiquitous ignorance compelled me to do something. While I could never go back in time, or for that matter, go back to work as a paramedic, I could reach out. So I sought for a way to connect with survivors who were living in Vancouver's Downtown Eastside; I brought food, they brought their courage.

I had the privilege of sitting with a number of survivors who allowed me to witness their heartbreaking stories. Many of their accounts were far too graphic to include in this book. Some of the survivors I got to know had never come forward to anyone with their truth. Their accounts need remembering. As Canadians, I believe need we to stand in the face of their truths and hold ourselves accountable for the atrocities that we allowed to happen. This self-reflection is necessary and just. It is also what holds us back from reconciliation with the Indigenous peoples of this great country. It takes courage to admit one's failings, but to transform our relationships with these communities each of us needs to take this first step or meaningful reconcilliation will remain elusive.

Although the crimes against innocent Indigenous children where directly perpetrated by the members of various religious orders (Catholic, Anglican, United, Presbyterian) I categorically believe not every nun, brother, priest or reverend are guilty of such cruelty. In fact, many of these people have done admirable things in this world.

snow that crowned the surrounding mountaintops, and it cascaded down his back in a long, elegant braid. His typical attire was simple, yet practical; a denim shirt, plaid quilted jacket, blue jeans, deerskin belt and moccasins, and a red bandana knotted loosely around his neck. His face exhibited the deeply etched lines of wisdom, accompanied by an unusual expression; an intriguing grin that made you wonder what great secret he guarded and understood. Throughout his lifetime, he had shown unflinching integrity and grown in wisdom by earning an abundance of knowledge, particularly regarding spiritual matters. All of which meant that the People considered him a man of great wealth.

Grandfather was always talking about the mountains. Even at his advanced age, he would often leave for a day or more to visit the sacred places up there, though Mother worried about him when he was absent. Grandfather knew this and had tried reassuring Mother his treks were safe. "My dear, there's no reason to worry about me," he said smirking. "Because you know I'm actually part mountain goat."

He cherished Mother and would never mock her concerns. He had taken her hand in his. "Remember, if I don't return it's because I've met Creator in the way that was intended." Nonetheless,   Mother remained skeptical, still not satisfied the old man's adventures were acts of sanity. So she had petitioned Father to intervene. "Can't you talk some sense into him?"

Father had one firm, but loving, response. "Grandfather knows who he is."

Without warning, a raucous giggle fest fell through the front door of their unpretentious home with Father and George stumbling over each other, their bellies sore from laughter. Vaulting off her stool, Mary bounded over to greet them.

"Father!" she yelled, leaping into his muscular arms and all but disappearing into his hug.

Sprinting into the kitchen, George pounced on Mother, grabbing her around the waist and squeezing her from behind like a vise. Mother gasped, having been knocked off balance by her youngest's enthusiastic greeting. "How are you, my son?"

George answered by snuggling her.

Father walked towards his wife swinging Mary back and forth while collecting giggles as a fee for the trip. Lowering Mary to the floor, he kissed her cheek and asked, "Would you please go and get the fish from outside?"

"Okay!" she cried taking off like a hawk after prey.

Father bowed to George. "Excuse me, sir, may I hug my wife now?"

George contemplated Father's request by wadding up his face for a moment. "Well...okay!" he yelled, dashing off to help his sister.

Mother merged into her husband's arms. "Hey! What're you doing chasing away my boyfriend like that?"

hemmed by gnarled stands of dwarfish Garry Oak trees whose constant fight against the elements left them deformed and leaning windward. Above the jagged shoreline lay several acres of maritime meadow which glowed brilliant yellow in springtime when the daffodils awoke into full bloom. This was the place that granted the two companions temporary asylum.

The echoes of red-winged blackbirds calling to their mates greeted Trevor at the shoreline. The delicate sound acted as a subtle cue for him to escape, both physically and mentally. As his brain registered the sweet melody, his breath loosened and his mind drifted away. He often fantasized about how he might build a place to live in the underbrush near the water's edge. He imagined constructing it using pieces of driftwood stacked upon each other for the walls. *I could find some cardboard for the roof, some carpet pieces for a floor,* he mused one afternoon as he sat tossing pebbles into the water.

The mere idea of escape, no matter how impractical or ridiculous, imbued Trevor with a much-needed, if only faint, sense of safety. More importantly, it provided him with a glimpse of hope. Hope he could eventually have some form of permanent respite from his day-to-day hell. Nevertheless, for right now, It would have none of that. Monster did not like her playthings to stray.

Though if somehow Trevor had managed to carry out his bizarre plan by building himself a hermit's shack, it never crossed his mind he would be missed.

In his heart, Trevor never expected anyone to have a concern for his welfare. That deep and abiding conviction was at the root of his fascination with TV news stories about the extraordinary lengths people took to search for a lost child or to save another's life. Those were alien concepts to Trevor, and they baffled him for the longest time. Thus, one relentless, enigmatic question rolled through his mind; *a life had value?* Ultimately the conflicting evidence between his personal experience and the caring others showed their own kind spilled over, creating an inner dissonance, which demanded a resolution. For a long time, Trevor grappled with the very idea of a human life being valuable, something worthy of cherishing. Eventually, that notion morphed into a robust mirror, one that challenged the worthlessness that had been beaten into him. And it was to become the touchstone of his greatest epiphany.

Trevor had been leaning against a twisted oak watching the ocean that drizzling Saturday afternoon when it hit him. And the profound insight had hit him hard. In a flash of supreme clarity, at the ripe old age of nine, Trevor grasped a universal truth. It became plain to him. The fact was, most parents actually loved their children and didn't try to beat them into oblivion. That revelation struck him like a lightning bolt, crystallizing the seeds of a new identity. *Maybe I'm not so horrible after all,* he thought. *Maybe...there's something wrong with her!* That was the moment Trevor knew, at the nucleus of his soul, all doubt erased, there was something fundamentally wrong with his family.

Trevor sat under that crooked oak tree, dumbfounded from the bombshell of truth. He had glimpsed his true nature, and it had altogether jolted him. Yet as Trevor felt the crushing weight of self-hatred lift away, its absence forced him to acknowledge what remained underneath, the overwhelming, stinging sense of betrayal. But before the hurt became unbearable, as if by grace, Trevor matched his breath to the rhythm of the waves and allowed the dramatic shock of his transformation to settle. He could never have put into words his experience of that startling shift. Though in fact, Trevor had claimed a resurrection. With his withering essence reborn, he forever renounced his former existence and its unjust, toxic indictment, vowing never again to sit on the brink of suicide.

From that day forward, an unstoppable transition gained momentum, and the remnants of his self-loathing continued to morph into something better. Each small act of human kindness he witnessed further commuted his spirit. He disavowed all the lies the brainwashing had forced him to believe, "You're lazy. You're an inconvenience. You have no right to exist". With focused intent, Trevor jettisoned the false veneer It had forced him to wear. In its place, he embraced his hatred; no longer of himself, but of Monster.

But despite his profound awakening, Trevor's living conditions hadn't changed and time moved at a glacial pace. Day after day, his body weathered a hurricane of abuse. Not a minute went by when he didn't wear a full spectrum of bruising. The purple, green and brown he could manage. It was the slimy malevolence and its energetic contamination that made him feel soiled, making his daily pilgrimage of renewal all the more vital to his well-being. But for now, at least, his fledgling spirit and mind were protected from further erosion, shielded by the knowledge of his actual worth. Regardless of how much mistreatment he lived through, it all fell away once he was able to see Her, to feel Her, to smell Her. Trevor would sit next to Her for hours, watching Her gentle waves caress the pebbled shore and listening, though for what, he did not know.

Chapter 3
One Year Later - Spring 1966
Bella Coola, British Columbia

Father would sit next to Her for hours, watching Her gentle waves caress the pebbled shore and listening, though when the warning would arrive, he did not know. In reality, his humble act was a crucial part of safekeeping the children, to prevent the police from taking them away. Balanced on a chunk of driftwood and lulled by the water's delicate melody, he sat listening. He remained motionless for many hours, concentrating, just like Grandmother had taught him. She had once kept the same vigil for him. Years ago, when Father was no more than a toddler before the police came to confiscate the children, Grandmother would sound the alarm throughout the reserve. She and others sent their little ones into hiding immediately. This spared some children, though many others were not as lucky. Grandmother had hidden Father well. She concealed him so well in fact, even after years of repeated raids, the police never found him, so he was never removed from his family. Grandmother always knew when to take action. She knew how to listen and had heard the warnings. She passed this wisdom on by instilling within Father a profound respect to "always heed the whispers on the ocean."

But that was only one example of a myriad of barbaric practices that needed stamping out. Such idolatry and witchcraft had no place in a civilized society. For this reason, thousands of years of wisdom and sacred practices, whose underpinnings had allowed the Indigenous Peoples to develop societies that coexisted in balance with their surroundings, to develop unique and highly evolved art forms and whose inherent social structure valued both genders equally, became demonized and marked for extinction.

"*We* will tell *you* what things are sacred. The blood of Jesus, not the ocean! Certainly not trees or animals! Idolators! Such things are devoid of spirit! There is only one spirit that is holy!"

So, where no problem existed, one was created by nothing more than the egocentric, self-righteousness of white Christians, rationalized by good intentions and constructed via a thoroughly toxic, moral superiority complex. "We're taking those children away from their families for their own good. After all, their parents are dirty, uncivilized heathens. Not to mention 'Indian culture' is a contradiction in terms."

The solution was simple: send the youngest to where they could become legitimate, assimilated members of Canadian society, namely, Christian society. This was the birth of the state-sponsored religious school. Thus, since 1920, Canadian federal law had declared every Indian child aged six to fifteen was legally obligated to attend a government-funded, church-run residential school. And that law was enforced with a brutal efficiency.

Though the federal statute was unambiguous, stating an Indian child must be a minimum of six years old, typically children as young as two were taken. Most kids were sent off to schools situated hundreds of miles away from their families and communities thus inflicting a devastating, and purposeful, cultural isolation. Classes were held ten months of the year, and it was virtually illegal for parents to visit their children at any time other than during the summer break and one week at Christmas. But visitation had one proviso; the family could reunite only if the parents came to get their children. Given the distances involved, this was a financial impossibility for the bulk of families who already struggled with living in poverty. With these onerous restrictions in place, the net result of attending a residential school was long-term incarceration. As a consequence, the severed families spent many years apart and quite often parents did not recognize their own child when they returned home, more precisely, *if* the child returned home, as many of the schools' mortality rate hovered between thirty and sixty percent. In contrast, at its peak, the 1918 worldwide flu pandemic only claimed five percent of its victims.

In Father's case, by the time the authorities found out about him, he was too old to be taken away. Father was forever grateful for this and thanked Creator daily for sparing him. And as the years rolled by, that appreciation grew more profound as he saw the repeated results of the schools' "education". Any child who did survive to return home was never the same.

To graduate, the children had to master a curriculum that instilled in them a deep sense of shame, of their race, their language and their culture. After enduring years of indoctrination intentionally designed to "kill the Indian inside the Indian," by necessity, they forgot who they were. Many now lived for the bottle after having had their unique human potential reduced to nothing more than a broken shell crammed with self-disgust. Though at the time, their choice had been simple enough, graduation or graveyard.

Early on, Mother had also been spared, but when she was nine years old, one who needed a bottle betrayed her. She had spent years in absentia, and even after having been home for more than a decade, she was still not quite herself. Every so often, Mother would tell Father about her time at the school. George always knew when Mother told her stories. George never overheard the chilling memories, but he read the signs. He would watch his parents go off by themselves and sit together by the ocean. Once there, Father would hold her, often for several hours.

At those times, Grandfather knew the particular importance of being close to his grandchildren. Today was one of those days. So, while their parents were off trying to heal the wounds inflicted by church and state, Grandfather stepped in and took on the children's lessons. Mary sat weaving cedar bark while Grandfather helped George to see and feel what was hiding in an otherwise innocuous piece of cedar, assisting him in how to use his knife to help it emerge. The first image George ever saw in the wood was Frog. Grandfather smiled at him as he took the bit of cedar in his wrinkled hands and scrutinized it. "Very good George, I see Frog too. Now, let's help Frog escape."

George possessed a natural gift for carving. With surprisingly little coaching from Grandfather, he was able to read the wood's grain, coax small pieces of it away, and produce uncommonly advanced figures for such a young man.

"Well done, Grandson. You are listening to your Spirit. It speaks to the spirit of the wood, and together they help the knife to move in just the right way."

It was well past noon when Mother and Father returned from the shore. Mother's eyes were swollen and red, but she seemed a little lighter, and Father was able to make her laugh. On entering their ramshackle home, George and Mary ran to greet them. "Mother!" George cried. And a spontaneous cascade of hugs and tickles followed.

The next day was bright and sunny, although an ethereal chill hung in the air. Mother was preparing a lunch of bannock and jam for the family while Father and Grandfather sat in front of the house mending some tattered fishing nets. Having done well with their lessons that morning the children had scampered off for some much-needed playtime before their chores started after lunch.

The sun was almost directly overhead when Grandfather tensed. "Listen," he whispered.

Father froze, closing his eyes for a few precious seconds before springing into action and yelling to his wife. "Where are the children!"

Caught off guard by her husband's panicked tone, Mother ran to the door. She stood petrified in the entrance and stuttered. "D...d...down...at the beach."

In a split second, which seemed eternal, husband and wife's eyes became riveted, knowing this could be the last time they might see each another.

"Go!" Father yelled.

Mother didn't want to leave. She hesitated, unable to break her beloved's gaze.

"Go! Now!"

Mother burst out of the doorway, off to warn the others in the village.

Father ran too, but in a different direction, sprinting down to the beach where he knew he would find his children. His feet were swift, and they didn't falter on the loose soil and large rocks littering his path. Within moments, George and Mary came into sight. Father yelled. "The boat is coming!"

Brother and sister, whose life moments before Father's panicked cry had been carefree now stood motionless, alarmed by the sight of their father racing madly towards them. The danger was closing in on them rapidly, and no one knew if it was too late to put their plan into action.

Using his muscular frame to full advantage and barely slowing his pace, Father scooped them both up, one under each arm and darted up the shore towards the riverbank at breakneck speed. He needed to hide his precious treasures fast. Within three minutes, he reached the first prearranged hiding place, an empty stink box. An old, well-used structure made of cedar planks, six feet square by three feet tall, which sat on the riverbank well away from the village. The traditional container was one of several used for fermenting the Ooligan fish the Nuxalkmc harvested, hence the name.

With panic gnawing in his gut, Father pulled back the lid and lifted Mary into the box. "Promise me you will not move until one of us comes to get you."

"I promise Father."

Taking a deep breath, Mary ducked into the stink box as Father kissed her forehead and pulled the lid back into place.

Grabbing George again, he raced further up the riverbank darting into the forest exactly where he knew to go. Traveling another few meters, he found the second hiding place, an old rotten cedar stump; hollow in the middle but still intact from above. Helping George to crawl into the stump's cavity through a narrow crevice off to one side, he kissed his son and gave him the same admonishment. "You stay right here until we come for you. Understand?"

"Yes, Father."

Pulling a nearby fallen log across the slender entrance to the stump, Father rearranged the nearest sword ferns to look undisturbed and brushed over his footprints with a cedar bough, completing the camouflage before rushing back to the village. This was the third time the family had undertaken this risky scheme. Thus far, they had been successful. But this did not lessen its terrifying effect on everyone involved.

The ominous sound grew louder as the boat drew closer. The pilot of the craft responsible for the noise was Sergeant, a tall man with a large build, thin nose, closely set dark eyes and salt and pepper hair. He had joined the RCMP at the tender age of nineteen and in the last fifteen years had truly found his niche. But what distinguished him from the rest of his peers was his conspicuous appetite for power and control, an obsession that was rarely sated. And the geographical isolation in which he worked only served to fuel his hunger for ultimate authority. He felt omnipotent, and in this place, he was. His job was to circulate throughout the Indigenous communities dotting the rugged coastline of this remote wilderness and enforce the law. One singular law; *all Indian children were to attend residential school, no exceptions.* Those daring to resist met with this particular officer's brand of swift, unrestrained brutality.

On this sunny but unusually cool day, Sergeant stepped onto shore with one specific mission, having "acquired" information about a family in this village who was hiding children. Sergeant had extorted this tidbit through systematic intimidation of several Nuxalkmc men who had been across the channel in the white village several days prior. Therefore,

Sergeant knew exactly where to go and who to look for.

Father arrived back home without a moment to spare. To his relief, he discovered Grandfather had also followed their emergency plan. At first, the elder had objected to the scheme, but after careful consideration had agreed to flee into the mountains because the octogenarian could not afford another beating. You see, on Sergeant's last visit he had targeted the elders, leaving a wake of broken bones in his path. As a result, Grandfather had almost died from pneumonia, which had set in after his ribs were fractured. And although leaving his family and hiding were contrary to every deeply-rooted instinct he had to protect his grandchildren, admittedly, Grandfather knew it was the most practical measure to take.

Father regained his breath shortly before the uniformed sadist reached the doorstep of their shack. Resting on the steps, Father kept as calm a composure as he could manage, mending a fishing net on the outside, praying on the inside. This was not the first meeting between the two men. Sergeant had accused Father of hiding his children once before. However, after an extensive search, several unprovoked strikes to Father's face, and no end of blistering threats, Sergeant uncovered no proof, forcing him to leave empty-handed. It was a grand humiliation and one the officer did not intend to repeat.

This time there were no words of greeting between them. Father raised his head from his mending to have it met with a crushing blow from Sergeant's right fist.

"No children! That's what you claimed last time, wasn't it! No children!"

The sucker punch knocked Father off balance, and he now sported several loose teeth. But Father knew better than to engage this man in a fight. Instead, he looked upwards at Sergeant and spoke calmly. "As I've said before, there are no children here."

That response was akin to throwing a grenade into a sea of gunpowder. Sergeant erupted, retaliating by punching the opposite side of Father's face. Father choked out a guttural moan from the second blow. It took every ounce of character he possessed to not return the vicious strikes. But he held fast, spat the blood from his mouth and was unflinching in his response. "There are no children here."

The officer was livid. "Liar!"

There would be no more discussion. Sergeant snapped. Grabbing Father's hair, Sergeant threw him to the ground, slamming his face into the gravel. The fall's force knocked the wind out of Father, and he lay there seeing stars. Before he could recover, Sergeant used his body's full weight to land his knee squarely on the back of Father's neck. Whisking the handcuffs from his duty belt, he bound Father's wrists behind his back, yanked him to his feet by his hair and dragged him summarily towards the waiting boat.

Sergeant took another bite from the sadistic smorgasbord in front of him by cinching the handcuffs until they could tighten no further. By the time he had hauled his quarry the few hundred meters to the dock, Father's hands were blue.

"Fucking chug," he said before spitting in Father's face. "I hope you enjoy prison because no judge is going to believe a lying chug over an officer of the law."

Sergeant made sure to punctuate his spiteful decree by kicking Father in the back, sending the bleeding man crashing face first over the rail and onto the boat deck. Father's bound hands were useless in breaking his fall, and his chin took the plunge's full force. Blood was spewing from his nose and mouth. Father lay there dazed by the unprovoked and continued abuse but regained his equilibrium within a few minutes. He analyzed his plight and decided it was best he did not move from the place where he had landed. Using his legs to prop himself upright, he leaned against the edge of the craft so he could face his assailant who was climbing triumphantly onto the deck.

"Don't fucking move," Sergeant threatened, grabbing his baton and pointing it in Father's face.

Sergeant went to the stern and untied the dock line before swaggering to the wheelhouse to engage the engines. The diesel motor let off a cloud of acrid black smoke with its unholy rumble. Sergeant expedited his departure by gunning the engines and thrusting the boat into gear making it lurch away from the dock. Everything this man did was calculated. And by making such an example of Father, he hoped his message was clear. Pointing the vessel towards Bella Coola, he threw the throttle wide open and leaned forward as the bow jerked upwards. Once he cleared the immediate shoreline, Sergeant slowed the engines' pace, allowing himself ample time to relish in his latest victory.

The vessel gradually made its way back across the channel, and the hypnotic rhythm of riding the waves seemed to settle Sergeant's rage somewhat. During this lull in the officer's mood, his eyes met Father's. In the chasm separating the two men, beyond the barrier of racism, lay an unlikely opportunity for empathy. One Father couldn't help but attempt to bridge. Through the searing ache of his fractured jaw and without breaking eye contact, he spoke in earnest. "If they were your children...what would you do?"

Father's words sliced through the ether of hate and hit their mark. Somehow, he had managed to find–and pierce–the remnants of Sergeant's soul. And it rattled the tyrant. Sergeant tore his eyes away from his prisoner's. The two had shared that glance for only milliseconds, which, as short as it was, made the officer squirm in his core. Sergeant stood at the helm stunned, staring out the front of the boat and mumbling. "I...enforce...my...job...the law."

The two spent the rest of the trip submerged in an aura of icy tension, nourished by a germinating seed of emotional dissonance taking hold in Sergeant.

Within a quarter of an hour, they arrived in Bella Coola harbor. Sergeant cut the motor and allowed the boat to drift to its berth. Once moored, Sergeant showed Father no mercy. His thirst for retribution remained unquenched, and if anything, his mood had deteriorated.

"Get up you fucking forest nigger!"

Father was dizzy and nauseated.

"Let's go chief. I don't have all fucking day."

Father struggled to stand. He wasn't fast enough for Sergeant. True to form, Sergeant wrenched Father from the deck, inducing further injury. After towing his prisoner to the police station a block away, Sergeant shoved the battered man into a cramped cell where Father waited to go before a judge the next day.

Father's experience was not unusual. Over the decades, the government and churches' tenacity for enforcing residential school attendance became legendary. The day Mary was born, Father had pledged to go to prison to protect his children. Although he dreaded the notion, he had always been willing to trade his liberty for theirs. Their freedom, at least temporarily, was what his sacrifice had bought.

Chapter 4
An hour later...

His freedom, at least temporarily, was what the end of the shift brought, though Sergeant considered it a fleeting liberty. He had married her just five short years before. But these days, he felt suffocated and trapped. Their marriage had initially been one of mutual convenience, the second for both parties. For her, it forestalled the specter of financial destitution and restored her ability to feed her daughter. For Sergeant, it meant cheap household labor. Nevertheless, over time his attitude about the union had steadily deteriorated, morphing from ambivalence into outright contempt. As far as Sergeant was concerned, home was merely a place where his needs got met, regardless of the cost to anyone else.

That evening he left the police station later than usual. Ordinarily, that wouldn't have bothered him because he enjoyed the tedious processing of prisoners. But this latest captive was different. This one had stirred up a hornet's nest inside the officer. The soft-spoken Nuxalkmc man had incited a struggle between Sergeant's sadistic tendencies and the residue of his soul. And in so doing, Father had undermined the deep satisfaction Sergeant usually got from jailing an Indian parent. But Sergeant had made sure that offense didn't go unpunished. It was going to be quite a while before that broken arm saw a doctor. And he made sure Father would recount his "accident" accurately by tapping his palm with a baton as he spoke. "You should learn to watch where you're walking. That dock gets slippery."

But even that savory bit of street justice couldn't gratify Sergeant. He was consumed with resentment, having had his slumbering humanity disturbed by an unwelcome whiff of remorse.

So it was axiomatic that Sergeant was fuming as he left the station house. He plopped himself into the driver's seat after stomping to his car and slamming its door. Neither action appeased him. No matter. Reaching under the seat, he pulled a near-empty whiskey bottle from its lair and inhaled the remaining mouthful. It didn't suffice. Reaching under again, he found nothing and punched the dashboard. "Fuck!" Storming out of his car, he hurled the door so hard the noise reverberated down the street. Five minutes later Sergeant had the steering wheel in one hand and a fresh bottle in the other. With the car's engine rumbling he cracked the bottle open and like a newborn calf took greedily to its stubby-necked teat. Several gulps later, he threw the car into gear and spun out of the parking lot with the same vigor. He sped home, drinking more heavily than usual and straining to tamp down the waging battle within. But the liquor only compounded his bitter rage.

"God damn fucking Indians!...What would I do if they were my fucking kids?...I tell ya what I'd fucking do!...If my fucking kids were subhuman papoose, I'd ship 'em off to a place where they'd get fucking civilized!"

Sergeant chased those venomous remarks with another long swig. He was too distracted from ranting at an invisible audience to notice he was zigzagging down the narrow country road. And he didn't spot the oncoming headlights. A split-second later screeching tires and a blaring horn cued him to swerve at the last second.

"Fuck me!...God damn fucking women drivers!...Fucking bitches!...Shouldn't be allowed to fucking drive!..."

The near miss didn't slow him down or give him caution. For the remaining few miles, Sergeant continued treating the centerline as a loose suggestion rather than an absolute rule.

His residence stood inland several miles from the hamlet of Bella Coola, further east in the valley. The home's isolation provided Sergeant with all the camouflage necessary for his private cruelties. The house had been built at the end of World War II and sat on twenty sprawling acres; once the home of Norwegian farmers who had established early settlements in the valley a century ago. Formerly a pretty shade of pastel green, the two-story farmhouse was now dilapidated and wrapped in rotting clapboard whose naked grain was peeking from beneath the peeling paint. Through years of continuous neglect, inch by inch, nature was reclaiming the once fertile farmland surrounding the cottage. Vines and brambles now covered the ancient, abandoned farm equipment, yielding a wild, lonely outline on the landscape. And not unlike an old man, whose march to the grave is made dignified by virtue of his wisdom, the farmhouse exhibited a solemn beauty in its decay. But inside, was anything but serene.

Sergeant usually arrived home in a foul mood, though tonight he was extra nasty. In the beginning, the beatings were few. Like snow in springtime, they had been random and unpredictable. Though the passage of time drew a definite pattern, more whiskey equaled more violence. It was his new wife who took the brunt of Sergeant's anger. She sacrificed herself willingly to protect her precious daughter, Wendy. But this was not what she had envisioned or bargained for in the marriage. Her first husband had been killed in a logging accident nine years ago when Wendy was just a baby. As a new widow with an infant daughter, she had few prospects and no available work. With destitution brewing on the horizon, she found herself in an impossible situation. She struggled for four years in poverty, before resorting to another marriage. For this reason, with small hopes and a desperate "I do," her life went from precarious to dangerous. Her existence now centered on keeping her nine-year-old safe from her stepfather and his insatiable rage.

Then there was Stuart, Sergeant's son from his first marriage. At twelve, he was three years older than Wendy and already an accomplished bully. Stuart could do no wrong, at least according to his father who indulged the budding narcissist at every opportunity. Sergeant had spent the last dozen years fostering his son's toxic vanity to the exclusion of any trace of empathy, remorse or guilt in the boy. At present, Stuart was busy crafting his own brand of misogynism, with Sergeant's eager approval. The little cottage in the valley housed a world that revolved solely around the two's base desires. Entitled, arrogant, selfish and cruel; like father, like son.

Stuart had always despised the idea of having a sister, but a sister like Wendy drove him mad. He envied everything about Wendy, her intellect, her authentic gentleness, and her mother's love. But his animosity did not end there. Early on, Stuart had vowed his mission would be to torment and antagonize Wendy at every possible turn. And he obliged his oath as if it was written in blood.

As expected, Sergeant stumbled through the front door grumbling orders with the same air of omnipotence he secreted at work. "This floor needs washing...Where's my newspaper!...I'm hungry."

The evening meal was set and waiting for him, as were his family. Seated around a small, wobbly table sat the nervous women and Stuart, the oblivious prince.

Sergeant fell into his chair at the head of the table. "Dinner better not be cold."

Mother and daughter began eating in tense silence.

"Did you learn anything from that useless teacher of yours boy?" Sergeant asked.

"Naw. She's so stupid! She gave us the same homework again."

"Jesus Christ! Why doesn't she just go get pregnant...like she's supposed to...and leave the teaching to men?" Inhaling another mouthful of whiskey, Sergeant continued, "I threw one of those fucking chugs in jail today. He'll be there for as long as it takes him to obey the law and hand over his feral spawn."

Since buying it in town, the bottle had not left Sergeant's grip. And its vile essence perfused him, goading his rancor with a pitchfork. After five minutes of strained quiet, Sergeant glared across the table at Wendy. The women held their breath as hostility filled the air and his glassy-eyed focus intensified. Without warning, the aggression climaxed. Sergeant bolted upright, aimed his dinner knife across the table and shook it menacingly in the little girl's face.

"And you!...You better make sure you stay away from those fucking Indians!" he slurred.

"Yes, sir," Wendy peeped, staring down at her half-finished dinner.

Sergeant's unpredictable behavior terrified Wendy, making her appetite evaporate. But through her mother's subtle urging, Wendy forced herself to finish the meager meal before cautiously asking, "May I clear the table now?"

Her mother nodded approval and Wendy scurried off to the kitchen with whatever she could carry, grateful to put some distance between herself and the men. She was glad to help her mother in this way. Wendy was worried about her. Over the past few months, her mother had developed a persistent cough, and she seemed to be tired all the time. In fact, she had become so fatigued their daily walks to the beach had stopped altogether, which was a shame because the shoreline was the one place where the two women could relax.

Not long ago, Wendy had asked, "Mommy, why do your clothes look so big?"

"It's nothing sweetheart. I've just lost a little bit of weight," she had replied, downplaying her daughter's concern.

But the pit in Wendy's stomach was screaming, *Yes! It is something!*

That night, as always, after helping with the dishes Wendy went straight to her bedroom. Once there, she read, voraciously and intensely. Helpless, she struggled to focus her attention on the pages, instead of the noises. She dreaded the noises, dull thuds, thumps and often yelps. She knew what Sergeant did. Wendy had lost her naiveté to her mother's bruised face long ago. And she hated him for it. At nine years old, Wendy saw Sergeant for the bully he was. What she hadn't understood yet, was that all bullies are cowards.

But all trees bear fruit. And a few days later, with a surreal atmosphere shrouding the house, the inevitable came to pass. Wendy had heard her fall down the stairs. And it was Wendy who had initially run to her aid. "Mommy!...Oh no!...No!..."

The attendants had to pry the little girl off her mother as they wheeled her into the black hearse that doubled as the community's ambulance. They found cancer the same night they admitted her to hospital.

She was riddled with it. And it didn't take long for the trauma of the fall to overwhelm her already fragile health. She slipped away the following Saturday morning with Wendy at her side.

One week later, a numb little girl stood affixed next to a flower-covered mound of freshly dug earth. A gentle April rain caressed her cheeks as if pleading for the release of her hostaged teardrops. Wendy shed not a single one. She felt nothing. The ordeal had left an empty cavern in the center of her chest.

The funeral was well attended despite it being no secret as to who was responsible for hastening this death. Though there were none courageous enough to step forward and speak the truth, except for Wendy's Aunt Laura. Laura had driven the thousand kilometer trek from Vancouver to attend her sister's funeral. And she brought with her a list of blunt questions surrounding the circumstances of her sister's "accident." Laura arrived demanding answers but quickly realized nobody in the hamlet was about to accuse Sergeant of assault. So, for Wendy's sake, she backed off the subject.

Laura was a Godsend for Wendy, preparing meals, running the household and providing a buffer between Wendy and the bullies. All while fighting to hold back the contempt she held for Sergeant. The two had never seen eye to eye. Sergeant considered her an uppity woman who didn't know her place, and Laura saw him for the savage he was.

On that dreary spring morning in the cemetery, Laura tried comforting her devastated niece by holding her close. Wendy's pale, expressionless face hung poignantly from her limp frame as she watched her mother's casket lowered into the ground. Standing next to Wendy, Sergeant's face looked the same as it always did, vacant eyes with a glint of rage at the ready.

Following the graveside service, Laura steered Wendy away from the fresh burial and towards the waiting car. Mustering up a contrite tone, Laura laid a blunt suggestion at Sergeant's feet. "Under the circumstances perhaps it might be best for everyone if Wendy came to live with me."

Sergeant responded by ripping Wendy out of Laura's arms. "It'll be a cold day in hell when I let a woman tell me what to do." He about-faced and began dragging Wendy towards the cemetery gates. "Stupid bitch...Thinks she knows best..."

Craning her head backward Wendy stared at Laura, her anxious eyes screaming, *Help! Don't leave me!*

Sergeant wrenched her arm. "What're you lookin' at! Let's go!"

In the weeks and months following, Sergeant continued deriving his sustenance from the bottle, while Wendy drew nourishment from the peace of the ocean, where she and her mother had often walked the shore together. Wendy's heartache would not heal. She longed for her mother's presence if only to ease her intolerable loneliness. Yet, there were times when Wendy was certain she could hear her mother's voice wafting in from over the waves. But she dismissed it as wishful thinking. During the summers of years following, Wendy would slip away and sleep there overnight, cradled next to a scarred driftwood log and swaddled in a moth-eaten sleeping bag. Sergeant never noticed her absence, though Stuart missed his plaything. The ocean became the singular thing Wendy could count on. She was her one and only comforter.

Chapter 5
One Year Later – Early Spring 1967
Victoria, British Columbia

She was his one and only comforter; silent, vast and cold, yet so full of life; the ocean. Those first steps upon the beach always exhilarated Trevor. He reveled in the glorious sounds of brittle seaweed crackling against the smooth pebbles as they gave way beneath his feet. He had an exceptional connection with the place, and he craved Her presence, especially when he was away from Her. In many ways, She was his first love. And every time he returned, Trevor felt instantly bonded to the water's heartbeat. This was where he learned what it was like to have a loving home. On stormy days, when the ocean pummeled the rocky shoreline, he still found comfort in the water. Even when those mighty waves tried forcibly enticing a speck of rock to join with them, the land never took offense. Trevor knew it was merely the way of things. Unlike his everyday existence, this display of power was not destructive, only natural, and impersonal.

What Trevor loved most was the ocean's smell. Every breath of salty air resonated within his soul. To him it was sublime, and the only meaningful nourishment the young boy ever experienced. With Shadow by his side, he would sit on the driftwood and inhale her delicious aroma, allowing the intoxicating scent to reach the smallest recesses of his body. When Trevor exhaled, he felt cleansed, though there were days when even that didn't help, days when he felt like he was permanently soiled.

Those few acres of land married to the shore were Trevor's precious refuge. He knew every hidden recess of that unpretentious corner of his world. Over time, he developed a detailed mental inventory of every gnarled oak and patch of brush, of each bit of ancient lichen that sprawled over the bedrock fissures, of every tidal pool and piece of driftwood. For hours, he studied the gulls gliding on the restless air currents above, contemplating the way they fed themselves and their young. Through his patience, the tides and currents gladly shared their otherwise silent secrets with him. Nature taught him to read her signs, and in doing so, she gave him what none of his own kind had cared or bothered to, an experience of love and peace. This place had taken him to her bosom as no human ever had, without judgment or expectation, without annoyance or loathing. She took him in and gently protected his spirit while his body endured the unendurable elsewhere.

Indeed, She taught him many things his own kind had not; or perhaps could not. She showed him change was infinite, inevitable, and even predictable. Trevor studied that lesson carefully. He never fully grasped its meaning, but he did get glimpses of understanding, moments when he saw that life and death were in perfect balance and the profound wisdom that underpinned that harmony. Strangely, those moments of insight gave him hope.

She was always a patient and committed teacher. She taught him everything in creation had its purpose and that no matter how small, every raindrop had its rightful place. That one notable truth was why Trevor struggled so hard to reconcile his own existence. Thus far, he had no rightful place. Oh, he labored to find it, but without success. So as a last resort, Trevor attempted invisibility. But try as he might to diminish himself, he never felt welcome outside of his beach, which was why returning home was so impossibly onerous.

Since discarding his self-hatred, Trevor had unwittingly accepted a new dilemma. You see, sometimes personal insight comes at a price. In Trevor's case, he had traded suicidal thoughts for a burgeoning anger that was on track to surpass even Monster's intense rage. But unlike Monster, the genesis of Trevor's anger stemmed from a righteous sense of injustice. And it began to preoccupy him.

The constant persecution Trevor underwent gave rise to a question that trespassed in his brain almost hourly. *Why won't she just leave me alone?* Every time the question trudged through his consciousness, his outrage grew. Sure, he could recognize sadism for what it was, its virulent, narcissistic need to hurt. And he also knew the Beast had no sense of fairness or integrity, only an all-consuming greed unto itself. But Trevor's real problem was his total lack of an outlet for his growing wrath. He had no escape from the mounting pressure within. Even in his dreams, Trevor found himself screaming, *Just leave me alone!* His desperate plea would continue demanding a resolution. And inevitably at some future point, it would either implode or explode. Only time would tell.

With a knot in his gut, Trevor knew it was almost time to leave his sanctuary by the sun's disappearance behind the horizon. Tonight it reflected a fiery red against the clouds, fringed by an ethereal mix of blues and pinks, but at its core, fiery red. Fiery red. The chilling irony wasn't lost on Trevor; fiery red–just like Monster's eyes.

He carried that dreadful image in his head on every journey home. As repulsive as the thought of going back there was, Trevor dared not be late. It was foolhardy to be late for dinner, though dinner was a pretty loose term for the ritual. The fact was, it was time for It to feed. Trevor felt like slop in a trough. It feasted on his pain, his cries and the torture It inflicted. She beat him before, during and after dinner. This wasn't a mother feeding her child; it was a child nourishing a sadist.

The dulling evening light prompted Trevor to start preparing for that emotionally arduous walk. Having no alternative, including suicide, he braced himself to leave his earthly mistress.

"Come on Shadow. Time to go girl." The dog let out a slight whimper and hung her head a little bit lower before obeying her master.

But before the shoreline left Trevor's sight he paused at the top of the rise, turning around to take in one last breath of respite, one last time, as if he expected never to return. Fortunately, but more likely by grace, a piece of Her found its way inside Trevor, forever merging with his psyche. What remained in his heart was Her voice, the ocean's gentle song.

Chapter 6
Meanwhile...

What remained in his heart was Her voice, the ocean's gentle song. But it was not the only soothing and delightful thing Father dearly missed. Prison was the antithesis of his former life, and was not, by any measure, agreeable to his nature. He found himself thrust into the midst of a brutal climate whose cruelty was self-perpetuating. Unaccustomed to the smells, the sounds, and the savagery, he struggled to adapt to the feral habitat. But it was the unbridled and ferocious racism that became his real nemesis. Unlike the reserve, here there was nowhere to hide from it, or from the other inmates and the guards. As time wore on, Father wondered if he would survive to finish his sentence. For this gentle-natured man, poverty was one thing, brutality quite another.

Father often stared through the three-inch crack that served as the window of his cell, in his unending search for some trace of beauty with which to counteract his harsh surroundings. Save for a few distant cedar trees, he saw little that was comforting, or familiar and he spent his daylight hours of confinement staring out the sliver of a window and praying.

Creator, Grandmothers and Grandfathers, I ask for the strength to be in this place. I ask for this not to be in vain. I ask for protection for George and Mary, for my beautiful wife, and for Grandfather. Help them to keep my children safe. Help them to grow up healthy and happy. I ask you to help the children who have been taken away. I ask you to send kindness into the hearts of the people here...

As Father languished in his prison cell, hundreds of miles away from his loved ones, Mother and Grandfather cautioned the children repeatedly to be extra vigilant now they had one less protector.

Regardless of those explicit warnings, a month later the inevitable happened–the sound returned. The People knew the sound. It echoed like thunder across the water and struck the village with a devastating intensity that lightning could never match. It was the sound of stolen children.

That fateful day, George and Mary were playing on the beach and in their delight had not paid as close attention as they should have. Before the siblings realized, the sound was right on top of them. At the last moment, the boat's tenor sliced through Mary's joy and awoke her to action. She gasped, "The boat!"

Grabbing her little brother's arm, she shoved him to the ground. With strength beyond the capacity of her small frame, she deftly rolled a hollow piece of driftwood on top of George before bolting up the beach in search of concealment for herself.

By this time, Sergeant had alighted the shore and begun pursuit. "You! Stop! Come back here!"

Sprinting from panic, Mary clambered over the maze of logs lying scattered between her and the safety of the woods. Without looking behind, she heard her pursuer narrowing the gap.

"Stop you fucking little squaw!"

Mary needed to get to the cover of the forest trail where she could disappear. Sergeant was closing in. With her heart pounding and lungs burning, she scrambled madly to reach her escape route; just a few more yards; she was almost safe. This life and death race was about to end. Mary was within two strides of the forest trail, with only one log separating her from freedom. *I can make it,* she thought. So she jumped– and lost her footing, falling hard and headfirst into a large rock.

More than an hour had passed before Mary began to stir from unconsciousness. Torrential rain poured from a dark gray sky, pelting her, stinging her face and arousing her further. Opening her eyes, she found herself lying sprawled face down on the boat deck, her head encircled by a puddle of coagulated blood. She groaned. Reaching up to her pounding head, she discovered thick, warm ooze flowing from a gaping wound. Slowly, her awareness grew. She felt the small craft swaying back and forth as it sliced through the rough ocean waves. Shivering from the wet and cold, and through the haze of her injury, Mary found it daunting to distinguish between reality and dream. Holding her bloody hand up in front of her eyes, she stared at it insensibly, watching the raindrops slowly dilute the gore. Inside, she waged a psychic battle of denial against this living nightmare. *This isn't real...This must be...I must be dreaming...I'm not really here...This can't be happening...*Mary refused to accept the veracity of her situation; until she remembered the chase. In that flash of nauseating lucidity, she grasped her predicament. The dire implications wrapped a stranglehold around her belly and she vomited.

Still hidden away, George lay paralyzed, afraid to make even the slightest noise; never before had he been this close to the boat. His ears had soaked in every dreadful sound. The vessel landing almost on top of him, Sergeant jumping ashore on the dry seaweed, and every surreal moment of the chase that had ensued. He listened to the officer's clumsy, frenzied footsteps as he yelled at Mary, swearing, and cursing. And the little boy had borne silent witness to Sergeant's depraved laughter when he had captured his prey lying injured and unconscious behind the nearby logs. All of it left his young mind creating pictures to match. Several hours had passed since that horrible event, yet George remained frozen under the makeshift ramparts, which his sister had lovingly provided. Still fighting back his urge to vomit, he dared not move.

I have to go home. I have to tell Mother. With those distressing thoughts, George began digging himself out from under the log with the woeful echoes still reverberating in his head. Tentatively emerging from his refuge, he stepped into a shroud of dismal silence along the shoreline. Chilled to the bone, his limbs numb, and engulfed by a traumatic fog, he cried out weakly for his sister. "Mary...Mary..."

The call of a lone gull overhead was his only reply. It was a bleak affirmation of his worst fears.

In a deadened stupor, somehow George managed to find his way home. He broke the horrific news with nothing more than the hollow expression on his face. Distraught, Mother collapsed to the floor wailing. She was powerless to stop her family from being ripped away from her, one precious soul at a time.

In the days following Mary's kidnapping, Mother withdrew into herself. Her once radiant face emitted no more than a vacant stare. She refused to eat, consumed by, and spiraling ever deeper into, the desolate abyss of grief. Grandfather was afraid her spirit had left her. He knew what was needed and pleaded with her. "You must come with me to the mountains."

But she was lost to her mourning and beyond the reach of his words.

The next day Grandfather took George to a sacred place in the mountains. It was there, camped amongst ancient cedars, old and young listened to the sounds of the forest. In front of a small fire, Grandfather drummed and sang medicine songs as George, only vaguely aware he was present, stared lifelessly into the flames. All at once, it happened. George began to cry; deep sobs that felt like they came from another plane. Grandfather continued drumming and singing. The fire glowed, and George wept and came home to himself, released from the curse of unshed tears.

The next morning, the pair trekked back down the mountain. George returned feeling a great deal lighter. His young face once more beamed with life and his glorious smile had returned. He had taken the first and most crucial step in coming to terms with Mary's loss, aided by an otherwise unremarkable man who carried a deep and abiding connection to the place of their ancestors.

Arriving at their dilapidated house, they found Mother in the same spot as they had left her; sitting in a small wooden chair, hunched over and staring blankly out the cracked window, still clutching Mary's sweater and swaying back and forth on her rickety perch. Fresh tracks of tears clung to her gaunt face, defining withered features that two days before had not been there.

At first, George was startled by Mother's haggard appearance. Grandfather sensed the little boy's reluctance to approach his mother's increasingly cadaverous form.

Grandfather whispered, "It's all right George."

Reverently, George drew near to her. Inching closer, he gingerly slipped his small hand into hers and leaning in whispered in her ear. "I brought you a present Mother. To cheer you up."

Gleefully, George produced a posy of multicolored wildflowers from behind his back for her approval. That gesture was small, yet momentous, bridging her chasm of grief and coaxing her back from icy solitude. Slowly, she turned her head toward her youngest. George smiled at her. And a gentle spring rain began to fall. At that moment, Mother stepped away from the brink of her despair and throwing her arms around her son embraced George so tightly he thought he would snap in half. They clung to each other as Mother rocked her little boy back and forth. Eventually, she let George loose from her grip. At the same time, a slight hint of a smile arose on her face. "Thank you, my son, for these beautiful flowers."

George threw his arms around her neck one more time, giving her a big kiss on the cheek. Just as quickly, he was off to find a drink of water for Mother's gift. Grandfather watched their reunion at a respectful distance with grateful relief and a silent, *Thank you.*

Regrettably, Mary was not the only child seized that tragic spring day, though she was by far the oldest. Even though Canadian law was explicit, stating a child must be at *least* seven years old before going to residential school, the decree was rarely respected. That same day Sergeant made a clean sweep through the village, taking every child who wasn't in diapers. As a result, in the days following the children's exodus, Mother became the object of envy. After all, George had been spared. Although jealousy was not the People's way, and as hard as those bereaved parents tried, they simply could not help themselves even knowing it was just a matter of time before George too would come to know the sound of the boat.

Boundless sorrow descended like a thick cold fog over the reserve, and the People became swallowed up by its palpable, exhausting emptiness. Admittedly, there was no defense against the thief who had stolen their joy.

Chapter 7
Two Weeks Later - Late Spring 1967
Bella Coola, British Columbia

Admittedly, there was no defense against the thief who had stolen her joy. All Wendy could do was sit at the ocean's edge hoping for that elusive visitor to return.

In the year since her mother died, Wendy had struggled to keep up with the demands placed upon her. She did her best to clean up after the two bullies and to prepare meals from the meager rations provided. The only true abundance the house knew was whiskey. There was always lots of whiskey and its insidious counterpart, violence.

Winters were a veritable prison sentence for Wendy. The bitter cold was her jailer, which confined her for long periods inside the house. But at last spring had arrived and the elements had softened enough to allow Wendy a much-needed reprieve. Taking full advantage of her parole, she escaped to the beach where she perched quietly on an ancient log, allowing the water to work its magic until she felt calm, clean and settled.

Wendy's daily existence evolved into one of necessary invisibility. The ten-year-old did her best to keep up the household, hoping Sergeant would have little to find fault with. She even resorted to preparing a bottle for him. Each evening she would place it gingerly, as if it was a sacred offering, next to his armchair where it waited like an impatient master for its slave. Once the stage was set for Sergeant's arrival, if she could, Wendy would disappear. She figured Sergeant couldn't hit what wasn't there. The strategy was sound, but it only worked three seasons of the year. During winter, Sergeant repaid Wendy's efforts with regular beatings.

The summer was Wendy's true savior. The warm weather allowed her to spend most of her time at the ocean's edge. It was where she reunited with her own aliveness, parted away from the necessary numbness of her daily existence. It was also where she met a highly improbable ally.

Their first encounter was etched in Wendy's mind, and she found even many years later she could recall it in great detail. There was nothing special about that late-summer evening. Wendy was sitting on the beach, tossing pebbles into the water when she heard light footsteps behind her. Surprised by the unexpected noise, she whirled backward and found herself face-to-face with a petite, elderly Nuxalkmc man. Being this close to an Indian rattled Wendy. Since she was little, she had been brainwashed into believing Indians were lazy drunkards who were dangerous and untrustworthy. And now, here she was *alone* with one. Spooked by the man's sudden appearance, Wendy thought her heart was about to explode. And not knowing what to expect, her body tensed.

The old man sensed Wendy's discomfort. He spoke in a deep, raspy voice. "I'm sorry if I startled you. I've had a very long walk today. Would it be all right if I sit and rest my old bones? Over there?" he asked, pointing a withered finger to the farthest end of the log.

Fearful and uncertain about her plight, Wendy simply nodded, readying herself to run at the first sign of trouble. He shuffled ten feet away and sat. The minutes passed. Nothing bad happened. And Wendy calmed down enough to realize this aged man was no threat to her. She discretely sized him up and guessed the better part of seventy years separated them. Besides, she figured she could run faster scared than he could angry. So, Wendy decided to stay put and allow the startling scenario to play itself out.

Even though Wendy tried to keep her distance and act nonchalant, an enchantment began inching over her. There was something about this man, something extraordinary and captivating. So she investigated. Surreptitiously, she studied his features. His face was dark, and the lines ran deep, framing smallish eyes, a broad nose and full lips, which displayed an intriguing grin. He had a weathered but wise expression, bordered by snow-white hair, braided neatly and running all the way down his back. He wore a denim shirt, plaid quilted jacket, blue jeans, deerskin belt and moccasins, topped off by a red bandana knotted loosely around his neck. Yet Wendy's focus was always drawn back to his eyes. Never had she seen such compassionate eyes. They were mesmerizing. But more than that, Wendy was attracted to his grounded presence. The elder projected a potent aura of calmness, a contagion that happily infected all who were near, including Wendy. The whole package took quite some getting used to, as this man did not fit the stereotype Wendy was accustomed to hearing about.

Enthralled by this human relic, she watched him inhale deeply several times like he was stretching his lungs. Staring straight ahead at the ocean, he exhaled slowly. "You picked a very good place to sit on such a beautiful evening."

"Oh, I come here all the time," she blurted, wincing at her indiscretion and thinking, *Ahhh...What am I doing! This is my beach, my spot. Why did I say that!*

"Uh huh...It is a good place. Especially to listen to the ocean. A very good place indeed...You know, I used to come to this same spot when I was about your age."

Charmed by her new companion, without thinking she blundered, "Wow! That must have been a hundred years ago."

To which the enigmatic man responded with the boldest laughter Wendy had ever heard. In fact, he began laughing so hard she was convinced he was going to keel over and die right there on the beach. Wendy was so stunned by his hysterics her mind raced to think of a plausible explanation in the event he did actually croak right there in front of her.

But he didn't die, though he did continue laughing for what seemed like forever to Wendy. And despite all her misgivings, she began snickering along with him. She couldn't match his performance as he was clearly in a class of his own. But Wendy surprised herself, spewing forth several spontaneous, well-formed belly laughs. She honestly couldn't help but giggle; his laugh was that infectious. For Wendy, this was like being overcome by a sickness, except it made her feel good. In fact, Wendy couldn't remember having felt this good for ages. Gradually, the explosive laughter subsided, and while still chuckling to himself, he admitted, "You're right, I *am* old."

Following their somewhat clumsy introduction, all of Wendy's trepidations fell away. Afterwards, they sat together, that most implausible pair, in the presence of that place. Wendy tossed the occasional pebble in the water while the venerable senior sat sporting a thoughtful grin. The two relaxed in the comfortable silence until Wendy noticed dusk falling. Knowing it was time for her to leave, she stood and turned to her new acquaintance.

"Okay...Bye."

The elder smiled before asking, "Is it okay with you if I come to sit here again another time?"

She didn't hesitate. "Yeah sure...Okay...See ya."

Truthfully, she was hoping he would return. He had made her feel calm, shown her respect and made her laugh. To Wendy that was the trifecta of friendship. She sprinted off home, unaware she would indeed see him again. In fact, she would see him many more times to come.

When Wendy arrived home that evening, there was no mistaking Sergeant's profound resentment of her. His tirade that particular night focused on how

Wendy was the "Bitch daughter of that slut who tricked me into marrying her...And now I'm stuck with you!" Though the truth of it was, Wendy was just the valve Sergeant used to release his rage. Yes, he hated her, but she was also good, satisfying fodder.

During her visit, Laura had also borne the brunt of his various outbursts. Since returning to Vancouver after the funeral, she had phoned regularly trying to keep Wendy's spirits alive and to beg, coerce or otherwise persuade Sergeant to let Wendy come and live with her. The answer was always a resounding "No!" Followed by, "Who the hell does this bitch think she is trying to tell me what's best in my house!" But besides, Sergeant enjoyed torturing Laura. He reveled in denying her her "bleeding heart ways."

Still, as satisfying as his sadism was, Sergeant was also tormented. Laura and Wendy plagued him because he recognized in the two women a spark of joy that refused to be tamed or extinguished. And the more he tried to do just that, the more intensely he experienced the pain of their delight. Wendy's smile, rare as it was, still came far too easily for his taste. The mere threat of her joy was too painful for Sergeant to bear. He simply could not tolerate it. You see, it was her innate sparkle that underscored how much he had endured himself. Her grin stood in stark contrast to of a way of life that had long ago been eradicated in him, one that had become smothered in his experience of abuse and loss. The pitiful irony of his traumatic past had come full circle. He loathed

Wendy for still being capable of smiling and laughing, as he had once done. A raging parent had beaten that out of Sergeant at an early age. And like an ogre lurking in a secret cave within, he despised, and begrudged, anyone who was happy.

But he had not always been this way. Sergeant's first wife had seen beyond his invisible bruising. She had dared to peek inside, behind his gruff exterior, and found the vulnerable, wounded soul she fell in love with. She had pulled the tattered armor off his heart and through her patient compassion helped him rebuild his emotional foundation and recapture his happiness. She nurtured his healing, allowing Sergeant to fall in love with her, and with life. But it was all for naught. She took her last breath as her son took his first. Sergeant never forgave her, or the universe, for their betrayal.

Instead of grieving his losses or acknowledging his hurt, and especially in place of forgiveness, instead, Sergeant chose jealousy, anger, and cynicism. His self-righteous, bitter resentment coerced him into inflicting revenge on the world in any way that was in his power. So without the benefit of a judge or jury, he imposed sentence, banishing himself to a prison, not of brick and mortar, but of hatred and fear. And he wallowed in the mire of that dark place. He fed each fear-based emotion relentlessly, nurturing each one until they grew strong enough to demand the same allegiance from him as the whiskey did. Inevitably, like the memory of his dead first wife, the tiniest wisp of joy was unbearably reminiscent of what he no longer possessed; his wife, his joy, and his humanity. He hated seeing Wendy happy.

Chapter 8
Eighteen Months Later
Late Summer 1968
Victoria, British Columbia

Monster hated seeing them happy. The slightest hint of a grin would trigger a merciless barrage of humiliation and abuse upon any perpetrator of that vile, forbidden act. Accordingly, the children learned early on how to hide their emotions. Their survival depended on it.

Emotions were just one of the many taboos in that household. Acts of kindness were also outlawed, as Terry found out one late-summer evening. Tess was struggling in school, due in large part to the abuse she endured, and was having difficulty with her summer school homework. Terry had been secretly tutoring his sister in her room, but they were found out. He had committed a wicked transgression in his bid to mitigate her suffering, suffering from which Monster derived great pleasure. With Terry's fatal indiscretion as ammunition, It concocted a fantasy, a thinly-veiled excuse to fulfill its mandate of perpetuating misery. Monster accused him of attempting incest. The rest of the night was filled with Terry's screams.

Shortly after dawn, a humid breeze sent salty air wafting through the house like a vagabond seeking a meal. Those early morning hours were typically quiet, and they bore as faint a resemblance to peace as the house would ever experience, though the pervasive tension infusing those walls lay lurking just below the surface, poised to erupt in an instant.

Trevor lay on his bed, wide-awake from the early summer sun and the apprehension in his belly. He was tired. He was always tired. Sleep never came easily, and when it did, it was restless. Last night's attempt had been all but impossible. All he could do was lay there–listening. There was hope dawn's arrival would offer a distraction. Now Trevor could try to fixate on the summer morning's sweet sounds, instead of the deafening silence in the next room. But the exercise made him feel like a pauper trying to exchange lead for gold. Nevertheless, Trevor lay there taking in the natural melodies drifting freely through his window, grateful for the lilting songs of red-winged blackbirds and herring gulls greeting the new day. Concentrating on the birdsongs, he attempted to block out the competing sounds of his memory, the sounds of his brother's last beating.

Terry was in his room. Monster had flung him in there late last night, like a discarded rag doll, after battering him with the fire poker. When Monster slammed Terry's door shut, Trevor pressed his ear against the plaster wall, but he didn't hear any noise. Not a sound–all night–not even a whimper. Trevor thought Terry was dead.

Thoughts poured into his mind. *What if Terry's dead?....The police would have to find out...Wouldn't they?...Maybe they'll arrest her...take her to jail...*Toying with the idea of his own emancipation through his brother's death nauseated Trevor. He was far too conflicted about profiting from the event to carry on with the fantasy. His mind continued running amok, succumbing to desperate reasoning. *Maybe I should just take off...I could leave and live in the forest by the beach...yes...I could build a shelter from driftwood...catch fish...*Trevor's delusions were cut short when the awful stillness emanating from Terry's room broke, and he heard his brother carefully moving about. His heart raced. Terry was *alive*. He wanted to run to Terry's room to see how he was, but that would be a suicidal dash through a minefield. Monster slept until noon and disturbing the beast before then would lead to an awful fate. Waking It was to be avoided at all costs.

Instead, tentatively cracking open his door, Trevor peered out through the small fissure down the hall towards Terry's room. Seconds later, Terry emerged and began creeping down the hallway towards Trevor's room. Trevor yanked open his door, waving frantically for Terry to enter. Watching Trevor's sobering eyes invite him into the bedroom, Terry froze. He was intent on leaving but succumbed to his little brother's silent pleadings by ducking inside and closing the door with haste behind him.

Trevor noticed his brother was limping and what he could see of Terry's body showed swollen purple, black and blue mottling. Yet Terry had an eerie peacefulness about him, and from it, Trevor felt a gnawing dread growing in his belly. The disquieting calm radiating about him was one thing, but there was a sense of sadness in his eyes Trevor had never seen before. As bad as things were in that place, as many beatings as Terry had endured, there had always been the trace of a flicker in his eyes. When Trevor was younger, he thought the flicker was Terry's defiance of the pervasive evil in their lives. Years later, as an adult, Trevor would come to know better. Eventually, Trevor would see the flicker many times, and just as often, he would also see it extinguish. Today, while staring at his brother's swollen, purple eyes, was the first time Trevor ever saw the glint of hope die.

Relieved to see his brother alive, but anxious something was wrong, Trevor whispered, "Are you okay Terry?"

"Yeah...I'm okay,"

Terry's bleak reply made Trevor pause to study his brother's face for a moment before begging, "Let's just get *outta* here Terry. You and me."

Shaking his head, Terry gave a grim sigh. "We've got nowhere to go."

Trevor knew he was right. There was no escape. But where was Terry going?

"Look, I'm going out for a while. You need to stay here. Okay, Trevor?...Don't follow me...I'll uh...be back in a few hours."

With that admonition, Terry turned and left. It was the last time Trevor saw him alive.

They found his body two days later, floating face down in the ocean. Officially, they ruled it an accident, surmising the bruising had resulted from him slipping off the cliff and falling into the water. Both Monster and Trevor knew better.

A late summer rain cloaked the mourners as they departed from the graveside. Ironically, Terry's death had allowed the two surviving siblings to feel a modicum of safety. After all, Monster couldn't beat or abuse them in front of witnesses. However, the reality was such that those who grieved for Terry wouldn't be around for long. And after such a long fast, Monster's appetite would be ravenous.

With Terry gone, Tess knew she would owe Monster a more considerable portion at feeding time. She had little left to give. Unbeknownst to Trevor, Tess had made up her mind to leave while watching Terry's casket being lowered into the ground. She vanished after the funeral, leaving not a trace behind, a well-executed departure for a girl of fourteen. Trevor would wonder about her for the next five years.

Trevor would have left too if it weren't for Shadow. But he couldn't have lived with himself if he had abandoned her. Even though both of his protectors were gone, he vowed to stay and safeguard his dog. In the midst of so much dreadful change, Trevor resolved he and Shadow would still be each other's confidant. Amidst their home's predatory atmosphere, he pledged to provide Shadow some relief. And he honestly believed he and Shadow could still escape into their blissful oblivion, even if it were only for a few precious moments each day. Trevor trusted that much wouldn't change.

But Trevor's trust was misplaced. On a Friday afternoon, within a month of burying his brother,

Trevor became the target of a blistering treachery. Returning home after school at his usual time, he nudged open the front door expecting Shadow to come bounding out. But she didn't. Trevor was besieged with silent panic and began a frenzied search of the house to find his friend, doing his best not to arouse Monster in the process. He turned up nothing. There was no sign of her, not even her food dish. The dog had vanished, and all traces of her had been eradicated. And it had been made to look as though Shadow never existed.

Trevor felt like he had been punched in the gut. He sat on the front steps with a whirl of emotions clambering for his attention. But he couldn't cry or scream. *My dog...what did she do with my dog?...Why?...* Trevor knew this was an act of revenge. *What did I do!...I've been good...I didn't do anything!...*

Trevor's first mistake was that he thought there were rules to this game. His second mistake was believing that those rules actually applied. He had naïvely assumed if he didn't cause trouble Monster would leave him alone. That was fiction. In the void of Shadow's absence, Trevor comprehended It's true nature; Monster's unquenchable need to inflict pain. It was hungry and required feeding. And It's nourishment came from watching him languish. The irrefutable truth was Trevor was just a means to an end. He was a piece of meat, a smorgasbord, the gutter from which It dined. Right or wrong, his actions didn't matter. Rules didn't matter. He didn't need to behave in order to avoid punishment. The fact he drew breath was enough for Monster to let loose her resentment. And the fact Trevor had love in his life, simply by way of a dog, made It salivate with a treacherous jealousy.

Now all bets were off. At twelve years old, Trevor allowed himself to feel it, his raw, unadulterated rage. More significantly, he permitted it to surface. And the fury emerged from its cocoon fully matured and seeking accountability for its deformed condition. As it marched into Trevor's consciousness, he acknowledged its unmitigated genesis–profound betrayal; of safety, love, trust; the very debasement of motherhood itself.

Through his numbness, a strange invigoration seized Trevor. Without thinking, he got up, walked inside, entered the living room and grabbed the same perverse took It had used against him and his siblings. Using the stealth of a python and a tight-fisted hold on his weapon, he crept up behind his sadistic tormentor as she sat watching television. It was as though a force beyond him had come to life, springing forth from the center of his being, possessing him and shrieking commands. He obeyed by wielding the fire poker with deadly intent. In quick succession, he struck once, twice, three times. Dazed by the powerful opening blows, Monster fell to the floor insensible.

Those first strikes drained Trevor of any further impulses to destroy It. Yet the memory of Terry's swollen, battered face flashed before him, spawning a second wave of emotions that both overwhelmed and reenergized him. Another volley of rage burst forth, spurring him on. He straddled her limp body, ready to deliver a last deadly blow to her head. Sizing up his target, he raised the poker high with both hands. He paused, tensing his muscles and perfecting his stance for his final strike, and It's final breath. But as he looked at her face, a veil lifted, allowing Trevor a glimpse beyond his hate. The truth of who she really was had broken through the adrenaline. Right then all he could see lying before him was a pathetic human being. Out of nowhere, part of him took pity on her. The steely grip he used to wield the poker softened, and the weapon fell from his hands.

In that fragment of time, Trevor would have undoubtedly walked away if not for the images that began parading through his mind again. Helpless, he became swept away, engulfed by an emotional tsunami borne from years of repressed anger, hurt and humiliation. The tug-of-war between his humanity and his rage was lost, obliterating his mercy. And as if commanded by the universe to expunge the evil lying stunned before him, Trevor obeyed, while the memories in his mind played on in an endless loop. Pouncing on top of It, he wrapped his hands around It's neck and squeezed. He leaned heavily, pressing his entire weight on Monster's windpipe, watching as the color in It's face transformed from pink to purple. Trevor stared into It's eyes, transfixed, witnessing It's essence fade. From the slow exodus of life from It's body, Trevor sensed a wondrous, intoxicating freedom.

He was only seconds away from killing It when a flash of panic struck him from an insight so abysmal and repulsive, it made him fling himself off her. "No!"

Horrified, Trevor scurried away, scrambling over himself and stopping only when he hit the room's far wall. He came to rest staring at her, with his heart pounding, his body shaking and tears streaming down his face. His rage had both terrified and disgusted him. Was he capable of similar acts of cruelty and hatred? Surfacing into his head was the most repugnant thought imaginable. *Am I just like her? Could I be...* With his mind spinning from the sickening possibility, Trevor crawled a few more feet before puking.

Trevor didn't know it at the time but, after today, his mother would never touch him again.

Chapter 9
Meanwhile...
Bella Coola, British Columbia

George didn't know it at the time but, after today, his mother would never touch him again.

Wisps of feather-like cloud, painted orange by a late-setting sun, were still visible on that warm summer's evening. And a weak breeze was rattling the cottonwoods, coaxing the forest melodies to transition from day to night. But as twilight lingered, a perilous vibration drifted from across the water, and the call of the loons fell silent. The boat was coming.

It was imminent. Another officially sanctioned terrorist act was about to be unleashed. For generations, this pitiful game of cat and mouse had played out. Political and religious power had always won. For almost a century, church and state had used their unholy alliance to abuse their authority in the attainment of one goal: cultural assimilation. *You will believe what we believe, wear what we wear, and talk how we talk.* All in the name of solving the "Indian problem." Those who survived their residential school incarceration inevitably turned to the bottle for comfort. Today was no exception. Today, the path that lead to betraying a youngster and forsaking one's own people was where the road of desperation met a fifth of whiskey.

And so it was Sergeant knew precisely where to go and who to look for. Stealth was vital. So he cut the boat's motor early, allowing the craft to glide into shore and landing himself undetected on the beach.

He held a bristling contempt for the People. The fact "those fucking chugs" always lied to him about their children, fueled tonight's quest for vengeance. With hatred as his accomplice, Sergeant hunted down his intended target, arriving at the ramshackle dwelling in short order. He didn't knock. Without missing a stride, he kicked in the flimsy door with his gun drawn and his finger poised on the trigger. Strutting towards Grandfather, and without provocation, Sergeant backhanded the elder with a brutal blow across the old man's face, knocking him off his chair. The officer's callous dance continued with a sinister pirouette, kicking Mother to the floor while shouting, "I'll shoot you both if you so much as twitch!"

Time slowed for Sergeant. He basked in his sense of omnipotence through the climate of fear he created. These were the moments he lived for, the moments he craved. This was the zenith of his addiction to power and control, and he apologized to no one for savoring each delicious and intoxicating morsel of suffering.

Calmly, he swaggered across the bare wooden floor towards a cowering George, his boots echoing an ominous prophecy. With cold-blooded calculation, he paused before grabbing George by the hair and yanking him furiously from the floor. George screamed a mix of panic and pain as Sergeant extracted him with a bold and premeditated cruelty.

Mother groveled on her knees. "No, no, please no. Don't take my boy. Please! Don't! Please!"

The cold metal of his revolver meeting her face was his brutal reply.

Sergeant left the house without delay, holding fast to his screaming quarry by dragging George by his hair. Moments later Sergeant heaved the child on the deck of the waiting boat.

"Shut up or else!"

George complied not because he understood what Sergeant said, but because he understood Sergeant's tone. George only spoke Nuxalt'mc. Huddling on the open deck, he peered up at the angry white man in the scary-looking uniform paying close attention to the big club hanging from Sergeant's belt. George knew what it was for because he had seen the weapon used on other children in past raids. Powerless and shaking from fear, George stared through glassy eyes until he relinquished his body to numbness.

The craft rocketed away from the beach as soon as George was dumped on the deck. Until then, George had been in love with the ocean's smell. He loved the water in part because Mother always taught him to cherish it. Time after time, she said, "Water is the giver of life." But George hated this smell. This was a profane, nauseating odor, an adulterated mix of diesel fumes with nary a ghost of nature's scent remaining. The noise the boat belched forth was just as harsh, drowning out every subtle melody that typically filled this pristine wilderness. As minutes passed, the little boy watched helplessly as the shoreline of his home grew faint on the horizon. Soon, darkness welcomed the stars. George looked upwards, seeking to grasp onto something familiar. He couldn't know it at the time, but in the following years the constellations would become the only tangible anchor to everything George had ever known and loved.

Overwhelmed and in profound shock, George remained crouched in the corner of the boat, rocking back and forth with his arms wrapped around his knees, trying to wake himself from the unfolding nightmare. His head throbbed from where his hair had been so viciously pulled out of his scalp. And he couldn't fathom why the big white man was so angry with him. Through his numbness, George did the only thing he could think to do. He shoved aside his disbelief and dismay and prayed to Creator for help. He was cold, scared and bewildered. In that moment of sheer emotional exhaustion, George felt it, an ethereal chill.

Chapter 10
Twenty-Two Years Later - Autumn 1990
East Vancouver

In that moment of sheer emotional exhaustion, Trevor felt it, an ethereal chill. Not the kind of chill that makes you seek out warmth. No, it was the sort of chill that made you keenly aware of a mournful emptiness within; a vacant landscape that demands acknowledgment. One seemingly endless night shift was all it took to beckon its intangible, coercive aura. And it always arrived coupled with the helpless sensation of being drawn into its infinite suffocating void. A void Trevor inched closer to with every cry of pain and violent act he witnessed. It was the inevitable, obligatory destination of any paramedic who came to the job with an intact human presence. It was the chill of his soul being eroded.

That morning Trevor didn't remember the drive home. Sweet dissociation behind the wheel was the other unavoidable consequence of fourteen hours of back-to-back calls. But the commuting coma lifted as soon as he pulled into his parking space back home. Trevor dragged his spent body through the door of his unassuming East Vancouver basement suite. He put down his backpack, kicked off his boots and allowed his breathing to relax ever so slightly.

Trevor's home was sparsely decorated and for the most part empty, save for two tattered pieces of furniture and a spindly philodendron in the far corner of the living room. Humble as it was, it was still a far cry from where he had come from. It was clean, it was warm, and there was always food in the refrigerator. Trevor made sure of that much. He had pledged to make his home the antithesis of the filth, despair, and deprivation of his youth. And he was good to his word. The only thing missing now was a dog. But there was a good reason for that.

Trevor could not forget his childhood. Even after being on his own for more than a decade he fought with his past, resisting the memories that pressed on his consciousness. For Trevor, falling into yesterday was all too easy. And there was no such thing as self-induced amnesia. So, over time, he developed a coping strategy. Trevor convinced himself the best way to forget yesterday, would be to create a today bearing no resemblance to it. That involved declining all invitations to stroll down memory lane, hence, no dog. Trevor reasoned if he could forget, he could finally be free. His logic was sound. But putting the theory into practice proved impossible. Too often all it took was a vaguely reminiscent noise or circumstance to throw open the doorway to his former, miserable existence, to the past he had been trying to bury for years. The worst culprits were simple odors. The smell of fresh rain, usually the stuff of poetry, was the sort of trigger that propelled him back to those miserable bygone days. And last night's shift had been littered with ugly nostalgia.

As a consequence of those sounds and smells, Trevor needed help assuaging not only his anxiety but also the ensuing chill. His first stop was the kitchen where he had his sights set on a half-full bottle of vodka sitting on an otherwise empty countertop. He slopped several generous fingers worth into a coffee mug that did double duty, vodka before sleep, caffeine after.

With bottle and mug in hand, Trevor sauntered wearily into the living room and plunked himself down into an overstuffed armchair that was older than he was. A decaying telephone book supported its front corner in lieu of a missing leg, broken off a generation ago. The upholstery was dark brown, which spoke to Trevor's practicality because it hid stains nicely. He really didn't give a shit what it looked like, the chair's high back and sides wrapped around him perfectly, embracing him and providing an innate sense of protection. The fact it was comfortable was all that mattered. Several mouthfuls later, the vodka had worked its magic, giving Trevor's exhaustion permission to take over. Letting down his guard, he sank into the timeworn cushions and luxuriated in the sanctuary of his modest home. Gulping another dose of self-medication, he muttered to himself, "Ahhh...Breakfast of champions."

Albeit temporary, Trevor savored the relief from the chaos of last night's shift. Without a break he had gone from one call to the next, tending to a variety of overdoses, stabbings, and psychoses. For fourteen long hours, he had had a front row seat viewing a relentless parade of people at their worst. Every single call challenged both his medical and interpersonal skills. Thank God he had spent the shift with Wendy.

Though Trevor hadn't always felt this way about his current partner. Oh, quite the contrary. Gratitude had certainly not been his first response. You see, Wendy's reputation had preceded her: mouthy, aggressive and annoying, your basic bitch. So, when she transferred to the station as his new partner, let's just say Trevor was less than happy about it. Recoiling at his predicament with a knee-jerk reaction, he went whining to his fellow male paramedics. "You gotta be out of your fucking mind to want to work with a woman. And now I gotta work with *her*? Fuck!"

Trevor automatically believed her rumored reputation and had assumed she couldn't handle the job's physical or intellectual demands. She was female, and therefore, he predicted she was incompetent. But Trevor's greatest fear was she would jeopardize his safety by pissing off their clientele, thereby making him a target of retribution. Until he actually worked with Wendy, Trevor was blissfully unaware of how much prejudice he was an unwitting accomplice to.

At the beginning of their partnership, Trevor had tested her repeatedly. Generally, he didn't trust women, and this one needed thorough vetting. Though Wendy always managed to pass every bullshit, next-to-impossible task he sent her way. It was what her entire career had been built on and what Trevor didn't understand. Since the day she graduated, at the top of her class, Wendy's daily reality was straightforward;

be at least twice as skilled as any male to garner any semblance of acceptance, never mind respect.

But as the shifts passed and they worked several serious calls together, one by one Trevor's preconceptions and doubts fell away. He came to realize she knew who she was and loved what she did. On top of it, Wendy was a talented paramedic. Eventually, "mouthy, aggressive and annoying" morphed into erudite, passionate and steadfast. And it hadn't taken long before Trevor could see exactly how smart she was. Wendy's secret weapon was her logic, which fueled an intimidating intelligence; a well-honed sword she wielded, as she saw fit, according to her moral compass, no one else's. Understand, if she knew she was right, there was no way she would let it go. This hardwired sense of right and wrong drove her to be a vehement patients' advocate, a trait that Trevor had never seen in any other paramedic. Wendy's motto was straightforward. "I'm not pro this or pro that. I'm anti-stupid."

It took several months to earn Trevor's respect, but more importantly, she won his trust. That was huge. Hell, why wouldn't he trust her? Her balls were clearly bigger than his and most of their peers. This made Trevor realize the likely reason why Wendy's male coworkers so despised her. *They* envied *her* penis. She was a strong, competent woman in a man's domain. Translation: she wore a permanent target on her back. Watching firsthand, Trevor became appalled at how much nasty abuse she endured. Everything from name-calling, to threats and physical shoves. So, by necessity, the "bitch" stood up for herself. On a good day, Wendy's workplace was sexist, though most days it was just plain old-fashioned misogynistic.

Although Trevor would never admit it to himself, Wendy was a force to be reckoned with, which was likely why they worked so well together. Their medical skills were equal, but Trevor avoided conflict at all costs. Wendy, however, did not. To be clear, she never looked for a fight or picked one just for the sake of fighting. On the contrary, she chose her battles quite carefully. But the conflicts Wendy did engage in were always meaningful to her. Deep down Trevor admired that about her and secretly wished he could do the same. Since dropping the fire poker, conflict always overwhelmed him, rendering him nauseated. Not only did Trevor learn a great deal about himself by watching Wendy in action, but he also lived vicariously through her.

Three years had passed since their pairing and much to Trevor's surprise he grew to like her–a lot. Yet, he was unprepared to acknowledge his growing fondness. Ironically, after all his initial misgivings and bigoted rants, he now dreaded working shifts with anyone else. But tonight she would be there, and that fact gave Trevor a great deal of peace.

In the meantime, Trevor sat cradled in his favorite chair physically and emotionally exhausted and pondering his work schedule, *Three shifts down, one more to go.* Tonight was going to be just as hectic and Trevor needed to be back at the station, rested and ready for action, in less than nine hours. The remaining vodka found itself inhaled, spurred on by a singular imperative echoing in his head. *I gotta get as much sleep as I can before tonight.*

Chapter 11
Meanwhile...
Vancouver's Downtown Eastside

A singular imperative echoed in Mary's head. *I gotta get as much sleep as I can before tonight.* But, here it was still light outside, and she was still awake. She had managed to doze off and on for a couple of hours. The real barrier to sleep was the pain that woke her.

Struggling to roll over, she groaned before thinking, *Damn johns. Isn't it enough I do everything they want?* Apparently not, this last one had used a beer bottle.

True to her nature, Mary relied on humor to shrug off her unappealing work. *How many ways are there to suck a dick anyhow?...I guess I should've asked him to show me how it's done,* she mused, chuckling to herself while imagining the scene she had conjured.

At last, Mary settled into a position that caused her the least discomfort and once more attempted to court sleep. She let out a sigh and began drifting off.

The sheets she lay on were covered in blood, mostly hers. In the grand scheme of things, it hadn't been a lousy night, even though the last john had substituted a beating for payment. Mary was alive, hadn't overdosed and had a place indoors to sleep. Measured by the yardstick of the Downtown Eastside, life was pretty damn good, at least for the time being.

Through partial awareness and half closed eyes, Mary stared at the cracked and stained plaster ceiling. The accommodation hadn't changed much since the rooming house was built in 1895. Its original purpose was to house a robust population of transient, seasonal workers, loggers and fishermen mostly. The cubbyhole rooms had only space enough to harbor the most basic furnishings. A metal-framed single bed, a hot plate sized table, one wooden chair and a sink that looked like it was shrunk in the wash. Measuring a cramped ten feet by eight feet, they were the budget motels of their day with just enough room for sleeping and whoring. But with the transom windows long since smashed and boarded up, and countless layers of paint obscuring the once decorative millwork typical of the era, these rooms were now the lairs of the modern-day poor.

It took a while, but finally, Mary slept and dreamt; it was her only real escape. But it wasn't to last. From deep within her, an alarm sounded. Remembering what day it was Mary awoke with a start and a fresh sense of purpose. "I'd better get my ass out of bed."

Fighting against the pain, she rolled off the sagging mattress and onto the cold, peeling linoleum floor.

It was Tuesday, one of two days of the week that really mattered. The other was Sunday. But today was the day Mary went to buy groceries for Marjorie, her elderly neighbor who lived in the adjacent room. Mary had offered to do this for the old woman after she fell and broke her hip a few months earlier. As a result, the senior's mobility was impaired, and the injury was taking its time to heal. Mary never considered this to be a chore, but an honorable, sacred duty. She had learned Father's lesson well. He had taught her to take care of the elders. This humble act of service also did wonders to prop up Mary's self-esteem. It may also have been the universe's way of slowing Mary down on her path of self-destruction.

At first glance, the friendship between the two women seemed improbable. Mary, a drug addict, who turned tricks to support her habit and Marjorie, a former domestic servant and English war bride, who'd been widowed twenty years ago. But in reality, they shared a great deal in common, much more than a casual observer might imagine. Fundamentally, they were both members of the sisterhood of marginalized women whom society didn't value. Despite their divergent backgrounds, their fondness had grown for each other over the last decade. Today, each prospered from a relationship that had been cultivated over untold cups of Earl Grey tea, always served alongside a generous helping of each other's kind spirit and sharp wit. Consequently, the friendship now rested soundly upon mutual respect.

However, respect was not about to stop Marjorie from worrying when Mary went on her "dates." Mary's profession was not a secret to the senior, and though they never spoke of it directly, Mary knew that she knew. Marjorie never commented, except to implore Mary to take safety precautions. Though it was Marjorie's complete lack of judgment, moral and otherwise, that had drawn Mary to the woman in the first place. In Mary's world, a kind, accepting soul was a rare and precious thing.

Marjorie was a tiny woman, whose physical size belied the capacity of her heart. She was also the building's indisputable matriarch and the unofficial glue that held the framework of that little village together. To those who subsisted in that microcosm of shabby, time-forgotten surroundings, she was the grounding force. Her presence was always light, cheerful and accepting, but certainly not naïve. She loved her neighbors and showed it by setting and maintaining strict boundaries. Make no mistake, wake her up at three o'clock in the morning and you'd hear about it. But she was one of those folks who could tell you where to go and have you look forward to the trip. Yet above all else, she was forgiving. And that most people in the building called her Mom, was a fact not lost on her. She was the magnet of unconditional love that bound the building's denizens together by setting the standard for living within its walls. And in the strangest of ways, this kept the destructive nature of street life from completely consuming those apartments. White or Indian, gay or straight, pensioner or hooker, addicted or clean, the community of folks dwelling within would rather die than disappoint Marjorie. The compelling influence of Motherhood, implied or otherwise, should never be underestimated.

So, with her duty in mind, a stiff Mary limped over to the ancient porcelain sink. Forcing herself upright, she peeked at her face in the cracked mirror hanging precariously on the plaster wall. Her left eye, sporting an ugly shade of eggplant purple, was almost swollen shut and her battered reflection shocked her. "Shit!"

Mary allowed her fingers to delicately explore the injury before commenting aloud. "Didn't feel like I got walloped that bad."

The bruised face staring back at her was an inevitable hazard of her job, a tragic fact to which Mary had long ago resigned herself. Most of the time, she worked when she was high. Understand the heroin had a twofold effect. It helped to make the degrading acts she performed more bearable, and it killed the pain of the beatings she received all too often as payment.

Mary leaned over the sink, waiting for the stained basin to fill with the cold, and only water supplied in her room and began gingerly washing her face. With the last remnants of dried blood wiped away, she put the kettle on for a cup of tea. Easing herself into the creaky chair that sat below the small window, she waited for the water to boil. Mary cupped her hands around the kettle's base, trying to warm herself while peering outside, eager for a glimpse of the familiar snow-capped North Shore Mountains.

Chapter 12
Late Summer 1968
Straight of Georgia

George rubbed his arms, trying to warm himself while peering over the bow of the boat, eager for a glimpse of the familiar snow-capped mountains. But instead, his eyes discovered a strange new vista revealing itself in the early morning light. George had never been this far away from his home, and he kept wondering, *Where are my mountains?* Unbeknownst to George, his mountains were several hundred miles away.

That morning the sea had a mirror-like calm, reflecting a ghostly pink hue from the mist above where the dawn's light sprang forth. A pale blue horizon merged seamlessly with the sky and the water, creating dazzling purple highlights that danced on the light ocean ripples. But soon the exquisite colors faded into bright daylight, exposing an alien panorama. The new landscape felt peculiar to George. Though foreign, it held its own wild beauty. Instead of tall green peaks, he found himself surrounded by islets of fissured gray bedrock covered in sporadic blankets of green and yellow lichen. And struggling to grow from the rock's shallow cracks were spindly, orange-barked trees with green oval leaves and deformed limbs tilting permanently leeward from the violent winter gales.

The morning sun continued burning away the marine fog, further exposing the exotic setting. The increasing light allowed George see the faint outline of a point of land wearing a familiar shade of green in the near distance, giving rise to a hopeful thought; *Maybe I'm not too far from home after all.* But the boat sped on, and George's hopes plunged.

Disappointed, George tried escaping back to sleep, to no avail. Before daybreak he had dozed for a few hours, lulled somewhat by the monotonous rumble of the boat's engine. Though in reality, he had only slept because the daunting experience had left him exhausted.

That night, the ominous craft had made several stops on its oppressive pilgrimage, each with the same outcome. Another terrified child rounded up and dumped onto the boat's deck. George relived his nightmare with every addition to Sergeant's pitiful cargo. At ten years old, he was by far the oldest of the human freight. The youngest were twin girls from his reserve. They were barely four. Other than to threaten the children occasionally if they whimpered or cried Sergeant had left them alone during their voyage. Now, after having journeyed throughout the moonless night, the new orphans found themselves approaching a wharf jutting out from a barren, gray bedrock island.

Standing on the dock, awaiting the boat, were several people dressed in long black robes. George had never seen such people before and to him, they looked like specters. From what George could see, there were two types, those whose heads were covered by a flowing black veil with a white stripe, gender unknown. And the others, obviously male, who had white collars and bare heads. George prayed these people would be kinder to him than his current captor. But the instant his eyes met the lead specter's icy stare that wish evaporated.

Sergeant guided the boat alongside the berth, and at last, the diesel engines went silent. He wasted no time grabbing each child in turn and heaving them onto the dock like sacks of potatoes. Once they landed on the pier, most of the little waifs were crying. Some were bleeding again, their fresh wounds having opened up from the rough treatment. But even a frightened, bleeding child did not stop the specters from chastising the new arrivals. George didn't understand the specter's words, but he couldn't mistake their menacing demeanor. Though still letting out the occasional sniffle, he stopped himself from crying by wrapping his arms around his chest and staring at his feet.

Frightened as he was, George's curiosity remained intact. For a split second, he peeked past the shoreline and beyond the adult's intimidating glares. That was when he first saw it, the monstrous red bird made of stone.

The red brick school had three distinctive parts. A central, taller section that pushed out from its two adjoining annexes, which flanked the center on either side. All George saw was a dominating structure complete with head and wings. Its red skull possessed lifeless windows resembling fierce eyes that seemed to leer down on him. Below those empty eyes, a large wooden set of double doors framed a hungry mouth where its tongue emerged as the narrow gravel pathway to the dock. George was filled with dread and got queasy from the idea they were going to being led up the walkway directly into its imposing craw. The edifice secreted a ravenous hunger that frightened George, and he feared if he entered, he would be swallowed up forever. He was right. The goal of assimilation had begun. His induction into the Plint Island Indian Residential School was nigh. A curt snarl from one specter snapped George's attention back, and they began their forlorn march. Like a funeral procession, the black robes herded the little ones straight into the jaws of the great stone bird.

Inside, the children were immediately marched to the shower room. The objective: disinfect the little savages. The decontamination process started with confiscating and burning all the little heathens' possessions. That meant everything. Including clothing adorned with painstakingly hand-stitched beadwork. Into the fire they went, thereby obliterating all tangible ties to their families. George saw what was happening. Standing there naked and holding his clothes, he reached into his coat pocket and grabbed Frog just before they ripped his clothing from his hands. George realized he was clutching contraband. He tried hiding the little figurine, but his actions had not gone undetected. A hooded specter marched up to George.

Shoving her open hand in George's face, the nun commanded, "Let me see that!"

Not understanding a word of what she had said, George simply stood there.

She scowled, motioning for George to show her what he was hiding. He had no choice. Grudgingly he opened his grasp, revealing Grandfather's craftsmanship. The sight of the little cedar carving cradled in his palm must have scorched her eyes because she screamed, "No! No! No! You will not worship satanic idols here!"

Her arm swooped down, slapping George's face so hard he became momentarily dazed. By the time George regained his senses, Frog was off to meet the same fiery fate as all the other children's belongings. Either by accident or design, her violent outburst served to intimidate the little throng into an instantaneous, fear-based submission. And that submission would turn out to be their best survival strategy.

A cruel assembly line formed next where the little sinners' hair was cut off. Each braid hacked from its owner's head was tossed away with audible disgust. George's people only cut their hair when someone close to them died. For George, having his braid lopped off meant someone in his immediate family was gone.

"Do you know who it is?" a frantic George asked in Nuxalt'mc.

He asked again, "Alhnapicwa Waks? Waks?"

"Get over there!" yelled a specter pointing to the shower stalls.

"Twa! Alhnapicwa Waks?"

The hooded specter cuffed George's ear. He winced and raised his arm to protect himself. She tried slapping him again, but George ducked. This time she grabbed his ear and dragged him to the shower stalls. He still didn't know who had died.

The nun shoved George towards another of her kind who was waiting with a stiff-bristled brush and a bucket of ice-cold water. She scrubbed George relentlessly. This particular hooded specter scolded him the whole time she scrubbed him, grumbling "filthy Indian" repeatedly. In fact, she said it so often, George presumed she was frustrated because his skin remained the same color even after all that scouring. When she was done with him, his skin was raw.

The final phase of initiation entailed them donning different clothing. Gray in color, ill fitting and threadbare. Any sense of individuality, but especially cultural identity, had been stripped away. The first lesson on "How to Be White" was complete.

In the days and weeks following, George struggled to adjust to his new life and its bleak surroundings. He understood almost nothing that was said to him and was beginning to forget what it was like to be warm and to have a full belly. Since arriving, he had been shivering almost nonstop, and though he had eaten what was put in front of him, it wasn't enough, and he was always hungry. George was housed with the rest of the children in large, unheated, gender-segregated dorms. A few fearless little souls crawled into bed with one another for warmth; only attempting this reckless and severely punishable act well after the lights went out.

However dreary and desolate this place was, it did offer something of value to George. The friendship of a boy named Joey. He and George were the same age, but Joey was considerably smaller. Three years prior Joey had arrived at Plint Island the same way as George, and the physical toll of his short incarceration showed in his gaunt cheeks. Joey was also the only person who spoke George's language.

Compared to the words the specters spoke, George much preferred the rhythmic tones of his own language. It reminded him of his family, of where he came from–of who he was. But Joey panicked as soon as he heard George speak. "Shhh! You can't talk like that, or they'll punish you real bad," Joey warned.

George stared at Joey and told him he didn't understand. "Axw alhnapits wa stl'yuk-nuts."

Joey sighed and looked all around to be certain they were alone before repeating his warning, this time in hushed Nuxalt'mc. Now George understood. He had already been cuffed about the ears for talking; he just never put the two together. It wasn't *that* he was talking, it was *how* he was talking. George tried to understand why it was wrong for him to speak the words of his ancestors because it didn't make any sense to him not to. So, he kept asking Joey the same question, over and over, "But why can't I speak my words?"

Joey's reply was always the same. "Because if you don't stop, they'll punish you real bad."

That wasn't a satisfactory answer to George. He wanted to know why he shouldn't speak Nuxalt'mc. He continued pressing the issue until Joey showed him what could happen. Joey opened his mouth and stuck out his tongue, revealing a partially healed, gaping wound. As punishment for speaking what those fine Christians called "the devil's language," the nuns had held Joey down while a priest hammered a large nail through his tongue.

On seeing Joey's tongue, the color drained from George's face, and he abandoned his search for a logical explanation. From that moment forward, George kept his mouth shut, his words falling silent in front of priests and nuns.

Even despite the risks, the young allies still spoke their own words, but only late at night. In daring, hushed whispers, they each recounted the stories of their Grandparents. George always recited his favorite, the story of Raven the legendary light bringer. An epic adventure about a big black bird who brought light to a cold, dark world. George could only imagine the nuns' reaction to a story like that. He knew the punishment for such blasphemy was severe, including everything from beatings to being forced to stand outside all night in his underwear. But the stories soothed him, and to George, it was worth the gamble.

The next lesson George learned, he learned perfectly. And it served him well. He learned they wouldn't hit him if he always answered "Jesus," even if he didn't buy it. Regardless of what his keepers said about Jesus being love, it seemed to George Jesus was a pretty angry guy. If Jesus was supposed to be so loving, he reasoned, why were his representatives mad all the time? George may have only been ten years old, but he knew hypocrisy when he saw it.

For a young boy who is cold, hungry, and basically punished for breathing, time moves slowly. *It feels like I've been here forever,* George thought. But it was just late September. After being at the school for a little more than a month, George was already losing hope, until one afternoon.

George spied her from across the open field, standing near the wharf. The sight of her halted him in his tracks. He held his breath. *Could it be?* he wondered. George knew better than to yell at her. Instead, he pretended to ignore her while moving nonchalantly closer to where she and the other girls were hanging laundry to dry. He could hear his heart pounding in his ears. Inching closer, his desperate eyes sought hers. *Please look at me!*

Mary must have felt the intensity of his silent plea. Looking to her left, she was astonished to see her little brother and his riveted gaze. A sea of mixed emotions engulfed her: happiness at seeing George, remorse because he was here, and enormous guilt for not having been home to protect him. She muddled through her reactions quickly. With a furtive glance she nodded at George to follow her, she prayed at a respectable distance, to the school's far wing where the bathrooms were. Girls and boys were not to be seen together, ever.

George slunk into the dark alcove that preceded the entrance to the boy's bathroom and fell into the first loving hug he had received since leaving home. It caught him by surprise. Melting into his sister's embrace, he couldn't help but start crying. Mary whispered in Nuxalt'mc, "Shhh, my little Georgie. We have to be careful. If they catch us, they will send one of us away."

Heeding Mary's words, George pulled himself together, and the siblings managed a fervent conversation in all but silent murmurs.

Mary said, "You must learn the white words as fast as you can. And you have to keep pretending you don't know me."

George's eyes were brimming with tears. "When do we get to go home?"

Mary had no answer except for her expressionless eyes. Until he saw the look on Mary's face, George didn't think his heart could sink any further. He was wrong.

Reaching her arms to her little brother and hugging him tightly Mary said, "We can't meet like this again. It's too risky."

The pair parted less than five minutes after their clandestine reunion, avoiding being caught together. Their meeting had shocked, yet buoyed, both of them. Reuniting with Mary gave George hope he could survive this place, though it did nothing to lessen his suffering. That night while lying in bed and shivering under the tattered, moth-eaten sheets, George was single-mindedly trying to figure out how he could steal some extra food.

Lying in the cot next to him, Joey must have read George's mind. "I can't take it anymore. We gotta get some food."

George didn't know how to do that. Instead, he closed his eyes, hoping a good dream would overtake him. George tried to sleep, but his consciousness lingered, tormented by the sounds of the youngest ones crying from hunger.

Chapter 13
Twenty-Two Years Later - Autumn 1990
The Roosevelt Hotel
Vancouver's Downtown Eastside

George tried to sleep, but his consciousness lingered, tormented by the sounds of the youngest ones crying from hunger. Whenever he closed his eyes, it was all he could hear. Falling asleep sober was impossible. The one thing that squelched the crying ghosts was booze, and lots of it. All the same, sleep still evaded him most nights. Last night he had managed three or four hours, but this morning he was still dead tired. So, George made one last attempt to drift off. The sagging mattress squeaked as he rolled over, faced the cracked plaster wall and prayed for sleep's sweet respite to overtake him.

It was six a.m. and except for the muffled sounds of scurrying rats in the walls, the Roosevelt Hotel's corridors were silent, its denizens having already stumbled home from another evening's chaos of drugs and booze. These were considered the fortunate ones because they had shelter. But in this context, "shelter" was an exceptionally loose term.

The building hadn't always been this way. In its heyday at the dawn of the twentieth century, the Roosevelt Hotel, known then as the Graycourt, was considered state-of-the-art lodging. Sitting in the former heart of Vancouver and built with the finest of materials, the narrow five-story structure enjoyed a bathroom on every floor and rooms complete with a sink, window, and transom. She even boasted an elevator whose glistening brass cage gently lifted her guests to their quarters. Or, choosing to walk up to your room, a magnificent staircase guided your journey, fashioned from thick Carrara marble, flanked on the open side by decorative ironwork that was topped by a sturdy oak handrail. The same rich marble covered the opposing wall, rising four feet high and crowned by medallions of delicately hand-carved oak dogwood flowers.

When the bygone guests reached their floor, their feet glided upon a river of countless, tightly knit, snow-white octagonal tiles flowing down the long passageways, resembling a rink that beckoned them to lace up their skates. A narrow margin of polished ebony tiles contained the long white river on either side, lending a refined tuxedo-like quality to the floors. At every room's entrance hung a sturdy wooden door hewn from ancient Douglas fir and fitted with ornate brass knobs shimmering in the glow of electric light. In those early days, the entire building had oozed class and civility, surrounding her first guests with graceful artisanship.

Though within a decade, the fashionable part of Vancouver had moved elsewhere and the neighborhood, including the Roosevelt, began its slow, inevitable slide into decay. Her elevator hadn't worked since the late sixties, and the stairway's resultant overuse had made the marble treads seem to sag, worn down by countless footsteps. Year by year, the hand-carved oak dogwoods surrendered their fine detail to repeated layers of cheap paint. The most recent color, a putrid turquoise, made them look more like cancerous growths than expertly sculpted decorations. The once glistening hallways were now mostly bare wood, pockmarked by a few remaining bits of porcelain. Lining the stinking aisles was a hodgepodge of cheap replacement doors whose transoms had long since been smashed and boarded up. Nowadays the lath plaster walls, reeking from years of accumulated filth, provided better shelter for the vermin and cockroaches than the building's human occupants, whom they vastly outnumbered.

Those poor souls who called the Roosevelt home relinquished their shelter allowances every month in exchange for shamefully inadequate housing, resulting from chronic and willful neglect. Each room's miniature sink hadn't worked for more than a generation. Of the original five bathrooms in the building, three hadn't functioned for twenty years. The single toilet on George's floor stopped working six months ago, which meant the building currently had one working toilet and bathtub for more than fifty people. Housed like animals, people defecated in the hallways. Tenants subsisted at the mercy of their parsimonious landlords who had no incentive to make repairs of any kind. Who was going to make them? After all, this was where Vancouver kept its human discards. "Survival of the fittest" was the canon that fed the prevailing social attitude of, *If they don't like it, they can go sleep on the streets*. Many chose to do just that, routinely enjoying better sanitary conditions outside in the alleyways. But be it alley or slum, there was never a vacancy in either place.

Another day loomed at the Roosevelt, another six a.m. All was quiet within the forlorn building except for the occasional rat darting down her fetid passageways.

George continued tossing and turning while the crying voices boomed incessantly in his head. The soundtrack had played all night. Still, he persevered courting that elusive stranger called slumber. But morning had dawned, and George recognized any further attempts to sleep as futile. He surrendered his pursuit and resigned himself to getting out of bed. Opening his eyes wide he drew in a deep breath, exhaling gradually and mentally preparing himself for the journey away from his room. Through the wavy, cracked glass of his window, George watched the light breaking over the city. Soon, hordes of office workers would start streaming into the metropolis. *Oh well. If I get up now, maybe I'll get a good spot to panhandle.* Whatever he told himself, it was still hollow consolation for chronic insomnia.

Rolling out of bed, George gathered up his clothes and arranged them on his drooping bed for efficient dressing. He worked from left to right: three T-shirts, one tight fitting pair of khakis, a larger pair of blue jeans, two pairs of wool socks and a pair of discarded high-top work boots he had rescued from the trash. Starting with the T-shirts, he clad himself in layers and struggled only when pulling the blue jeans over top of the khakis. Last week he had "scored" a well-fitting pullover sweater, which he ably donned over the three T-shirts, followed by an old wool overcoat that he chose purposely for being two sizes too large. Topping off his ensemble was a previously discarded baseball hat whose team insignia was obscured by filth. It wasn't that the weather called for such thermal precautions, George simply valued what little he owned. Wearing his entire wardrobe was necessary stratification. He knew if he left anything in his room, the feeble door lock could never guarantee his things would still be there when he returned. For all practical purposes, he was homeless.

While wrestling into his overcoat, a worrisome thought surfaced. George realized he had already drunk the last mouthful of rice wine he had bought last night. His head dropped, and he groaned through his fatigue, "Shit."

So, in an all too familiar mix of disappointment and resignation, he forced a smile, gave out a weary sigh and mumbled, "Well, I guess I'd better hurry up and get to work."

It was unusual, but this morning George actually felt hungry. But that would have to wait. If he didn't get a drink soon bad things would start to happen, uncomfortable, potentially life-threatening things; otherwise known as the scourge of withdrawal. George couldn't count how many withdrawal seizures he had had over the years. The worst part about the seizures was how vulnerable they made you. When you had one, you never knew what people would do to you, or where you might wake up, sometimes in detox, sometimes in hospital–sometimes robbed. All of which made this morning's mission self-evident. Get a bottle and get it fast.

The last item to accompany George was his carving kit; four blades of varying styles inside a beat-up leather case whose zipper only closed halfway. It had taken George years to collect just those few blades, and it was his one valued possession. It was also the one delicate link to who he was. *I can't forget you,* he thought grabbing the sheath and wedging it between his coat and sweater.

Just as George finished zipping his overstuffed figure into his overcoat, he spied a pair of giant cockroaches hiding in a darkened corner. *Aww, jeez.* At first disgusted, his reaction promptly morphed into one of compensatory amusement. "Oh, hey Spot, hey Rover. Wow, you guys got big enough to guard this place. Would you do that for me? Yeah? Thanks. Okay, have a good day."

After bidding his repugnant sentries farewell, George readied himself to wade through a minefield of excrement in the hallway. Stepping carefully outside his room, he used his full weight to wrench on the warped door until it closed. Once it wedged shut, he plunged his hand through his many layers to fish out the key that dangled on a shabby string around his neck. George grabbed the key quickly, but his newly trembling hands fumbled with the door's padlock, underscoring how time was running short.

He trudged down the eight flights of stairs to the street below and hurried out of the building's enclave to avoid the oppressive stench of stale urine. Taking a sharp right onto Hastings Street, he kept a surprisingly brisk pace towards his intended piece of sidewalk. Dark clouds were gathering overhead, and George thought he smelled rain coming. It didn't matter, be it rain from the skies or sweat from his wardrobe, he would get soaked either way. Upon reaching some prime real estate, he sat on the pavement and swallowed another generous portion of his dignity. Within a couple of hours after placing his grungy baseball hat on the concrete, he had amassed enough nickels and dimes to exchange for a few more seizure-free hours. He didn't dawdle.

With the harbingers of withdrawal biting at his heels, a shaky George shuffled off to a dingy market two blocks away in Chinatown, whose vendor traded primarily in seizure relief. There he could barter the two dollars in his pocket for a bottle of rice wine; a clear, heavily salted cooking wine with an alcohol content greater than forty percent. It was cheap and accessible. But it tasted foul. Though it wasn't as nasty as some of the alternatives: Lysol, aftershave or rubbing alcohol. But when all was said and done, it staved off withdrawal, halting the seizures as effectively as Napoleon brandy.

With a tight grip on his purchase, George stepped out of the market and basked in the tremendous sense of relief flooding his body. Lingering was not an option, and he left Chinatown as quickly as he had entered it, knowing he had worn out his welcome as soon as his money was spent. But George didn't waste his steps. On his way back to Hastings Street, he stopped in an alley behind one of the Chinese bakeries to inspect its dumpster. As if it were a newborn, George placed his new bottle carefully on the ground away from harm before ascending the garbage bin. "Don't you go anywhere. I'll be right back."

Luckily, the dumpster was full, and George struck pay dirt, or rather, pay pastry. "All right!" He crooned lifting a small cardboard tray and its contents from the top of the heap before descending back to the pavement a happy man. So far, George's day was shaping up to be an exceptional one.

Thanks to his multilayered attire, he bent over awkwardly to inspect his treasure. He was ecstatic and stuffed several of the less moldy pastries into his overcoat pockets without delay. Retrieving his bottle George prepared to leave the alleyway, helped along by the local merchant's disapproving glares. He was just grateful they hadn't thrown garbage at him this time or chased him away with a broom like a rabid pigeon.

Walking further up the alley, the clouds broke apart, and George noticed some faint warmth on his face. Pausing, he looked skyward and sighed with contentment.

Yup, today is going to be a good day indeed, he thought.

Once he had cleared the gauntlet of contemptuous stares, George set his mind to the morning's last essential task. The first chance he got, he ducked behind another dumpster in an adjacent alley and at the makeshift altar of his no-win situation, he consecrated his addiction. Steadying his tremulous hands, he cracked open the bottle and took a deep breath before gulping down several vile mouthfuls from its slender neck. Getting drunk was not his goal. George hated that feeling. For him, drunkenness was an unwelcome side effect. The revolting liquid was a straightforward means to an end, a way to stop the constant barrage of voices, images, and memories plaguing him.

Having met his day's objective, George's frenetic pace slowed dramatically. He was content for the moment knowing he was not going to have a seizure. With little else on his agenda, he pointed himself towards Oppenheimer Park and, figuratively speaking, a bench with his name on it. He even took the time to watch the skies along his way. Thus far, the clouds had only gathered enough to block the sunshine, no rain yet.

Invigorated from this morning's good fortune, George maintained his buoyant disposition, wandered up Dunlevy Street and saw from a distance his favorite park bench was unoccupied. The bench faced east, protected from the sun by the seventy-year-old chestnut trees lining the park's one block perimeter. The long-standing sentinels marked an invisible corral where society tolerated their less-desirables and their vices. The trees' colors were beginning to change, and the autumn winds had begun to awaken, bringing with them a taste of the chill yet to come.

George plunked himself sloppily, yet purposely, in the middle of his bench. He figured if he were to tip in either direction, the bench would interrupt his fall and prevent him from hitting the pavement below. He thought this a practical strategy and by doing so, hoped to avoid collecting any further scars on his head.

He sat motionless on his bench, clinging to his bottle and sipping from it at regular intervals, grateful for the numbed relief the noxious liquid afforded him. Even though the alcohol never completely silenced the soundtrack in his head, it did help it morph into a homogenous blur of yesterday and today, making the awful recollections stand less contrasted and somewhat more palatable.

Today the wind was from the east and smelled of nothing; just the way George liked it. For him, the smell of the sea was too reminiscent of days gone by. Between sips, he inhaled deeply, one breath after another, savoring the fresh odorless air, like Grandfather had taught him.

So on this crisp fall day, George sat on his bench using what means he had available to subdue his demons. Soon his tactics paid off, and the clamor of traffic became indistinguishable from the sound of leaves rustling in the wind or the voices in his head. Hours passed with occasional sunshine perforating the clouds. And George managed to forget.

It was late afternoon when a siren pierced the veil of George's intoxication. Finding himself vaguely aware of being sprawled on the ground, out of reflex he reached for his bottle. Instead, he found shards of broken glass. He didn't care.

A fellow corral mate staggered over, yelling at George, "I called them...I called them to take you away!...They're...they're gonna take you away!"

Through his stupor, George struggled to comprehend those foreboding words. But his mind's turmoil numbed any attempts at digesting their meaning. A minute or two passed before the message coalesced. That simple phrase had opened the floodgates of panic, and George was sitting directly in its path, helpless and chained to an anchor of fear. He started yelling, vacillating between sorrow and aggression. "No! No! Don't take me away! Don't...don't let them take me away!"

Wendy exited the ambulance and walked over to her patient whom she could tell was upset about something. Though she was unaware it was not of this moment. For safety reasons, she squatted beside George just beyond his arms reach and attempted to make eye contact with him. His head bobbed in her direction, and Wendy smiled. This wasn't the first time she had been called for George. "It's okay George, I'm not gonna take you away."

"I won't...I won't let you take me away!"

Wendy was patient. "No one's gonna take you away, George...Is it okay if we stay right here and talk for a while?"

George began to sense Wendy's presence. Her calm demeanor and tone were reaching through his emotional fog, coaxing him to come to the moment. With a heartbreaking sigh of surrender, George gave one last pathetic objection. "I won't let you...take...me away."

He made a weak fist, more symbolic than threatening and shook it at Wendy, his perceived tormentor.

Maintaining eye contact with George, Wendy smiled. "I'm not stupid George, I know you could whoop my ass."

"You damn right!" he slurred.

"You can stay right here if you want to, okay?"

Her reassurance settled George, and the anger in his voice was replaced by tears rolling down his cheeks. With his head at a drunken tilt, he stared at Wendy, pleading his case in a despairing whisper. "Please...don't...don't take me away."

Wendy's gut told her she was sitting next to a wounded person, someone whose vulnerability was in its rawest condition. Knowing this, she tread carefully. "I don't want to take you anywhere you don't want to go. Okay, George?" she said, giving the comment plenty of time to settle into the space surrounding them.

His fist unclenched.

Wendy began her assessment. "Do you know where you are, George?"

His head wobbled as he looked around. He stared at the ambulance and its flashing lights for a moment before turning back towards Wendy. His tired, bloodshot eyes met hers. She smiled at him again, and he grinned back, having recognized her. "I'm...I'm in heaven...and you're my...my guardian angel."

They both laughed. Wendy was relieved George had let his guard down.

"No, really, where are you?" she asked again.

"I'm...at the park."

"You had anything to eat today George?"

"Nah...I don't remember..."

Pausing, George recalled his morning's prize and reached into his pocket, pulling out a handful of moldy crumbs to display.

"Wow, okay. But when was the last time you had a real meal George?"

"I...I dunno..." he said, his voice trailing off and his face becoming blank.

"Mmm, well how 'bout getting some food from the nuns–"

George became agitated and cut her off. "No, no, no, no, no, no, no!"

Wendy backtracked. "Okay, okay, just a suggestion. Sorry, George."

"It's...it's okay...angels...angels think nuns are good."

"Can I check you out, George? You know, make sure your ticker's still ticking and stuff like that?"

"Yeah. I guess," he mumbled.

During this time, Trevor was standing guard behind the two, at the ready for whatever his partner needed. He knew Wendy could handle herself and he appreciated her ability to defuse tension. They both had the same philosophy; always better to avert a fight than to have to win one. Although when push came to shove, he had seen Wendy take down a guy a lot bigger than she was. Suffice it to say, Trevor was glad she was on *his* side.

While Wendy carried out her medical assessment, Trevor made small talk. "So where you from George?"

George paused before answering.

"Up the coast...Do you...you know Bella Coola?"

"No kidding? That's where my partner's from."

"Really! My...my guardian angel's from...from Bella Coola?"

"Sure am. You from the rez up there?" she asked.

Right away George's eyes welled up with tears, and his tenuous mood threatened to dissolve. "Yeah...Before...before..."

Wendy pulled the blood pressure cuff from his arm and immediately changed the subject. "Are you still livin' at the Roosevelt?"

The question stopped George from plummeting into emotional turmoil. "Yup...and...and I got Spot and Rover guardin' my place right now."

Wendy grinned, assuming he was facetious. "That's good. You need a roof over your head. Okay, hold still now. I'm gonna test your blood sugar, just a little pin prick on your finger."

"Ouch! Geez...Angels ain't s'posed to bite."

"Sorry George. There, all done. Now, how about a trip up to Detox? A nice warm place to sleep and a sandwich when you wake up? It won't be for long."

George knew the routine. And he knew he didn't really have a choice, but he appreciated at least being asked. It was either Detox or police the drunk tank. Detox was a much safer choice.

"Yeah, sure. It's...it's gonna rain soon anyways."

"Good. We'll call a ride for you," she said, nodding at Trevor to call for the Vancouver police wagon.

Hopefully, the wait for the VPD wouldn't be too long.

"You carving much these days George?" Wendy asked.

"Not...not...too much right now...I got this little one I'm doin'," he said, reaching into his soiled pocket, fumbling to retrieve a small, partly carved figure and handing it to Wendy.

"What will it be when you're finished?"

Looking up at Wendy, George leaned close to her, studying her face. Locking onto her eyes, he answered in a slurred whisper. "It's gonna be Frog...Did you...you know you got Frog medicine?"

His words caught Wendy off guard. She sat there mute, overwhelmed by a rush of memories pouring into her mind. She was trying to regain her composure when the wagon came to a screeching halt beside them. An overweight, unkempt officer of questionable hygiene emerged from behind the wheel. "This my customer?"

Trevor replied, "Yup. Give us a second to get him over there."

"Okay, George, your ride's here. We'll help you walk over there. Easy now," Wendy said.

Flanking George, the paramedics helped him to stand and walk over to the police wagon.

As George was crawling inside the confined space, the cop mocked him. "Another fine taxpaying citizen, eh?"

The portly protector seemed inconvenienced by the whole affair. Slamming the wagon's steel door closed, he narrowly missed George's foot before sauntering back to the driver's seat and muttering under his breath, "Fucking chugs."

He didn't think anyone had overheard him, but Wendy had. And the remark sickened her, though there was little she could do about it.

With the call completed, both partners climbed back into their ambulance. Once inside Wendy asked, "Do you ever wonder why they're like that?"

"Why who's like what?" Trevor mindlessly replied.

"You know, all these Native people down here."

"Who knows. I try not to think about it."

But Wendy pressed on. "And what was all that 'don't take me away' stuff about?"

Trevor wasn't thinking when he let slip, "Maybe he's starting the DTs."

"Oh fuck that, Trevor! If he were d.t.'ing I'd have treated him, and we'd be at St. Paul's already."

Trevor knew he had goofed as soon as those words left his lips. So being unable to ignore the conversation he tried tempering it instead. "Look, I don't know why they're like that, and at this point, I don't really care. You've worked the skids long enough to know that if you take this crap on you won't last down here."

"Well, excuse me for giving a shit."

"Hey, I'm just saying that 'giving a shit' is a slippery slope. If you let this place get into your head, it'll chew you up and spit you out."

A contemplative lull fell over them and the rising tension dissipated. After a few moments, Trevor broke the silence by teasing her. "Besides, I don't feel like breaking in a new partner."

Wendy smiled and pushed back. "Uh, exactly who broke in whom here?"

"Ah, come on, you know I taught you everything you know. Just not everything I know."

"Well, I see the delusions are back. It's like you think you could function on a call without me."

Grinning, Trevor suggested their next stop. "Waterfront?"

"Yeah, sure."

So, by necessary habit, Forty-Eight Charlie drove off to their oasis. It didn't take long before they were parked next to the ocean overlooking Burrard Inlet and the North Shore mountains. Except for the dispatch chatter on the radio, Trevor and Wendy sat in silence, processing the last call and waiting for the next one; mentally preparing themselves to work in this overwhelmingly ugly place by soaking in the beauty before them.

Chapter 14
Autumn 1970
Plint Island Indian Residential School

Nothing could have prepared Mary for such an overwhelmingly ugly place, so devoid of beauty. She ached for her family, her community. She longed for love. Real love, not the kind she was forced to engage in now. Above all, she yearned for Mother's touch, Father's gentleness and Grandfather's kind eyes.

The men came by boat from Vancouver, mostly businessmen with the occasional judge or political figure rounding out the clientele. And they always arrived at night. Whenever Mary was expected to perform, Sister would send her to the shower room and insist she scrub herself clean. She would give Mary a pretty dress to wear and usher her upstairs to a vacant, musty smelling bedroom directly above the priests' apartments. Steeped in a repugnant silence, Mary waited.

The men were always white, and always smelled of liquor. Sometimes they gave some to Mary. She despised the taste almost as much as the men themselves. But once she knew the liquid's effects, she openly welcomed its numbing help. They treated Mary like a piece of meat, soulless, inert and unfeeling. By necessity, Mary became just that. Her first few encounters had been the most repulsive. Initially, she had fought against the damp, clumsy hands that single-mindedly sought to violate her young body in ways that often caused her great physical pain. But it was her spirit that bore the greatest injury; driven away, bit by painful bit by the endless lascivious assaults.

Following each vile encounter Sister scolded Mary. "Get back to your dorm and keep your mouth shut. You filthy whore!"

Mary wasn't allowed to shower afterward, but that didn't really matter. She felt soiled in a way bathing could never cleanse.

One night there were no boats and Mary was left alone in the dorm with the other girls. The littlest ones had always been drawn to Mary's gentle presence. Over time, she took up a de facto mother role and tonight she assumed its mantle once more. You see, earlier in the evening a few of the youngest girls had received beatings for various infractions and were in desperate need of a caring touch. Mary blatantly defied the rules by cradling one of the more severely bruised girls in her arms, rocking her back and forth. In her own language, she sang a song Mother had sung to her when she was small. Mary's soft words filled the room soothing each child, lightening the atmosphere and chasing away the heartbreaking cries and whimpers.

But without warning a bucket of ice-cold water came crashing over Mary's head; another sadistic punishment courtesy of their virtuous caregiver. But Sister wasn't done. Reaching down she ripped the girl from Mary's embrace and hurled her to the ground. Furious and screaming, the nun chased the little one back to her own bed, kicking the little girl as she scrambled across the bare wooden floorboards. Terrified by their angry overseer the dorm erupted with crying and whimpering again.

Triumphant in separating the two little heathens, Sister marched back towards Mary where she lingered, glaring at Mary with an intense disgust. "You *will stop* speaking the devil's words!"

Satisfied with her pious decree, the bride of Christ strolled out of the room leaving Mary to sleep on the waterlogged mattress. There were no dry clothes for Mary to change into. Even if there had been, Sister would never have permitted it. The nun made her exit deliberately slow, her footsteps echoing in that cavernous, desolate chamber, underscoring how forsaken each child felt.

Shivering uncontrollably in the frigid room, Mary curled up into a fetal position and prayed. *Please, Creator, I beg you to help me endure this awful place.* She spent the night sopping wet and cold.

Chapter 15
Twenty Years Later - Autumn 1990
Vancouver's Downtown Eastside

She spent the night sopping wet and cold. The evening's rain was merciless but so was Mary's overpowering need for heroin. Tonight she had been on the stroll for more than two hours with nothing to show for it except the gnawing pangs of withdrawal. Her bones ached from a deeply-rooted fire, a pain so intense it made her want to scream. Nevertheless, Mary only grimaced occasionally, managing to hide her suffering by sheer will alone. In her solitary misery and in spite of regular waves of dry heaves, she forced herself to smile at the men driving slowly past her, leering, judging and choosing.

Mary needed a fix and the sooner, the better. Although for the past year, she had found it increasingly difficult to find a usable vein. Over time, the repeated injections created scar tissue rendering her veins like concrete and therefore useless. If that were not bad enough, she had developed a dangerous problem; an open, weeping abscess in her arm. But this was not Mary's first infection. Addiction inevitably meted out a penalty for fixing in a hurry and in less than sanitary conditions.

With a dissociated smile adorning her face, Mary stared down Cordova Street watching the traffic. She was deep in the throes of her personal hell when she noticed an ambulance driving towards her.

That night it was Wendy's turn to drive and Trevor's turn to attend. Or, if you prefer, Wendy was aiming, and Trevor was maiming. The shift was off to a slow start, and so the crew decided to do a little outreach work with the local sex trade workers. Wendy slowed the vehicle, stopping in front of Mary whose agitated behavior belied her plastic smile.

Trevor rolled down his window and greeted her matter-of-factly. "Hey, Mary. How's it goin'?"

Recognizing them, Mary smiled, happy to see a non-threatening face. "It's goin', you know? How 'bout you guys?"

"We're good. Night's off to a slow start," he said.

"That's good news right?" Mary asked.

"Yeah, except that it means I have to spend more time talking to my partner," he said.

Wendy rolled her eyes.

Mary forced a laugh and said, "Is this what you've got to put up with girl?"

"You don't know the half of it," Wendy said.

"What're you complaining about partner? You always get in the last word," Trevor said.

Wendy replied, "Yup."

"See," Trevor said to Mary.

The teasing helped Mary relax somewhat, albeit imperceptible.

Trevor had already assessed Mary, noticing both her junk sickness and her abscessed arm. So he asked Mary, "How 'bout I take a quick look at that arm for 'ya?"

Mary felt torn. She was both touched by his concern and anxious about losing sidewalk time, which would prolong her suffering. Trevor knew her predicament and tried reassuring her. "I promise I'll be quick, only a couple of minutes."

"Well...Okay...Just don't make me miss any of my regulars."

Trevor didn't hesitate. Sliding out of the front cab, he opened the side doors and motioned for Mary to follow him. "I'll be as quick as I can. Step into my office my dear and get outta this rain."

Mary sat down and wasted no time in presenting her swollen, painful limb to Trevor. He supported her arm as he gently cleaned the open wound. It was evident she was beginning withdrawal, but Trevor felt obliged to tell her the truth about the risks of her infection. He was direct but kind. "I think you need to go to the hospital, Mary. I know that's not what you want to hear but if this abscess bursts, you could get really sick, maybe even die."

Mary protested. "Aw...it's not that bad, is it?"

But Trevor pressed on. "I'm not trying to scare you, but I'm not gonna bullshit you either. This could turn into something quite serious."

"Can't you fix it up for me?" Mary begged.

Trevor shook his head. "Sorry, this needs a doctor."

"How long do you think I'd be up there?"

Trevor answered tactfully, knowing how powerful the heroin's stranglehold was. "Well, a few hours anyway. And you might need to stay for a day or two. It really depends."

That little tidbit was a deal breaker for Mary. "I can't right now...I, I just can't."

Under different circumstances, Mary would have jumped at the chance to get help. But right now, her life was not her own, withdrawal being a more compelling reality. Mary was under the whip of a cruel, unforgiving master named addiction who demanded total allegiance from its indentured servants.

Having no alternative, Trevor confronted the elephant in the room. "You're junk sick, right?"

She laughed nervously before copping to the truth. "Is it that obvious?"

"You're hiding it really well."

With mounting shame, Mary looked at the floor in response.

Trevor understood addiction's all-consuming nature, knowing Mary was at heroin's mercy. So instead of forcing the issue, he counteroffered. "Tell you what. How 'bout I bandage you up, you go get a fix, and then you go to the hospital and take care of your arm?"

Surprised, she said, "Really?"

"Yeah. Really."

Mary was overflowing with relief. "Oh, yes please."

Trevor finished dressing her wound and Mary thanked him in part by spontaneously kissing him on his cheek.

"Thanks a lot...And thanks for not treatin' me like a piece of shit."

Trevor smiled. "You take care of yourself... Promise?"

"Yup, I promise!" she yelled, springing out of the ambulance and jogging back to reclaim her patch of sidewalk.

It took Trevor just moments to clean up the tiny workspace. Once seated up front again, Wendy shifted into drive and waited for a break in traffic. Cautiously she pulled away from the curb as Trevor stared into the mirror, watching Mary's figure recede into the rainy darkness of the night.

Chapter 16
Autumn 1970
Plint Island Indian Residential School

Brother Murphy receded into the darkness of the night as George slunk back his dorm, vigilant to remain unnoticed by the other boys. With stealth, he crept into his cold metal-framed bed and curled up into a tight ball. He wanted to disappear, to become invisible–to escape. Perhaps that was why George felt so numb.

Tonight the dorm was unusually quiet, except for the echoes of Joey's labored breathing and regular coughing fits. He had been sick for two weeks and hadn't eaten for almost as long. And it was taking a worrying toll. As the days wore on his small frame steadily diminished in size and vitality, revealing sunken eyes, which peered out from freshly skeletonized features. The illness weakened him so much he could no longer get out of bed. And he coughed almost continuously. George was sick with worry, yet the nuns didn't seem concerned. George overheard them talking about how Joey had something called TB. George didn't know what TB was, but he was glad when they had pushed their two beds together. The boys didn't understand why the nuns did that. They were just happy to be near to each other without the fear of reprimand.

Settling into his bed and pulling the threadbare sheet over his shoulders, George heard Joey's croaky whisper. "He got you...George...Didn't he?...He got you..."

George's stunned silence confirmed the unthinkable. Since becoming sick, Brother Murphy had left Joey alone.

Between coughing fits and gasping between his words, Joey pleaded with George. "You...gotta...promise me...George...promise me... gotta...get out...tell someone...tell them...promise me...George...promise..."

George was reluctant but felt like he had no choice. "Okay, I promise. I promise." In his core, George didn't want to make the vow. In his heart, George wished he were as sick as Joey.

Laying in that cold, lonely dorm, bereft of all joy, of any sense of safety and having had his body and mind violated in ways he could not have imagined, George began to pray. *Creator, I ask you to let me see Mother and Father again.* It had been three long, painful years since their separation and George feared they wouldn't recognize him.

Desperate, he squished his eyes closed and laid his heart bare. *Jesus, why do you hate us Indian children so much?* It was vital George understood what he had done to deserve this punishment. But he received no answer. So instead, he turned to the ocean. *Grandmother Ocean, please come and swallow up this place. Make it clean.*

George craved release from his suffering, and he frankly didn't care what form it took, emancipation–or death. He begged for relief, by any means. *Grandmothers and Grandfathers, please help me.*

At the exact moment George finished petitioning the universe for mercy, with a final exhalation, the coughing stopped. George opened his eyes to see Grandmother Moon's light streaming through the curtain-less windows, filling the room as if at midday. In the shadows of her gentle glow, he saw Joey's calm, serene face. Closing his eyes again, George pictured Joey's smile, heard his laugh and remembered the glint in his eye. He started sobbing, not as much for Joey as for himself. He would do anything to follow Joey into the Spirit World.

That was when the lingering shreds of George's spirit left him. Flowing from one small niche in his chest, he felt a vacuous deadness gain momentum until it filled every recess of his body. From that moment forward it was that deadness that replaced Joey in George's life. And it would be that deadness, that waking dream of dissociation that would now sustain his existence.

Since that morbid night, the days dragged into weeks, the weeks into months and George had virtually abandoned the notion his body could ever leave this horrible place. And his vow to Joey became a burden that grew heavier with the passage of time, taxing his fragile will to live. Where once a sparkling soul once dwelt, now all George could sense within was a permanent void.

Chapter 17
One Year Later - Autumn 1971
Plint Island Indian Residential School

Where once the hope of growing a sparkling soul once dwelt, now all Mary could sense within was a permanent void. She could see the stitches and feel the burning pain in her belly, yet the nuns hadn't told her anything about the operation, about what they did. All Mary knew was her body felt vastly different and she no longer experienced her moon times. That suited the priests just fine.

The operation was forced on her after her baby had come. They had whisked the child away moments after its birth and Mary wasn't permitted to see it. Stranger yet, she never heard it cry. It didn't live long enough to cry. The nuns made certain of that. They never allowed it to take its first breath. With malignant piety coursing through their moral characters, they took the tiny corpse to the basement and tossed it shamelessly into the furnace along with the rest of the day's garbage.

But Mary had dared to ask, "Is it a boy or a girl?"

Disgusted, the nun snarled, "Stop asking about that bastard child. You are going to burn in hell, you filthy whore!"

Mary loved children and her longing for the future was to have a big family of her own someday. They obliterated that dream when they stole her gift of life-giving. Never having felt more powerless, or worthless, Mary became as dead as her newborn. Numbed to all she experienced, she no longer cared about what they wanted to do to her, or how often.

Even after all the abuse, the repeated violations of her body, the betrayal of trust, after all of it, Mary mustered up one last courageous act of defiance by pledging to save the other girls from the same fate. Making a sacrifice of herself, she fed her body willingly to the dark beasts that lusted after her youthful flesh. And she did so with astonishing frequency. To Mary, it didn't matter anymore; she merely wanted to spare her sisters. Initially, her strategy worked, with her offering greedily consumed. But as Mary grew older, it became impossible to shield the smaller ones; pedophiles crave youth.

So, Mary trudged through the grotesque ordeal of her life with as much emotional distance as she could summon. Time blurred and seasons changed, until one day they stopped coming for her. Barren, used up and discarded like trash, she was all of fifteen.

Since arriving at the brutal school, Mary's dignity had been undermined by institutionalized bigotry. The natural result of the school's pernicious brainwashing was that self-loathing had supplanted the sparkle of her true identity. By design, the toxic curriculum had met its goal of washing away the fertile soil of Mary's self-esteem, replacing it with the bedrock of racial inferiority. The only things keeping suicide at bay were the little ones who surrounded Mary and her primal urge to protect them.

Not surprisingly, Mary slept little. She usually awakened in the middle of the night in a cold sweat with horrific images playing out in her head. Tonight was no different. Hoping to escape the nightmares, Mary slipped out of bed and crept to the window. Staring out at the moonlit grounds, she found it almost impossible to remember the sound of Mother's voice. But she kept trying. From the depths of her being, Mary grasped at the faint memories of Mother's gentleness and soft touch, and her breathing loosened somewhat.

But Mary's reprieve was short-lived. She felt possessed, a captive of her memories. Asleep or awake she dreamt of all the tortured little faces. And now, staring into the night, she heard their whimpers; those hushed, painful cries carried on the salty air. Burdened with the ghosts of a seemingly infinite past, a trancelike Mary found herself in an impregnable and despairing nimbus. Tonight especially, it felt like there was a drop of cold sweat for every terrifying memory.

Chapter 18
Autumn 1990
Vancouver, British Columbia

Tonight especially, it felt like there was a drop of cold sweat for every terrifying memory. Wendy's sheets lapped it up while she fitfully tossed and turned, caught up in an uneasy blend of dream and recent reality. It had only been a couple of hours since she fell asleep and now the nightmares had started up again. It was two a.m.

There wasn't anything Wendy could do to shake the images out of her mind, the little white T-shirt dripping with crimson, and the small blue sneaker clinging to the lifeless foot. Kiddie calls were the worst. But murdered children? Well, that is an evil so perverse it shatters your faith that goodness even exists in the world. Calls like those were like a snakebite whose slow-acting venom poisons your entire being. And its pernicious toxin doesn't diminish with time. Instead, it grows more potent, especially if its host already pulsates with the catalyst of preexisting bitterness. It had been weeks since that heinous call, and since then, the ferocious poison had sought out a foothold in Wendy's psyche.

Tonight, momentarily trapped between asleep and awake, she tried jolting herself out of her slumber's purgatory. Slapping her own face and forcing her eyes wide open, Wendy stared out the window, focusing intently on the torrential rain, her eyes locked onto the streetlamp which illuminated the drops falling fierce and hard. Listening keenly to the water spattering against the asphalt, with every inch of consciousness at her disposal, Wendy willed herself into the moment. She needed solid anchoring to the present if she had any hope of escaping tonight's tormenting onslaught of memories.

Defenseless, and without recourse, she bolted upright in bed with her heart racing and shirt soaked through. Throwing off the covers, she sat motionless on the edge of the mattress for several minutes, sitting on the brink of overwhelm and frozen from the barrage of mixed emotions springing forth from within; anger, disgust, horror–and grief. Tonight's images were especially vivid, and as a result, Wendy felt uncommonly shaky. Her tremors must have beckoned to their kin because just then an uncharacteristic thought perforated her tortured awareness. An outlandish idea so unsettling she became instantly appalled. *I need a drink.*

Ordinarily, the slightest smell of alcohol nauseated Wendy. Yet here she was actually suggesting to herself she have one to calm down. The fact she offered herself such offensive advice was what rattled her most. *Oh, my God! I must be really fucked up for that to have come out of my brain. Jesus!*

And so began the mental tailspin, Wendy was getting anxious about being anxious. On the verge of panicking, she grumbled, "Fuck it." And reached for her running shoes. Maybe she could outrun the flashbacks and the crazy-making anxiety. Maybe she couldn't. But she was damn well going to try.

Maybe it was enough that running helped her keep a firm grasp on her humanity. It definitely helped dissipate the anger she regularly amassed from seeing people at their worst, from watching them do brutal and vicious things to each other. It would have been all too easy for her just to say, "Fuck them. People are assholes. And if you fuckers get yourselves beat up or murdered you probably deserved it." Without a doubt, there had been enough occasions when the cult of misanthropy had come close to convincing her to join. But Wendy kept rejecting the convenient, repulsive invitations, choosing to die rather than betray her own humanity. She was at war with cynicism and wasn't about to give up the coveted ground of her compassion. So to keep from despising her own kind and to lessen tonight's torrents of anxiety, grief, and rage, Wendy fought back the only way she knew how. She went for a run–at two thirty a.m.–in the pouring rain. It was her way of trying to negotiate a truce within herself. And she would run until there was a ceasefire, regardless of how tenuous it felt.

Cynicism was the uniform of hatred's foot soldiers, and thus far, in the battle for her soul, Wendy had refused to wear it.

Chapter 19
Seventeen Years Earlier - Summer 1973
Bella Coola, British Columbia

Cynicism was the uniform of hatred's foot soldiers, and long ago, in the battle for his soul, Sergeant had agreed to wear it. Today, whiskey filled the void where his humanity used to dwell. First, it had been the little bottles, then the big ones. Nowadays, Sergeant wallowed in a river of it whose unpredictable currents swallowed up anyone in its path.

Sixteen-year-old Wendy was forever in the rush of those turbulent waters. When Sergeant wasn't beating Wendy in a drunken rage, he was screaming at her. He called her all sorts of demeaning things. Through his cruel violence, Sergeant blindly chased catharsis and its promise of a perverse salvation. Yet venting the sum total of his childhood beatings onto Wendy gave him no relief. The more he beat her, the less gratifying it was, and the more he reached for the bottle.

Wendy spent as much time as possible elsewhere, away from her home's prison. But there were no lasting means of escape or parole. So, by default, endurance became her sole survival option. And although she didn't know it at the time, another predator was stalking her, about to pounce from out of nowhere.

As Wendy slept soundly one August night, the doorway to a different personal hell was kicked open.

Her slumber shifted suddenly from peaceful dream to living nightmare, startled awake by Stuart's rancid breath hissing against her face. Muffled sounds of panting and moaning filled her room. Struggling, Wendy cried out.

"Stop...stop...no...no...stop...Please...no..."

Stuart responded by laughing with contempt.

"Please...no..."

Wendy continued grappling with him, and what was happening to her. Both were in vain.

After his triumphant fait accompli, he rolled off her and climbed into his trousers. Before strutting from her room, he spat on her. "Fucking slut."

There he left her, befouled, debased and plunged into a cavern of shame.

Wendy spent the remaining hours of darkness imprisoned there, curled up in a ball and rocking back and forth. Eventually, the shock receded in tandem with the breaking dawn. With the fresh light, Wendy broke free of her mental bonds long enough to dress and sprint out of the house towards the ocean. She soon found herself huddled on the beach. It was there, tucked away between two great pieces of driftwood, she wept inconsolably; her tearstained cheeks and contorted face appealing for deliverance. Wendy didn't budge from that spot for the rest of the day.

The sun hung low in the sky, painting the clouds a flaming burgundy when a faint breeze lifted off the water, sweeping softly over Wendy's anguished features. The salty gust was still swirling around her when a state of complete serenity fell over Wendy.

Having no rational explanation for it, she basked in its tranquility; grateful despondency's veil had finally lifted. In the midst of this new peace, Wendy found her gaze drawn downwards. Lying there at her feet, partially buried in the sand, she spied a harmless looking fist-sized rock, though the find would turn out to be anything but innocuous.

What's this? she thought. Picking it up Wendy discovered it molded to her hand perfectly and felt as though it was a natural extension of her arm. Its remarkable qualities captivated her, and she began studying it closely. Made of opaque white quartz, it had a heft to it she hadn't expected but apart from its custom fit its most notable feature was a gnarled clump of razor-sharp barnacles encrusting one side. Numbering more than a dozen, each menacing mini-blade protruded outwards, making the stone resemble a shrunken medieval mace. Wendy sat there mesmerized, cradling the intimidating find and pondering its implications. *I wonder...I bet this could give me a fighting chance.*

All at once, a startling shift occurred. Wendy's long-held helplessness disintegrated, and with its demise, a formidable inner strength revealed itself. Time and place had conspired to reunite Wendy with a long-lost part of herself. And it was just the beginning. That reunion had catalyzed a potent metamorphosis, transmuting her crushing despair into legitimate rage. But more importantly, Wendy realized she did indeed have a choice. That insight made her next decision easy. Rather than abdicating her power, abandoning her dignity or submitting herself for defilement, she renounced victimhood and chose to fight back. She screamed, "Never! Again!" And listened as her resolution echoed out to sea.

She wasn't going to tolerate rape, at least not without one hell of a fight. That evening a galvanized Wendy marched into combat, girded with a steadfast resolve and a tailored weapon. At first touch, the little mace became welded to her hand, and after returning home, Wendy slept with it concealed under her pillow, poised for battle until war broke out. But she was worried. *Jesus, this had better work.* She knew if her plan backfired, Stuart would use the weapon against her. *Fuck it. I'd rather die than be raped every night,* she thought. Her desperate plan was a last-ditch effort to protect herself. And she had armed herself just in time because that night, with vulgar intent, Stuart slunk back into her room. But she was ready.

Wendy lay in wait feigning sleep, her body taut with expectation. Careful to do nothing that would belie her trap, she ignored her deafening heartbeats and the panicked impulse to run, letting the predator get within striking distance. The moment arrived when she could hear the incubus's breath. Fueled by a mix of adrenaline and fury she exploded into action springing from the bed and bludgeoning him.

Slamming her mace into Stuart's head, she cracked his left temple open. Dazed, he staggered backward from the impact. Her ambush worked flawlessly. She pounced again. With every strike finding its mark, Wendy felt the barnacles ripping pieces of his flesh away. She didn't care. With a crimson river streaming into his eyes, Stuart staggered into the wall. He was still teetering when she landed another meat-ripping punch to his jaw. His stance faltered, and he fell to the floor. Wendy maintained her calculated offensive, macerating his bloodied head with repeated blows. "You...fucking...pig!" she cried between punches.

On his knees, Stuart tried shielding himself from the onslaught. But Wendy was unstoppable. Lost to her mission, she would never accept surrender–only annihilation. She was tireless. Every drop of blood was retribution. With an unwavering commitment to her dignity, she pummeled Stuart into unconsciousness. And to further guarantee her coup, she didn't stop wielding punches until well after he had ceased to move.

As suddenly as the battle had begun, it was over. Stuart's figure lay motionless on the floor, and a disquieting silence filled Wendy's bedroom. Breathing heavily, and shaking from the adrenaline, she paused to catch her breath. *Did I kill him?* Tentatively, she kicked him over on his back, watching him flop into place like a rag doll. Wendy found herself transfixed at the sight of her battered and vanquished enemy and the grisly red puddle amassing beneath his head. *He's still breathing,* she noted. Ignoring a growing revulsion of the unfolding gore, she chose instead to delight in her victory. Yet, there remained unfinished business. So, in preparation for vengeance against the fleshy weapon used against her, Wendy pushed Stuart's legs apart. Summoning every last ounce of strength, she stepped back and took two strides forward kicking him in the groin, with one specific objective. "That was to make sure you don't breed. You disgusting piece of shit." The mighty boot to his testicles made him wince through his unconsciousness.

Wendy was emotionally spent but continued her vigil. Straddling over Stuart, she watched intently to see if he would continue the struggle, still clenching the little mace that dripped with her rapist's blood. The ordeal had exhausted her. As minutes passed, her heart slowed, her rage abated, and the rock softly left her grasp. And with her victory, the last ghostly shreds of her despair crumbled away.

Stuart survived the encounter though he was quite different afterward. The terrain of both his face and persona had changed dramatically. Before long, ugly jagged scars replaced the bruises and avulsions. Wendy had made his exterior match his interior. And the bully's once arrogant swagger had been reduced to the awkward gait of a subjugated coward. By defeating him, Wendy had ripped away the flimsy veneer of Stuart's seething, narcissistic rage and revealed what a truly pathetic, empty young man he was underneath. Yet Wendy hadn't damaged Stuart enough he couldn't heed the cautionary lesson. Not only did he never lay a hand on Wendy again, but he also quit bullying her altogether.

An obtuse Sergeant paid little attention to his son's condition, blindly accepting Stuart's lame excuse of having injured himself from a fall at the beach. But for Stuart, the shame of such a beating was a wound that wouldn't scab. He didn't dare admit the truth to his father, his teacher, and mentor. He didn't dare admit to losing to an inferior, a mere girl. Sure, he could have made a big deal about the incident. He could have lied and made Wendy's life even worse. But he also knew he wouldn't get off so easily. The fact remained he had lost a physical fight with a female. A female. The lowest form of life whose right to exist was solely predicated upon serving two functions and two functions only–cooking and fucking. Stuart's defeat meant he had committed a mortal sin in the church of misogyny. Had he disclosed his crushing defeat, he would have been forced to kneel at its altar and openly confess his failings. And there would be no redemption from that untenable humiliation. For this reason, Stuart kept his newly disfigured mouth shut.

Wendy had conquered one brute, but she still shed many tears at the hand of the other. The beach was where she grieved, and she grieved often. Every tear was a straightforward, gut-wrenching plea, enough! With the fervor of a televangelist, Wendy prayed for relief, and she honestly didn't care what it looked like. She never prayed for happiness or joy, or even revenge. Her sole petition was for deliverance from the pain. Wendy had had enough, and in a blatant, unadulterated way, she begged the universe to make it all stop. What Wendy didn't realize was the ocean had also had enough.

It was late September, and autumn's days were waxing, on the night Wendy's life changed for the better. An unfamiliar RCMP officer knocking on the door delivered her reprieve. Sergeant was long overdue arriving home that evening. The cop was matter-of-fact. "There was a freak accident at sea. He drowned. I'm...uh...sorry."

She couldn't believe her ears. Sergeant wasn't coming home that night, or any other. In retrospect, Wendy would always think it strange the officer seemed confused as to whether he was delivering good, or bad news. Nevertheless, the tyrant's reign had come to an abrupt yet welcome end and with it, so too had Wendy's nightmare.

They recovered Sergeant's body within hours after the accident and arrangements were made without delay. Laura had dropped everything after Wendy called her with the news and she arrived in the early morning on the day of the funeral. Laura found her teenaged niece sitting alone, waiting for her at the edge of the ferry dock wearing an expressionless face and loose clothing that did little to conceal her skinny frame. Laura found Wendy's appearance disconcerting, but it didn't stop their wordless, heartfelt reunion. The two held each other for several minutes, surrounded by the salty air and an extraordinary calm. A raven's croaking calls in the near distance marked the end of their embrace and the beginning of their short walk to the community hall, which was doubling as a funeral home.

"I haven't seen him yet," Wendy whispered, as the two walked arm in arm towards their obligatory destination.

Wendy was filled with a sense of foreboding. She had spent the better part of twelve years trying to avoid Sergeant's presence. Now, contrary to her every instinct, she was voluntarily moving towards him. They said he was dead, but Wendy still wasn't convinced he couldn't persecute her from beyond the grave.

The auditorium was empty. The pine coffin was not. It sat at the far end of the hall with its lid propped open, waiting pathetically for mourners who would never arrive. The women's footfalls echoed in the lonely building as they approached the pitiful bier. With every stride narrowing the distance between living and dead, Wendy's trepidation grew until it became palpable. Suddenly she froze, hijacked by anxiety, just short of being able to see the contents of the imposing box. Staring at the floor, her hand trembled in Laura's grasp. Seconds later Wendy took a deep breath, withdrew from the safety of her aunt, and approached the morbid container alone. Wendy took those last few dreadful steps towards the coffin accompanied by a wrenching nausea in her belly. When its inhabitant came into view, she stopped, closely studying Sergeant's pale, lifeless face. Meditating on his condition, time became irrelevant for Wendy. At last, a remarkable equanimity arose within. "He doesn't look angry anymore...He looks...almost...almost happy...Don't you think?"

Nodding in agreement Laura reached towards Wendy and grasped her hand.

Wendy was right. Sergeant now enjoyed a certain serenity only death could have brought him. All at once pity had replaced fear and Wendy inched towards forgiveness.

"We can go now. I'm not scared of him anymore."

With that straightforward declaration, and relief ringing in her voice, Wendy wrapped her arm around Laura, and they left the barren hall.

Early that afternoon the whole town showed up for the service. It was a grand tribute to a brutal man. Wendy hated the smell of it, the stench of hypocrisy. Every single person in the community knew exactly what Sergeant was like both on and off the job. And not a single one of them could look Wendy directly in the eye. Wendy supposed it was the effect of collective shame, the village secret. Or perhaps they had been as oppressed as she. It no longer mattered.

The moment his box disappeared into the ground, sunshine cracked through the ashen sky, and the communal sigh of relief was practically audible. With the perfunctory ritual over, and without tears or words, the pseudo mourners abandoned the cemetery.

Laura turned to Wendy. "Are you hungry dear?"

The emaciated girl's answer wasn't surprising. "I'm starving! Could I have a cheeseburger, please?"

Laura smiled. "Of course you can. How about some french fries too? And a piece of pie for dessert?"

For the first time since her mother died, Wendy grinned.

Laura wanted to extricate Wendy from that miserable life as quickly as possible. After watching her niece wolf down a hearty meal, their next stop was the ancient farmhouse. There she helped pack Wendy's meager possessions in preparation for the move to Vancouver. They accomplished the task in under ten minutes as the teen's clothes barely filled half a suitcase. Moments later, on that early autumn day, Wendy walked out of the dismal little dwelling for the last time with her bag in one hand, her rock in the other, and nary a glance backward.

Aunt and niece were going to spend their last night in the village motel, which sat conveniently across from the ferry dock. Everything was in order for them to board the first departing vessel at dawn the next morning. The pair arrived at their lodgings with plenty of time left in the day. But when entering their room, Wendy gasped. "Oh no! I forgot to say goodbye to somebody."

Having never seen such a reaction from Wendy, Laura intuited whoever this person was, they were obviously important to her niece. "Well, off you go then. Say your farewells."

Wendy kissed Laura's cheek. "Thanks, Auntie. Be back soon."

"Take your time, dear."

Sprinting out the door the teen headed straight for one particular spot, on one particular beach.

It took years before Wendy could fully appreciate Grandfather's uncanny ability to show up just when she needed him the most. More often than not, he was already sitting there anticipating her arrival. Though on Wendy's more upsetting days he would only arrive after Wendy had finished crying, after her more vulnerable moments had passed. He had always appeared as if by magic when her morale was most in need of a potent counterweight to her routine misery. Those were the days when his stories were at their apex of power. The grand storyteller always did an excellent job of taking Wendy's mind off her troubles and lightening her mood. But more significantly, he showed her life was still worth living.

With only a few hours remaining before her departure, Wendy ran full tilt all the way to the shoreline expecting to find her dear friend sitting perched on their favorite driftwood. Wendy got there quickly though out of breath and suffering a stitch in her side from the sudden exertion. But the sight of a vacant log made her heart sink. For the first time since their enigmatic meeting six years earlier, Grandfather wasn't there on cue. However, in his place, and exactly where he should have sat, Wendy found an enchanting little carving. She recognized it as Frog.

The petite effigy had been placed atop of a piece of cedar bough where it sat waiting for her. A piece of paper under a small stone was next to it. Sensing it was a parting gift from her old friend, Wendy picked up the note and read it.

My dear Wendy,

I'm sorry I couldn't say goodbye in person. Frog is a reminder to use your medicine. Using your medicine reminds you of who you are. When you know

*who you are, you will always do what is right. Thank
you for your friendship and for the good life you will
lead.*

Grandfather

Reaching down Wendy brought Frog close to her
heart. It seemed to pulsate with love and vibrated with
Grandfather's essence. Bulging tears welled up in her
eyes. She cherished the gesture, but the gift had stirred
up mixed feelings. *How did he know I was leaving?
And why the heck isn't he here to give this to me
himself?* she thought, wiping her teardrops away.
Unbeknownst to Wendy, Grandfather had left the gift
two days earlier on his way up to the mountains,
where, at long last, he fell asleep under the cedars.

For the first time in years, Wendy sat on the
shoreline alone. Staring out over the water, she
struggled with the part of herself that knew she would
never see her dear old friend again. In deference to
him, she took several nice deep breaths and focused
on the little cedar gift. More tears came forward. She
allowed them to trickle freely down her face. Still
cradling Frog next to her heart, Wendy let out a sigh
of acceptance. A modest amount of her grief had been
cleared away but none of her disappointment.

Grandfather's absence did nothing to soothe
Wendy's nerves. To some extent she was still in shock
from Sergeant's death; not that she necessarily
grieved for him. It was just that for the first time in
recent memory she wasn't being abused, and she
found the liberation pretty unsettling. Wendy felt like
she was lost in uncharted territory; paralyzed by her

newfound freedom. Despite all the positive changes
happening in her life, she was reeling. Her roller
coaster of mistreatment had come to a screeching
stop, and it would likely take a while before the
emotional dizziness would calm down. Wendy pushed
her feet deeper into the pebbles lining the shore in a
vain attempt at managing her inner turmoil.

But before long, another layer of apprehension
made itself known; the move to Vancouver. The
notion of living with Laura exhilarated Wendy, but at
the same time, she found it impossible to relax, to be
less than perpetually vigilant. It was the tattoo of
chronic abuse and neglect. The lasting mark of an
education based in terror and intimidation, in hate and
disgust. And its scar tissue was a singularly resolute,
yet unconscious truth flowing within her. *Never let
your guard down because that makes you vulnerable.*
And to Wendy, vulnerability meant death.

For the final time, an unshackled Wendy pulled
her feet out of the pebbles, stood up and left her
beach. With scars in her psyche and Frog in her hand,
she made her way towards her new life.

The next morning the ferry departed before the
sun rose over the mountaintops, so the morning light
was ghostly gray. Still numb, Wendy stood on the
deck watching the hamlet recede into the morning fog.
When the last bit of familiar coastline became
swallowed up by mist, a pair of ravens flew overhead
performing an otherworldly aerial waltz accentuated
by their joyous, croaky melody. And as Wendy beheld
their playful dance, she awoke from her anesthetized

state and felt a spark of hope kindle inside her. She smiled.

Gradually over the next few weeks, Wendy adjusted to her new life in Vancouver. For the first time she could remember, she had a full stomach, proper clothing, and a safe, supportive home. Although the chaos of the big city did take some getting used to, Wendy enjoyed its mild climate, which gave her almost year-round opportunity to venture outdoors. And best of all, Laura's house was only a few minutes walk to the ocean.

It didn't take long for Wendy to settle in nicely there. She made herself right at home on her new beach laying unofficial claim to a distinctive stretch at the shoreline's far end where several driftwood logs quietly beckoned to her. The ocean smelled the same here as it had in Bella Coola and there were the typical gulls, ravens and harbor seals. Wendy's new sanctuary and its irresistible familiarity provided her with a welcome bridge for her transition to safety.

Mid-October brought a patchwork of orange and yellow pockmarks amongst the North Shore Mountain's usual palate of greens. Fall filled the air as Wendy sat ensconced in her driftwood barricade. While a crisp breeze off the water nipped at her face, she sat studying her little wooden Frog, tumbling the creature over and over in her hands, and pondering her elderly friend. Wendy missed him dearly.

She was fondly replaying one of his grand stories in her head when the city's dull hum melted into the background revealing a strong sense of his comfortable presence. In fact, the experience was so distinct it made Wendy turn around to see if he was standing behind her. He was not. Yet curiously, in that small sliver of time, Wendy swore she could hear his laughter drifting in from the water. The phenomenon evaporated as fast as it came leaving a tingling serenity sweeping through her. She noticed a remarkably calm ocean was what commemorated the moment.

Chapter 20
Autumn 1973
Victoria, British Columbia

He noticed a remarkably calm ocean was what commemorated the moment. Amidst all the chaos that day had brought Trevor vividly remembered how peaceful and still the ocean had been, just like glass.

The bad news arrived early that Sunday morning via a knock on the front door. Standing solemnly at the home's entrance were two police officers, accompanied by a woman in civilian clothing. Trevor secretly hoped, and assumed, they had finally caught up with his father. But the energy of their presence was familiar, too familiar. History was about to repeat itself.

The official trio promptly unloaded their somber message with their words straddling an emotional no-man's-land somewhere between perfunctory and kind. The ranking officer took the lead. He was blunt. "I'm sorry to inform you that your daughter Tess is dead. From what we can tell, it looks like she died of a narcotic overdose. She wouldn't have suffered."

And with the news, the police had inadvertently served up the choicest of buffets for Monster. Nothing fed It's appetite like the outpouring of sympathy from a dead child. True to its nature, It immediately bellied up to the trough presented to her with the zeal of a skilled professional. While the police spoke of the death of Monster's only daughter, the one who had borne the brunt of so many of It's brutal attacks, the dramatics appeared right on cue: moaning, wailing, even alligator tears. All in all, quite the performance, histrionics at their finest. The bogus emotion spewing from It didn't surprise Trevor, it just sickened him. He ran to the bathroom to vomit.

Immediately after Tess's funeral, Trevor stuffed his few possessions into a duffel bag and marched out of that house, slamming the door so hard he suspected it came off its hinges. He never looked back to see. Tossing his meager belongings into the back seat of his car, he started the engine and left for good, declaring never to set foot in that horrible place again.

That afternoon Trevor drove off with a single destination in mind. Moments later he parked his car and let his sober, deliberate strides carry him to the beach. Coming to the end of the gravel trail overlooking the water, he studied the landscape for the perfect spot to settle himself. Then he spied it. High up on the craggy bedrock well above the tide pools, thrown there by a violent storm years before Trevor was even born, sat an imposing log, bleached gray by the tidal elements. As if approaching a mystic guru, Trevor began his mindful ascent towards it with a sure-footedness that had been born on those same rocks. He climbed towards the summit and upon reaching his goal let his full body weight sink against the wooden relic. Gazing out over the cove that had provided him with the only respite his childhood knew he filled his lungs to bursting, gradually exhaled, and prepared to digest what was happening.

In the five years since Shadow's disappearance, Trevor had worked his ass off at whatever he could find; odd jobs, babysitting, lawn mowing. And every penny he didn't spend to feed or clothe himself he saved. He had paid for his car in cash, and although he was leaving sooner than he had planned, he knew if he stayed, this time he *would* kill her. Today he had a sleeping bag, a car, and a steady job flipping burgers. He figured it was more than he needed to survive. At seventeen-years-old, all his hard work had finally paid off, allowing him to move far beyond his desire for an imaginary driftwood shelter.

On that crisp autumn day, Trevor rested upon that timeworn log and permitted himself to be categorically present in the moment. He remained there studying the faint ripples that danced upon the sea and allowed their enigmatic presence to reach inside and soothe him. Before long, he became one with the place. Never had he felt the water's calmness as abundantly. Right then Trevor resonated more with his sanctuary than he had thought possible. Placing his hand on his heart and closing his eyes, he overflowed with silent gratitude. *Thank you, for everything.*

Dusk fell, and the clear blue sky began morphing to gray. As it came time to leave, Trevor descended back to the pebbled shore and approached the water's edge, drawn to its gentle lapping. He knelt on one knee and placed his right hand into what was for Trevor, a holy font. Instantly, he felt an energizing cold vibrate throughout his body in such a way that he momentarily lost track of time. Seconds later he found himself staring at his distorted reflection in the waves. He felt as though he had just seen himself for the first time, as if he knew who he really was. He withdrew his hand from the water feeling oddly renewed by the bracing jolt.

Standing up his mind began to whirl. Not because he was dizzy and not with dread or the usual cavalcade of anxieties and survival strategies, but with a wholly uncustomary feeling, one of hope. He was literally overflowing with possibilities; thoughts of things that could be, when he felt the chill that had permeated him for so long subtly begin to shift. At last, it had moved aside and allowed his breath to flow more freely than he could ever remember. What's more, Trevor noticed the long-held tension in his gut had vanished. He smiled. Having endured years of abuse and neglect the unthinkable, the unimaginable, had manifested at last. Escape was nigh, and like a fool spouting wisdom, it had come unexpectedly.

Chapter 21
Meanwhile...
Plint Island Indian Residential School

Escape was nigh, and like a fool spouting wisdom, it had come unexpectedly. On an oddly cold day, a group of white men wearing fancy suits showed up unannounced on the island. Their mission was simple enough, to deliver a message: the school was closing. Effective immediately all the children were to be returned to where they had come from. And the order was executed with whirlwind precision.

On the morning of the children's emancipation, dense fog shrouded everything but the closest of objects, framing the experience with a sublime surreality. One by one, each child stepped solemnly onto the boat that was to ferry them back to their respective communities. With numbed hearts and hollow expressions, they made little, if any, noise. There were no celebratory smiles, no excited chatter, and no fond farewells. The exodus may as well have been a zombie march.

After six long grueling years, Mary stepped off Plint Island for the last time with the ragged clothing on her back as her only tangible possession. Yet, ironically she was shackled to something more onerous than physical baggage. And that invisible millstone would prove increasingly problematic. At the same time Mary was settling onto the boat, she was fighting off an onslaught of images, the faces of all the little ones who didn't live to see this day, who didn't live to take this boat ride. She didn't stand a chance. Mary was now chained to a ponderous yoke and struggled to shoulder its ethereal burden–a legion of tiny ghosts.

Ever wary to deny their kinship, George ignored his sister as he too boarded the vessel that signified the end of his five-year sentence. Once its pathetic cargo was loaded, the boat glided away from the dock and towards the fog. George was too numb to do anything but stand on the deck and watch, transfixed, as the ominous brick building receded into the mist until all at once it vanished from the horizon. He panicked if he allowed his eyes to wander from the spot where he last saw Plint Island. The better part of him still believed the great stone bird would follow him. George feared that somehow it would take flight, hunt him down and swallow him up again.

His physical departure from that obscene institution was not at all like George had imagined. He had assumed escaping would make him feel better. In reality, he was just clinging to an intense need for hope. Hope that he could leave all the adversity behind. Hope that somehow he could emerge whole from the brutality, starvation, and rape he had endured. Hope that he could discard the infinite shadow of malevolence cloaking him. He was wrong. The numbness still accompanied him, as did the chill. He along with the few who survived to see that day had been irreparably changed, and not for the better. Though as far as the church was concerned, it had accomplished what it had set out to do. They had "civilized" those "heathen" children.

The boat left at daybreak and many hours had passed before that handful of derelict waifs was dumped onto the very beach from where they had been abducted in the first place. Where there should have been many, there were few. Untold numbers never returned. And unbeknownst to those who survived to reunite with their community, that stretch of pebbles and driftwood would be the only recognizable feature about their village.

Mary and George stood motionless on the shoreline paralyzed by the sight of the vaguely familiar landscape. Brother and sister exchanged secret glances until the boat was safely out of view before falling into each other's arms and sobbing.

Each child's reaction to its homecoming was unique and unpredictable. Some ran immediately into the village yelling for their parents. Others just sat curled up on the beach, arms wrapped around bent knees, crying while rocking back and forth. Those were the ones who had been taken away at such a young age they had no memory of this place where they now found themselves abandoned.

The siblings wiped away the remnants of their tears, gripped each other's hand and began their tentative journey up from the shoreline to the village. They were home at last. Provoked by the sweet-smelling air, the mountains and the river, a cascade of faint but happy memories ran through their minds as they made that short trek. George and Mary held out a courageous hope that life could return to the way it used to be. They had palpable, but precarious expectations.

News of the arrivals had spread quickly, and the People came out of their houses in disbelief, awed to discover their children back home. Many did not recognize their own sons and daughters. Most parents had not set eyes on them since they were taken many years ago. Collective grief followed those few awkward reunions.

George and Mary were dumbstruck by the changes that had descended upon their former home. To them, the village felt radically different. It was quiet, yet chaotic, calm, yet desperate.

The further they drifted through the rows of despairing houses, the firmer they gripped each other's hand. No one came to greet them. Empty liquor bottles lined the unkempt streets.

At last, they came to their house. Or what remained of it. It teetered at a distressing angle and, like a drunk trying to steady himself, leaned dangerously on the adjacent fence. Jagged bits of glass were all that remained of its windows along with a gaping hole where its door once hung. Without caretakers, the roof had caved in upon itself, allowing, even welcoming, its further decomposition by the elements. A glance was all it took to realize it was uninhabitable.

More distressing than the state of their rotting home was the glaring absence of its occupants. Apart from the crumbling building, there was no evidence the family had ever existed. The stark metaphor was an all too painful, but accurate, impression. George and Mary were alone. There were no eyes to bear witness to their return, no arms to embrace in reunion. Only a decaying heap of lumber and two people's shattered hearts.

Mary's face was blank and pale. George's stomach flip-flopped.

"Where are they?" Mary asked.

"I dunno..." replied George.

The pair stood there staring at what used to be, lost to their remembrances until George noticed his sister's stare and became concerned. Mary bore a look he had seen once before, on Mother. "Come on Mary, let's go, let's go..." he said, pulling her by the arm and leading her away from her dashed expectations.

The dispossessed pair wandered indiscriminately amongst the broken community until they came upon a gray weathered log, hewn partially into a canoe and lying abandoned by the river's edge. For a generation weeds and grass had been reclaiming it on Earth's behalf. Being neither log nor canoe, and without the power to transform itself either way, it welcomed them as its own. Brother and sister sat there trying to negotiate a groundswell of reality. The knowledge that they had lost everything they remembered loving. The hope that had sustained them and to which they had clung all those years now felt absurd. And by believing in it, they had played a cruel joke on themselves. Mary broke down crying tears of despair. George had moved past being despondent or heartbroken, he sat there staring at the river's mighty current and contemplating suicide.

Darkness was falling on that brisk fall evening when they noticed the outline of a man marching towards them. As he drew nearer, Mary recognized their Uncle. He had Father's eyes. Anxiety was ringing in his voice. "George! Mary! Is that you? Have you seen your cousins?"

Uncle had not seen his kids in over a decade. The teens both shook their heads in unison. Devastated his own children hadn't returned, Uncle's face dropped. All the same, his niece and nephew were back home, and he was grateful. He picked up his pace, opened his arms towards the emaciated young people, and invited them into his embrace giving them a loving, welcoming hug; something George and Mary had almost forgotten existed. Having no alternative, and at Uncle's insistence, the siblings accepted his offer to come and live with him.

Their new home was reminiscent of their old one and in a similar state of disrepair. But nonetheless, it housed an abundance of love. But it wouldn't be enough to counter the impact of what the siblings were to learn about the cruel truths of their family's fate. The duty fell to Uncle whose gentleness was most suited to revealing the somber facts.

Uncle sat George and Mary down, knelt in front of them and clasped each of their hands. His face was cheerless, and his words were tender. "By now you must have guessed that they have all dropped their robes...After you were taken George, your mother refused to eat and wasted away...Your father was killed in prison not long after he was sent there...And Grandfather...Well, one day this past summer he went up to the mountains and never came back."

It was confirmed. Mary and George had nothing else to lose. Heaving sobs followed.

Several days after the children's return, as was the Nuxalkmc people's custom, the community gathered for ceremony. Mary and George attended the gathering with apathy as their escort. The People drummed and sang their medicine songs. They danced their traditional dances and enjoyed a humble feast. And above of all, they gave thanks for the homecoming. But not everyone who returned from residential school attended the ceremonies. Forever loyal to their brainwashing, the vast majority of the older teens rejected the ancient rituals, calling it the devil's work and chastising the participants. "You'll all burn in Hell!" they chimed, quoting the exact scripture that had been beaten into them by the nuns and priests.

They had been taught well; taught a doctrine of fear; taught to be ashamed of who they were; taught racist propaganda by rote. What's more, they had been exceptional students. But of course, their teachers had been skilled in brutality. At least in this respect the government and churches had achieved their primary goal. They had killed the Indian inside these Indians.

By their own acknowledgment, George and Mary felt a great deal less burdened after the ceremony, after listening to the Elders talk about returning to your people and remembering who you were. "Speak your language," they said. "Remember your art and the sacred stories. They will call your spirit back to you and can make you whole again."

But as brother and sister left the meetinghouse that night, albeit a little lighter, they still carried within them the numbness. They courted it for a while, trying to welcome it, trying to turn it into an ally. But it refused to be tamed. Its allegiance was to darkness and darkness alone. It was utterly incompatible with the light. What little ground the two had gained in the war against despair soon evaporated, promptly replaced by nightmares and flashbacks. What followed was only inevitable, even predictable.

Life at residential school had affected everyone differently, but all were affected deeply. It wasn't long before the curriculum of fear and hate matured, manifesting outright in all aspects of their lives. Some raped, some stole. Like their teachers, some became cruel. But they shared a commonality. They all drank, and they all drank for the same reason. Drinking was the one thing that quieted the voices, muffled the screams in their heads, and blotted out the gruesome images. It was the one thing that made living somewhat bearable. Though at first, everyone fought the liquor's pernicious influence. But with time and growing desperation, one by one, each succumbed to its siren song. Alcohol became their medicine, filling the void left by the exodus of their spirits.

Mary, too, made a pact with the liquor, though she no longer possessed anything of value to sacrifice to her new idol, surely not the burnt offerings of her dignity or self-respect. She agreed to kneel at its altar of temporary relief in exchange for its sole demand, unconditional devotion. In return, the booze made it easier to sleep, its anesthetizing effects keeping the nightmares at bay, for now. That evening a drunken Mary plunged into a dead and dreamless abyss. For at least one more night, Mary avoided reliving the horrors of her past.

Chapter 22
Autumn 1990
Vancouver, British Columbia

For at least one more night, Wendy avoided reliving the horrors of her past. It was welfare payday, a.k.a. Mardi Gras. And a shift of back-to-back calls was exactly what she needed. The intense workload provided Wendy a welcome diversion from dwelling on her own crap to managing someone else's miserable existence.

That evening both partners arrived at the station earlier than usual expecting to work sooner than scheduled. They weren't disappointed. The dispatch phone rang only moments after Wendy had stowed her gear in her locker. Trevor took the call's details, and within moments they were off, code three, to deal with the Downtown Eastside's most ubiquitous call, "the man down."

Ninety seconds later, Trevor pulled up in front of the call and discovered a heap of familiar looking clothing sprawled on the sidewalk. It was George. Both paramedics slipped out of the vehicle effortlessly. Wendy got to her patient without delay and began her assessment while Trevor grabbed the jump kit from the back of the car and brought the equipment to his partner's side.

George lay slumped in the middle of the walkway as if he was a puppet whose strings had been cut. In the few seconds it took Trevor to bring Wendy the bag, she was reaching for the essential medical gear and asking for more. "His coma scale's not much better than a parsnip, *and* he's got a big gash on the back of his head," she said.

Trevor's lips barely moved. "Fuck."

Wendy sighed. "Yeah, I know. I hate that hospital too...But that's where neuro is."

They could both smell the unmistakable odor of liquor on George's breath, and it was obvious from the large gash on his head that he had hit the pavement with a lot of force. This, coupled with his diminished consciousness was concerning to Wendy. Was he simply drunk and needed some stitches? Or was he bleeding into his brain? Or both? Did he need a neurosurgeon or a few hours to sleep it off? Out in the field, it was impossible to tell. Even in the hospital, they would need medical imaging to know for certain. Since Forty-Eight Charlie couldn't rule anything out, they always erred on the side of caution, followed protocol and took the patient to the most appropriate medical facility. Every hospital in the city housed a different specialty. In this case, neurology was located at Vancouver General Hospital.

Forty-Eight Charlie worked like a well-oiled machine, each partner competent in their skills, rightly anticipating each other's needs. In the care of those skilled hands, George was carefully packaged, placed in the back of the ambulance and underway to the hospital in under three minutes.

En route Wendy paid close attention to George's rate of breathing. She had already inserted a tube down his throat to protect his airway but was still unsure what was going on. Was this an alcohol overdose, a closed head injury, both, or something else entirely? Fortunately, so far, George was still breathing on his own. Since their patient was in tenuous condition, Trevor notified the hospital so they had time to make preparations to receive their patient. Forty-Eight Charlie left the scene code three and in nine minutes delivered George to definitive medical help. Or so they believed.

Forty-Eight Charlie's reception was predictably frigid. More often than not, the VGH staff didn't call Wendy and Trevor paramedics, they called them "one of those skid road crews", whose marginalized clientele were judged by many of them to be less deserving of medical expertise than the rest of Vancouver's "taxpayers". At least that was the prevailing attitude of too many of the nursing staff working there. Several of the more brazen nurses were even openly hostile to Trevor and Wendy, calling them "garbage truck drivers" to their faces. The hospital staff shunned Forty-Eight Charlie and treated the crew as though they were trespassing. But there wasn't any point in the paramedics complaining about the toxic environment as their supervisors either took the same stance or were unwilling to take the hospital to task on the issue. The crew's only recourse was to avoid that place like the plague. Though in this case, not only was policy clear, George may have needed a neurosurgeon. Having no feasible options, Wendy and Trevor hoped for the best.

The crew wheeled their patient into the emergency receiving area, and Trevor assumed George's care. Wendy feigned a smile as she approached the triage desk, which was where the nurses prioritized patients, presumably based on the severity of their condition.

"Hi there. This is the patient we notified you about..." Wendy said.

The senior nurse stood up and craned her neck to look at their stretcher's contents. Once she got a glimpse of George, exasperation exploded on her face and she plonked back down, shaking her head in disdain.

Wendy continued undeterred, giving a concise, professional report, making certain to emphasize George's deepening unconsciousness, tenuous breathing, and uncertain neurological status to the two nurses, ending with, "I think you can see why we're concerned about him. " Finishing her report, Wendy expected to get the green light for the trauma room. But what happened next was to Wendy's mind a new low, even for this hospital. And the ensuing vitriol outraged her.

The whole time Wendy spoke, the nurse continued shaking her head and chuckling with condescension. Ignoring the medical report, she casually spun around to her colleague and groaned, "It's *obviously* just a drunk. Do we *really* want to tie up the trauma room just for that?"

Wadding up her face with acrimony, the junior nurse replied, "No, not really."

At this point in her career, Wendy wasn't easily shocked. Even so, she was having a hard time believing her ears. *What the fuck!* she thought. But to her credit, instead of reacting to the hateful rhetoric, she went to see how her patient was doing. The subdued look of rage in Wendy's eyes when she stepped into the hallway told Trevor everything he needed to know as to why they weren't in the trauma room yet.

In Wendy's short absence, Trevor had had his hands full.

"I didn't like his respiratory rate so I started bagging him...He's crashing fast."

"Shit. So I see. I'll be right back."

Quickening her step, Wendy returned to the triage desk. "Excuse me, but my patient's deteriorating and no longer breathing on his own. We're ventilating him manually."

This should have been all it took to get immediate medical attention for her patient. Instead, what spewed forth so incensed Wendy she would later say it was only through divine intervention that she didn't actually kill the soulless bitches on the spot. Those two nurses unified response to the deteriorating condition of that particular human being was arrogant indifference. "Yeah? Well, we don't want to waste the trauma room on this."

That was it, Wendy snapped. And she made a career decision. As far as she could tell, she had been left little choice. With the tenacity her reputation had been built on, she marched to the hallway, grabbed one end of their stretcher and growled, "We're going to a real hospital. Code three. Could you notify St. Paul's?"

Trevor grinned. "Okay."

They loaded George back into the ambulance and delivered their patient to a waiting, fully staffed trauma room within six minutes. Upon arriving at St. Paul's, George got everything he needed; a doctor, a ventilator, blood work and was prepped for a CT scan of his head; all in under fifteen minutes.

Shortly after the flurry of medical activity had died down, Wendy pulled the attending emergency physician aside. "I just wanted to give you a heads up that a shit-storm is probably brewing over this call and I take full responsibility for it." She went on to explain why she chose to bring her patient to him. "I'm sorry for complicating your day. But Frankly, I don't give a rat's ass what the fallout is. I don't apologize for providing good patient care."

VGH's attitude wasn't a secret. The doctor smiled and putting his hand on Wendy's shoulder said, "This guy's lucky to have you in his corner. Don't worry, it's all good."

"Thanks, doc. You guys are the best."

Wendy was resolute in her responsibilities, and to her, that meant providing the best medical care possible for her patients regardless of their mailing address. Today, she had upheld her values and met that goal. As far as she was concerned, both she *and* George could live with her decision.

Not surprisingly, the VGH nurses had wasted no time in lodging a formal complaint against Wendy. Dispatch notified Forty-Eight Charlie that a supervisor was on his way to meet them at St. Paul's and they were grounded until he spoke with them. But they weren't sending just any old supervisor. Nope, they sent John Phelps.

You must understand, John Phelps had an air about him. On first meeting him, you immediately disliked him. He was so unlikeable Gandhi would have slapped him. He was the kind of guy you just *needed* to smack. His repulsive aura oozed out of him, like a gangrenous, pus-filled abscess. But his personality was nothing compared to his skilled approach to personnel management, which consisted of a refined, yet eclectic, mix of sadism, glaring misogynism and general incompetence. That, coupled with his room temperature IQ, did not make him an effective problem solver. On any level, he was no match for Wendy, and he knew it, which made him hate her all the more. Phelps had been gunning for her since she started in the service, taking an immediate dislike to the capable, forthright woman. But he didn't have an excuse to "manage" her until several years ago when she claimed a nursing home was engaging in elder abuse. Phelps had taken great exception to her suspicions and dismissed Wendy's evidence outright, branding it as the ridiculous, hysterical rantings of a woman who didn't know her place. He gave Wendy an ultimatum, "Go apologize to the nursing home staff or face disciplinary action." Though she didn't use the words she would have liked to, she diplomatically told him to go fuck himself. And if he didn't do something about her concerns, she was going to go to the authorities herself. He didn't, so she did. As it turned out the police investigation vindicated Wendy, and it also protected a group of vulnerable seniors in the process. From that day forward, Phelps swore to do whatever he could to make Wendy's life a veritable hell until she quit, transferred out of the region or killed herself. He didn't care which. And Phelps made no bones about his goal. He just wanted the bitch out of his life.

Phelps pulled his vehicle into the far end of the ambulance parking lot and came to a squealing stop. The first thing you noticed as he slithered out of the car was the look in his eyes. All predators have the same look, especially when they smell blood.

Forty-Eight Charlie was standing at the back of their ambulance having just finished cleaning up from the call. Trevor was the first to notice the supervisor's arrival. "Huh...He must've gotten bored torturing small animals."

Wendy turned to see who it was. She sighed, and her fingers began tapping on the stethoscope in her hand. "Well shit, this is gonna be good. Why did it have to be him?...Hey, you wanna bet on what he accuses me of? Come on, I'll bet you coffee for a week."

"You mean accuses *us* of, right?"

"Delusions of grandeur Trevor? You're not in the crosshairs. *I'm* the one he hates...Come on, coffee for a week."

"Nah, sucker bet. He's gonna say A-you've got a shitty attitude, B-you did the wrong thing and C-you're gonna be disciplined for it."

"Yeah, yeah, obviously. So we bet on the *order* he does it in. A, B, C. If he goes C, A, B, you lose. Come on...coffee for two weeks."

"Mmm...Yeah, okay. But I get to collect as soon as you come back from your suspension."

"Deal," Wendy affirmed, just as Phelps came into earshot.

In reality, Trevor's guts were in knots. He knew Phelps was gunning for his partner, but he knew he was also fair game. This was just another instance when Wendy's ethics lit up the bulls-eye on her back. And Phelps didn't care if there was collateral damage.

Wendy's predominant trait, and the one that Trevor admired most, was how fiercely she stuck to her principles. She was one hundred percent faithful to her values. Wendy never went looking for trouble, and she never came off as self-righteous, but if in her eyes something were wrong, she would take it upon herself to make it right. Especially when it concerned people who were vulnerable and couldn't fight for themselves. Wendy was the self-appointed defender of the downtrodden. And when she took on a cause she was like a guard dog on a steak, nice and cuddly until you piss it off, then it won't let go. But she was tenacious because it meant something. Mainly it meant she could look at herself in the mirror, personal integrity at all costs.

Wendy prayed the conversation would be civilized. With that faint hope, she feigned her second smile of the day and watched her tone. "Hi John, how are you?" But to no avail, all that did was light his fuse.

Phelps launched into a screaming tirade in front of no fewer than a dozen civilian onlookers. "Why the hell did you whistle a patient from VGH! You were already at a hospital! You didn't need to come here!"

Wendy couldn't help herself. "I'm fine, thanks for asking. And my patient is also doing well, I'm sure he appreciates your concern."

Phelps continued screaming at her, almost blind with rage. "Your attitude sucks, Missy! I just spoke to the triage nurses at VGH, and they said they offered you a bed and you just refused it and left!"

"John, that's complete and utter bull. They're lying because they got caught practicing a little ethnic/social cleansing. They said, and I quote, "We don't want to waste the trauma room on a drunk," Furthermore, my patient was steadily deterior–"

Phelps cut her off and continued shouting, with his face bright red and veins bulging out of his temples. "You broke policy, *Missy*! That's where neuro is! As usual, you made another stupid decision! You should have just stayed..."

Watching the exchange from a respectful distance, Trevor knew his partner well enough to know she was just about ready to pop.

Wendy stood there tolerating the public dressing-down, cringing as Phelps droned on about her incompetence, her poor judgment, being a token female, and "Instead of pretending to be a paramedic, just do the public a favor and quit and go have some babies." Phelps would have continued vomiting his mommy issues all over Wendy until there wasn't anything left of her character to debase if she hadn't finally gotten fed up. When Wendy had had enough, she cut him off. "What, exactly, is my job description?"

Wendy hadn't taken his bait and remained on point. Unprepared for the query, Phelps got flustered, momentarily stopping his incessant barrage of insults. Wendy swooped in and took full advantage of the break in his rant. She took one compelling step toward him and, without raising her voice, began the pointless but necessary task of defending herself. Trevor leaned against the ambulance, anticipating the verbal bloodbath to come. Watching his partner, he raised his hand to conceal his smile. This was his guilty pleasure.

"Please correct me if I'm wrong, John. But as far as I'm aware, my job is to do everything within my power to ensure my patients don't die. I thought policy was pretty clear on that. In their complaint, did they happen to mention our patient wasn't breathing and needed ventilating? Or did they conveniently skip over that part? My understanding of legal negligence is that a reasonable person wouldn't let their patient sit at a hospital that was denying them treatment. And unlike those sanctimonious bigots at VGH, I don't discriminate as to who's deserving of medical care and who isn't. Furthermore, a neurosurgeon is a moot point if my patient dies in the hallway of *any* hospital because the nursing staff is withholding medical resources for someone they judge to be more worthy of receiving them. And because I know how important it is for you to gather all the facts, you should know that my patient is currently on a ventilator, having his head CT'd and very much *alive*...And one more thing. My name is spelled W-e-n-d-y."

Phelps was flummoxed by her. She was erudite and kept to the facts. But what pissed him off the most was she was right. The fucking bitch was right. He had had the same thing happen to him when he was working on car. Yet he never did anything about it. No bullets remained in his arsenal of wits, and without a feasible argument, Phelps defaulted to his usual bullying tactics. "You're lying! The invitation to your disciplinary hearing is on its way, *Missy*!"

With his parting threat delivered, he about-faced and marched towards the hospital entrance.

Wendy figured she was as good as fired, so she had nothing to lose. "Two words John...Elder abuse."

Phelps's head was already gyrating, and her reminder only infuriated him further, sending him storming off inside the hospital with one resolute objective: To root out someone–anyone–who'd be willing to crucify her.

Trembling from anger, Wendy walked back towards the ambulance and her grinning partner.

"Wipe that fucking smile off your face you asshole...Why *are* you smiling anyway?"

Still grinning, Trevor sighed, shook his head and asked, "Why do you insist on poking the bear?"

In return, Wendy shot him "the look." A gaze that only she could pull off. "The look," as Trevor called it, was an artful scowl that succinctly communicated all the following: "Are you fucking kidding me?...Have you lost your mind? (Because by saying this you are clearly suicidal)" and most importantly, "Keep it up, and I *will* get you for this."

"Well, I think I'd like alternating mochas and cappuccinos, *Missy.*"

"Now who's poking the bear?"

"I think *you* should make *me* coffee from now on. After all, that's what token females are for, right? It's the natural way of things."

A barely detectable, yet evil little grin crept onto Wendy's face before she whispered in Trevor's ear. "You value your nuts?"

But Trevor had made Wendy smile, and even if she had cut off his nuts, he figured it would have been worth it. He craved more of his partner, but she would have nothing to do with it. How did he know? They had had a conversation about it once.

That enlightening discussion took place one rainy night while they were parked in an alleyway guarding their people. Trevor had been testing the waters because he had to know one way or the other. But he tread carefully, knowing how much they both valued their working alliance. The last thing he wanted was to fuck that up. Trevor sat behind the wheel, sipping his coffee and working up the courage to broach the subject when at last he blasted from the hip. "You ever think about having a relationship?"

Spurting coffee, Wendy almost choked. "Yeah, right!"

"No, really. Don't you ever think about having someone to come home to, share things with?"

Wendy's reply was "the look."

Undeterred, and now sweating slightly, Trevor sat tall and forward in his seat before firing back. "What? Okay, so maybe not the happily ever after, story-time bullshit. But what about a genuinely flawed, passionate, real relationship."

Wendy used a tone she usually reserved for idiots. "With who, exactly?"

"Um, a guy. Unless I've read you wrong."

"Very funny. Don't worry, your gaydar's fine. And don't pretend you don't know exactly what I mean. No one gets us remember? The Normal people don't relate to us, and we don't relate to them. Might I remind you the reason they don't get us? Here's a hint, because we deal in hardcore reality, and they don't. And they never will, because our job is to protect all of them from having to deal with reality. Don't get me fucking started."

Deflated, Trevor slumped back into his seat. "Tooooo fucking late."

He was right. Wendy was on a roll. "Yup, I can hear it now, *Hi honey how was your day? Oh not too bad, just a murdered baby, a mutilated corpse and someone so badly burned we couldn't tell what gender they were. And I only had to take one extra shower today to rid myself of the feces I crawled through to save some sorry shit's ass.* Trevor, nobody gets us! Our worlds are just too fucking different. Christ, I thought you knew that."

Round two. Trevor marshaled his convictions and downplayed his intentions. "I didn't say go out and get yourself one of the Normals. I said a relationship. There's plenty of us around you know."

Wendy stared at him, wearing her patented expression.

"What's with the *look*! That's twice now!"

"Jesus freakin Christmas! That'd be like going from the frying pan into the fire."

But Trevor soldiered on. "Why? It's a warm body and someone who actually does get us. They've been there. They know."

"And they've got *baggage* Trevor! And what's worse, they don't know they've got *baggage*! At least I know I've got my own shit."

Trevor knew he was losing ground. "Oh come on, everybody knows they've got their own shit."

Wendy responded by taking out the big gun and aiming right between his eyes. "Yeah, maybe so but the Normal's divorce rate is fifty percent, and ours is ninety-five. And that's just for the first two attempts. How many of our esteemed colleagues are on their third or fourth?"

Trevor let a few moments of silence pass before firing his last salvo. "So you're going to be single forever then?"

Wendy sighed, reflecting an unexpected glimpse of her own ambivalence. "I dunno..."

She let his uncomfortable question settle into her mind.

That was the last they ever spoke about the issue.

Trevor resigned himself this was as close as he was ever going to get to Wendy. But that was fine. The fantasy was his. Trevor preferred indulging the dream of a relationship, even though it bore no resemblance to his actual life.

Chapter 23
Ten Years Earlier - Summer 1980
Vancouver's Downtown Eastside

The fantasy was theirs. George and Mary preferred indulging the dream of a better life in Vancouver, even though it bore no resemblance to their actual life there. In the end, moving far away had been a last-ditch attempt to escape.

Leaving Bella Coola had been a heartrending decision. Home represented every person, sight, sound, and smell they had ever loved. But since returning from Plint Island, those things evoked not love, but terror. George and Mary sought liberation from the endless throngs of memory triggers that dogged their every step back home. Whenever they heard Nuxalt'mc spoken, the evocative words sent sharp waves of panic careening through their bodies, flooding their minds with frightening images of nails and black robes. So by fleeing to Vancouver, they believed they could leave the vestiges of their traumas behind, having childishly convinced themselves their resident demons wouldn't follow. It was a pitifully naïve expectation.

Five years ago, with little more than the clothes on their backs and a fervent desire for a better life, brother and sister had made the long trek to the big city. Before they left, people said, "It'll be easier to find a job there." But work had been impossible to come by. Being Aboriginal didn't help. Being barely able to read and write also didn't help. Their schooling hadn't been about that. And when their optimistic plan backfired, life went into a downward spiral. Finding themselves shunned by ordinary society and without the means to afford decent housing, they landed deep in bosom of the Downtown Eastside; a small parcel of Vancouver relegated to its less-desirables and those willing to exploit them. The single ray of hope in their gamble for sanity was that soon after arriving they had each found lodgings, albeit courtesy of a particularly lethal batch of heroin the previous week. So, George settled in at the Roosevelt Hotel and Mary did the same at a rooming house about a mile further east. In spite of their disappointing new life, they persevered. Even as time blurred with each passing season, even when their optimism went on life-support, George and Mary remained loyal to their shared delusion of having a better life. Though with every rejection, with every job or opportunity denied, their hopes eventually faded into a backdrop of racism induced despondency, and alcohol-induced stupor.

One July afternoon, whatever happy future Mary envisioned for herself became forever annihilated. After weeks of searching, she had landed a job interview. But she never made it. As soon as Mary left her building on the day of her interview, they jumped her from behind and dragged her between two dumpsters in the adjacent alley. Throughout the ordeal, as she had done so often in the past, Mary surrendered to the repulsive violation of her body. She didn't fight back or scream, but that didn't stop them from beating her once the four of them were done. And she never went to the hospital. Instead, Mary crawled up eight flights of stairs to her room and hid in a corner. For weeks after the attack, she couldn't bring herself to leave, fearful of stepping foot outside her building. She told no one including, but especially, George. He brought her what little food he could spare and was surprised and troubled by his sister's unusual behavior. *I wonder why Mary never wants to leave her room. I hope she ain't sick.*

Since the gang rape, alcohol had failed to calm Mary's nerves or help her to sleep. And that lack of sleep only worsened her condition. Craving nothing except deliverance from her overwhelming anxiety ironically, or perhaps fatefully, early one August morning it knocked on her door.

Between raps, Mary heard a shrill feminine voice squeaking through the door. "Hey, girlie...You got a light I can borrow?"

Inside her room, Mary froze. A minute passed. Mary let out her breath, thinking the interloper had given up and left. But the invisible mouse-woman continued thumping and begging. "Com'on, I ain't gonna rob ya or nothin. I promise...I just need a light...real bad."

Mary kept silent, praying for the unwelcome visitor to go away, except the piercing voice persisted. "My name's Tanis, I live across the hall...I seen you around...I don't bite...Can ya help me out?...all's I need's a light...hey, that rhymes..."

By now Mary's attitude had shifted from fear to annoyance. She wasn't sure which she found more irritating, the fingernails-on-a-blackboard voice or its owner's tenacity. Still, there was something intriguing about this unseen woman. And that allure was enough to compel Mary to crack open her door, barely an inch mind you, to make sure it wasn't a predatory setup. With trepidation and a knot in her gut, Mary peeped through her door's narrow rift. But once her curious eyes met Tanis's, all Mary's apprehensions fell away.

Tanis sported a partially toothless smile attached to a near Lilliputian body. Her features were haggard and framed by thin blonde hair. She wore a white T-shirt, stained with age, and frayed blue jeans. Her atrophied physique swam in the clothing with the fabric dripping off her like a scarecrow without stuffing. Mary could see she had fresh bruising that hugged old scars tracing the veins running from wrist to elbow on the inner aspects of both her arms. Tanis's body may have belied one part of her story, but her gentle, bubbly nature beamed through her eyes and innocent grin. "There you are! I thought you might be dead," she said, winking at Mary.

Mary tried being upbeat. "No...No, not yet anyway."

"You got a light I could borrow hon?"

"Yeah...Sure...somewhere around here. Just a minute."

Mary closed and locked her door before rummaging around her room for something to satisfy her neighbor. Moments later she returned. Opening the door slightly wider this time, she slipped a soiled matchbook into Tanis's twitchy, nicotine-stained fingers. With that small deed, Tanis exploded with gratitude. From the display, Mary thought she had just pulled a drowning woman to safety. Tanis was spinning around in joy.

"Thank you! Thank you! Thank you! Bless you! Bless you!" she exclaimed, in an octave Mary figured only a dog should be able to hear. But Tanis was merely appreciative and overwhelmed with relief. Her parting comment to Mary was straightforward. "Thanks again. I was startin' to get junk sick. You know?"

With that, the harmless soul turned around and headed back to her room across the hall.

But before Tanis disappeared, a blunt question shot out of Mary as if her mouth were not her own. "Why do you do that stuff anyway?"

Mary surprised herself by asking such a bold and personal question of a total stranger. But in spite of her indiscretion, and her embarrassment, Mary waited to see if she got a response.

The query made Tanis lurch to a stop, preventing her from taking another step. Pivoting towards Mary, she began fidgeting, uncomfortable with the sudden reality check but feeling obliged to answer in payment for the matches. Tanis stood there in silence with her eyes fixed on the dirty hallway floor, shaking her head and struggling for a reply. In her heart, Tanis knew the answer. But she had never articulated it before.

As Tanis contemplated the riddle before her, the space between the two women filled with a raw authenticity few people will ever encounter. The poignant stillness felt interminable, but Tanis finally dispersed it by offering up a truthful, heartfelt answer preceded by a deep sigh. "It's the *only* thing...the *only* thing...that kills the pain in your heart...It makes you feel nothin'...It makes you forget..." Tanis's feet were no longer set in concrete and without raising her head or making further eye contact, she scampered back to the relative safety of her room with her debt fully repaid.

Mary couldn't explain where her spontaneous question had come from, except it seemed to billow up from her core and felt akin to vomiting poison. No longer obsessed with being attacked she stood motionless in her open doorway, paralyzed by Tanis's candor. Mary hadn't expected a meaningful response, much less such a captivating one. And that answer had not only rattled her but had summoned forth an intense emotional resonance.

Mary closed and locked her door while replaying the mesmerizing syllables in her head and plunging headlong into a trance. *It makes you forget...* They were enthralling words. *It makes you forget...* Could this be the pathway to peace? Soon those words began spinning a web of enchantment that would prove challenging for Mary to unbridle herself from. Wearing a deadpan expression, she sat next to her wobbly table. *It makes you forget...* She chanted the mantra over and over until she became spellbound. *It makes you forget. It makes you forget. It makes you forget.*

Mary had ample time to contemplate and digest Tanis's unforgettable words. George was out "binning," a.k.a. dumpster diving, trying to amass enough empty bottles and cans to trade for his day's supply of rice wine. If his luck were good, he would buy Mary a bottle too and wouldn't arrive for several more hours giving her plenty of time to court the prospect of a different kind of numb; enough time to ponder a life free of suffering. Alcohol wasn't working the way it once did. Mary needed to drink increasingly dangerous quantities to achieve the desired effect, to calm her anxiety, to dam the flood of appalling memories, or to simply fall asleep. Mary found the idea of finally securing the elusive relief she sought to be a tantalizing prospect. Sitting alone in her shoebox of a room, a solemn Mary toyed with the notion of relinquishing her final shred of pride, the pride of not being a junkie. Hours had passed before she had made her semi-free choice. In the end, Mary succumbed to its bait, entering into the enchantment's vestibule and locking its door behind her.

It was near sundown that summer evening when George returned from his day's work with not one, but two bottles. Providing for his sister, even in this dysfunctional way, gave George a great sense of pride and accomplishment. But it was soon to evaporate.

George knocked on Mary's door. There was no answer. This time he pounded. Still no answer. He yelled, "Mary!...Mary!"

He tried the doorknob, it turned, he pushed on it and the creaking door swung open. Upon entering Mary's room, his eyes took in the startling scene of Mary's lifeless outline on the bed. George's sunny mood melted into horror. He stood there stunned, bottles in hand, knowing his sister had become possessed. George recognized all the signs, the look, the feel, even the smell. He knew it was heroin, but he never imagined he would find it in Mary. George squeaked, "Mary?...You okay?...Mary?"

The limp form stirred briefly to her name but nodded right off again.

George's heart almost exploded. Leaping to his sister's side, he grabbed her arms and shook Mary in a frenzied attempt to bring her back to consciousness. She roused just enough to satisfy him she wasn't dead, at least not yet. He sat there cradling his sister and spent the next two hours maintaining an intense watch over her. During his vigil, George had plenty of time to think. *First, it was the boat, then the nuns and priests, then the endless stream of men, and now this. I've failed her again. Why can't I ever protect her? I'm such a loser.*

"I'm sorry Mary...I'm so sorry."

And so, from his wardrobe of helplessness George permanently adorned himself with the robes of shame.

When the heroin's effect wore off enough and George knew Mary was out of danger, he fell apart. His poignant tears sliced through Mary's residual high. "Oh my God Mary...No...no...no...Oh my God."

Hearing her sobbing brother, Mary wrenched herself from the thought-free nirvana she had embraced and began coming to terms with screwing up. She knew she had made a huge mistake letting George find her all fucked up like that. *Oh, shit. What've I done?* she thought.

Turning to George, she wrapped her arms around him, trying to comfort him. "Shhh, my little Georgie. Quiet now. It's all right. It's okay. Shhhh."

Eventually, George calmed down enough to sputter a plea, "You gotta...make sure...you don't o.d...'Cause...you're all I got...You're all I got left."

With that, George raised his head and riveted his gaze on his sister's face. His red eyes, swollen with tears, locked with Mary's. "I was so scared...so scared when I saw you just lyin' there."

In that brief instant, Mary caught a glimpse of how wounded her brother truly was. She saw a terrified little boy, ripped from the arms of his family, beaten, abused and perennially tormented. That flash of reality seared her heart like a branding iron.

By now Mary's high had dissolved away, and she spent the next hour reassuring George she would be okay. "I just wanted to try it, you know. To find out what it was really like. But now I know, and I promise I won't ever do it again."

"Oh, you gotta promise not to do it again Mary. It's no good. It's no good."

"I promise Georgie. I promise," she said, stroking his hair.

But Mary knew that was a lie and deep down, so did George. The relief was real, she liked it, and she had married it willingly and without reservation. Though what Mary didn't realize was that heroin never takes a honeymoon.

Though her experience that night was far from wasted. Because from then on, every time Mary picked up a syringe, her little Georgie's face was there. In a twisted way, it was what kept her alive. The memory of his distraught eyes kept her vigilant to avoid overdosing.

George was emotionally spent and physically weak. It was one a.m. "Now that I know you're okay, I think I'm gonna go back to my own room."

"Okay. I'm tired too," she said.

With more than a modicum of fear still resonating in his voice, George teased his sister. "Remember, we gotta date for coffee at the Ovaltine on Sunday. 'Cause you know I need checking up on."

Smiling, Mary gave him another big hug. Cupping his face in her hands, she kissed his forehead and walked him to the elevator to say goodbye. George pressed the button, but there was no whir or crack of machinery. He took the stairs instead.

Chapter 24
Ten Years Later - Autumn 1990
Vancouver's Downtown Eastside

Trevor pressed the button, but there was no whir or crack of machinery. They took the stairs instead. The hotel's elevator hadn't worked for several decades, so Forty-Eight Charlie ascended the Roosevelt via its worn marble treads. The crew had twelve flights of stairs to conquer with sixty pounds of medical gear in tow. Breathing deeply was compulsory, but the thick revolting odor of stale urine permeating the air made each breath obnoxious. Since they couldn't escape the smell, they climbed faster, hoping to outpace the sickening stench.

This place was little more than a barn for human beings. Like most rooming houses in the area, the landlords squeezed every cent from their tenants and spent little to nothing on maintenance. Miss a rent payment, and within twenty-four hours you were strong-armed to the street. Yet, there was no accountability for letting entropy consume the building and neglecting the tenants' fundamental human needs. Large chunks of missing plaster dotted a vertical canvas of peeling, cracked walls forever stained by the leaking roof and windows. The bathrooms functioned sporadically and were obscene in their filth. Typically, there was no heat supplied in the winter. These chronic, squalid conditions are what nourished a veritable petri dish of disease and desperation.

Laden with equipment Wendy led the hurried, single file climb up the narrow staircase. At about the halfway point she donned a devious grin and glanced behind at Trevor who was shadowing her every step. She felt overdue for some playful blackmail.

"You know Trevor, I ate an oversized portion of bean burritos last night."

"What, exactly, are you implying? Because that sounds like a threat."

"Just that you'd better be nice to me, or I'll let one fly. And since your head is at a precarious height relative to my ass, I'd heed that warning if I were you."

Trevor wasn't going to let his partner get away with such unbridled extortion or, God forbid, the last word. "It's against the Geneva Convention to let that kind of biohazard loose, and I'm fully capable of matching your firepower. So if you decide to nuke me, you're only guaranteeing our mutual annihilation."

"I'm not the one always spilling my partner's coffee, Trevor. Maybe this is righteous payback."

"Oh, so now it's my fault the city has potholes."

"Just sayin' don't piss me off, and I won't pull the trigger."

"I wonder what's it like to work with someone who doesn't abuse me."

"It's fucking boring."

The two were cognizant of the fact outsiders wouldn't understand the purpose of their ridiculous banter. So they were discerning about when and where they indulged themselves, ensuring nobody ever overheard them. Nonetheless, as unprofessional as some would judge it, all the gibes, teasing, playful empty threats and black humor served an important function. It eased their anxieties about working in such unpredictable environments. Understand, this wasn't just their peculiar brand of comical rhetoric, it was a survival technique designed to counterbalance the inevitable emotional toll their job's hazards took on them. This obligatory coping mechanism helped them defuse the constant state of tension in which they worked. God only knew what was in store for them on this, or any other call. Guns, knives, and violence regularly greeted paramedics. Normally the problem wasn't their patient, but their work's ever-changing landscape. On numerous calls over the years, they had inadvertently interrupted drug and arms deals, assaults, sex acts, robberies and other insanely volatile situations. Threats to their safety surrounded them around the clock, danger a constant threat. This made the job not just physically demanding but emotionally taxing. Their minds were continuously engaged in a mental balancing act between responding to what each moment presented and the risk of developing a crippling paranoia. Consequently, Wendy and Trevor had learned to live in a perpetual state of hypervigilance. While on duty it served them well, off-duty, not so much.

With only a few stairs remaining they wrapped up their verbal contest.

"So, do we have a truce?" he asked.

"You gonna give me a smoother ride from now on?"

"That all depends on your burrito butt."

Reaching the end of the climb, they were met by a short, grubby old man wearing several layers of sweaters and a frightened look. As soon as he could make out the uniform, he began pleading with the crew. "Hurry up! I think he's dyin'! He just keeps tell'in me to dig his grave."

Calm and professional Wendy took the lead. "All right sir, can you please show us where he is?"

With that, the crew followed their odiferous guide down the dank hallway to their patient's room. At the far end of the musty passage, the walking relic stopped next to an open doorway and began waving his arms as if directing an aircraft.

"I been try'in to feed him but he don't want nothin," he croaked.

Before following Wendy into the tiny space, Trevor praised the senior. "You're a good friend to try."

One glimpse inside the six by ten-foot space was all it took for Wendy to recognize their patient. He was gaunt, pale, and looked like shit, but it was George.

Wendy seized the chance to gather a medical history. "How long has he been like this?"

Thinking, the old man curled his face before mumbling, "Oh, I found 'im like this 'bout a week ago. He weren't gettin' no better, so I called you guys."

George lay shivering and moaning curled up on a worn-out mattress on the floor, his body veiled with a ragged, grungy sheet soaked in sweat. Kneeling down, Wendy grabbed her stethoscope and went to work examining George. Instinctively and without a word from his partner Trevor laid out the IV kit and prepared the stair-chair to haul George down the twelve flights.

Swinging her stethoscope around her neck, Wendy reached for the gear Trevor had readied and placed behind her. "Looks like he's got a nice case of pneumonia."

Wendy's words brought George to a fleeting moment of lucidity. Turning his head towards her, he sputtered a wheezing gurgle. "Hey...my...angel."

Putting an oxygen mask over his face, Wendy smiled at him. "Yes George, it's me. You and me, we're gonna go to the hospital. You've got a bad infection in your lungs." She hoped he understood. "You're gonna feel a little pinprick in your arm now."

Delirious with fever and severely dehydrated, George never flinched as the IV went in. These were the tricky calls. While lying down George's blood pressure was already dangerously low due to dehydration. Yet, the crew had no choice but to sit him upright to get him down the stairs, which meant his blood pressure could bottom out causing his heart to stop. In his current state, sitting George upright could easily put him into cardiac arrest. But there was no other way to get him out of the building, and he couldn't stay there because without further medical treatment he would be dead within a day or two.

Wendy strangled the IV bag with both hands trying to push as much fluid as possible into George as quickly as she could. She knew whatever blood pressure gains he would get from the IV were short-lived, hopefully buying the crew enough time to get him downstairs safely. Two minutes later, she reassessed his blood pressure and gave the nod to a waiting Trevor. "Let's go. Fingers crossed," she said.

The team worked in a graceful synchronization, unparalleled by less attuned partnerships. It was the primary reason they seldom spent more than ten minutes at the scene of a call. That was especially true today.

With George's shrunken frame in tow, the partners managed the challenging descent without incident. When they arrived back down at street level, the offers of help from passersby were almost nonstop. Trevor and Wendy had built up plenty of allies on the street, and as a result, they never worried an expensive piece of equipment would go missing if left unattended. It was quid pro quo.

Wendy followed the loaded stretcher into the back of the ambulance.

Trevor asked, "Need a hand?"

"Yeah, help me get him undressed."

"All right," he said, jumping into the back of the car and closing the door behind him.

As Trevor struggled to peel away the sweat-soaked jeans, Wendy double checked George's blood pressure, the IV drip rate, oxygen flow and took off his T-shirt. The sticky denim finally gave way, and Trevor was folding the pants when all of a sudden a small item fell from one of its pockets, hitting the floor with a dull knock and rolling underneath the stretcher.

"I'll get it," she said.

On her hands and knees, Wendy grabbed it off the floor. But as soon as she looked at it, she gasped. "What the..."

She was staring at a little wooden frog that was almost identical to the one Grandfather had left for her almost twenty years ago.

"What's wrong Wen?"

"Um...nothing...it's a...nothing...the floor's really grungy."

"Okay, he's naked. You got this now?" Trevor asked.

"Um...Yeah...Yeah. Let's go."

Trevor slid up front, and Forty-Eight Charlie left for St. Paul's Hospital.

It took a minute or so for Wendy to extricate herself from the river of memories that she had been swimming in. But as she tucked the carving into George's belongings, she regained her emotional footing quickly. "ETA?"

"Traffic sucks. Probably fifteen. You want me to step it up?"

"Nope, just wondering why the ride was so smooth."

Trevor gave her the finger in the rearview mirror.

Meanwhile, in a far corner of the Ovaltine Café, Mary sat nursing an hour-old cup of coffee, her stomach tightening with every passing minute George wasn't there. *Where the heck is he?* she thought.

Halfway to St. Paul's, Wendy found herself momentarily without medical duties so turned her attention to her paperwork. But before she made a single notation, George became agitated, mumbling the same phrase over and over. Wendy attributed it to the delirium of his high fever. After all, what else could it be?

"Hurry up...Dig...Hurry up...Dig the hole..."

Chapter 25
Eighteen Years Earlier - Autumn 1972
Plint Island Indian Residential School

"Hurry up! Dig the hole!...Or else!" Brother Murphy snarled, standing at the edge of the growing fissure, hissing threats, belt at the ready and towering over George who labored in the pit below. Aside from the thirteen-year-old's size and build, Brother Murphy had one particular reason for selecting George for this task, self-serving intimidation.

Plunging his shovel into the dense soil and compelled by blind obedience, George dug the hole as fast as he could manage. With only a splinter of light from the waning moon as his helpmate, he struggled to dig in the darkness. It was grueling work. But to avoid the sting of leather he persevered, toiling clumsily in the pit and struggling to heave the shovelfuls upwards and onto the pile lying above his head. Thankfully, the mixed bouquet of damp earth and salty air conspired to mask the disturbing smell of death that lay next to the growing mound of dirt.

Today's toll was a considerable one, resulting in three little ones needing burial tonight. The first was from TB, the second a suicide, and the third, and youngest, having been kicked down the stairs by a nun. Three bodies. One hole.

Tonight's excavation wasn't far from Joey's. George knew the spot from how the moonlight threw long shadows across the ground, highlighting the sunken soil and delineating the contour of each tiny, unmarked grave; many holes, many more children.

One by one, George awkwardly rolled the little corpses into the earthen cavity. Each made a dull thud as their flesh hit the clay, and each other. George didn't want to look at their faces. But he had to know if Mary was one of them, so he forced himself to peer into the abominable cavern. Once he spied the gut-wrenching sight, he yanked his head away in disgust. That split second was enough for the gruesome scene to be emblazoned in his mind permanently. It was the high price of satisfying his curiosity. And the fact Mary wasn't among the night's dead did nothing to assuage George's growing revulsion. Nonetheless, he carried on sealing the little ones in their tomb. As soon as he spread the last shovelful of dirt on the mound, he dropped the spade, scurried a few feet away and began vomiting.

Brother Murphy rushed after his young slave. While the boy was still retching on all fours, he seized his hair, wrenching George's head backward at a dangerous pitch. George believed the monk was about to release him from this world by snapping his neck. And in place of fear George embraced the idea of death, welcoming its promise of relief. Instead, Brother Murphy bent over, his menacing eyes glaring at his plaything, and pinned George at that vulnerable angle until reaching his extortion's apogee. "If you say anything about this, I will make you dig your own hole!"

213

Unclenching the terrified youngster, God's dedicated servant raised his belt in the air as a warning. "Get the hell back to bed!"

As Brother Murphy's commandment pierced the darkness, George remained crouched on the ground, petrified and having long since left his body. The boy just stared at the ocean in the near distance while his grief and horror melded into an all-embracing numbness that eclipsed his capacity to cry. His soul's lingering fragment was busy courting the woeful salty air that was beckoning to him, coaxing him to join Her, offering an alternative to his dismal existence. In that blissful, dissociative moment, and in earnest, George considered Her invitation; run, run into the ocean. But the cruel sting of his taskmaster's belt jolted him back to his senses. George ran all right, directly to his dorm.

Minutes later, as George had done so often in the past but for other deporable reasons, he snuck into his bed, careful not to wake the others. It was cold in the dorm tonight, so cold George could see his breath. But the frigid air wasn't what kept him awake and staring at the ceiling. Not tonight. Tonight his mind was spinning out of control, obsessed with the priests' and nuns' incessant words. The Holy Ones' perpetual droning about why all the children were going to Hell. That was how George got sucked into a vortex of absurdity and became swept away by all the reasons he was damned. *They say I'll go to Hell if I don't believe in Jesus...and because I speak my language...and because I honor the memory and spirits of my ancestors.* It seemed to George everything he had been raised to believe was a sin. And as he lay in that barren room ruminating on his Christian education, he became increasingly convinced that Jesus was undoubtedly sending him to Hell. Aside from being Nuxalkmc, what was George's crime? A few days earlier George had stolen a handful of food scraps and given them to the smaller children. When a nun had confronted George about it, he had lied. *They say I'll go to Hell if I lie, cheat or steal. But I only stole to help the little kids. Besides, I didn't know how to do any of those things before I came here. Anyway, how bad could Hell be? It couldn't be any worse than this place. Maybe it'll even be better than this place.*

Sleep didn't come easily that night, or any other for that matter. For George, it had ceased to be an effortless state for several years. With this one opportunity for respite denied, George tried imagining dreams instead. But even that was futile.

You see, George was preoccupied, baffled by an enigma named Jesus. Try as he might, he couldn't reconcile that guy. Over the years, George had tried his best to believe in Jesus, though motivated primarily out of fear. Nonetheless, George figured if he could truly believe in Jesus, then one way or another, Jesus would make this place better. After all, they kept saying Jesus was love. And they always said Jesus loved the little children. *But wait! It wasn't what they said. It was what they didn't say!* Then for George, the meaning coalesced. *They said Jesus loved children...but they never said Jesus loved Indian children.*

Thus, his mind began fabricating fact from fiction. *But my family loves me...Don't they? Didn't they?...I can be loved...Can't I?* For untold nights, George had sat on this precipice, straddling time and on the verge of losing the agonizing tug-of-war between the forces of yesterday and today. But tonight the hostilities ended. George hadn't been overpowered or outflanked, but infected. They had used biological warfare. A matured, virulent contagion of self-doubt had taken hold and was flourishing. And George had no immunity to the deadly virus of self-hatred.

What sprang forth from George on that moonless night was a false epiphany, which nourished itself on the rotting carcass of his self-worth. It didn't matter his conclusions arose from flawed reasoning, abuse, and unscrupulous dogma. To George, it became an irrefutable truth. It simply had to be true. It was logical, even obvious. *I'm so awful even Jesus can't love me. How could it be any other way? That's why they always beat me, starve me and rape me! Now it all makes sense. It's because I'm worthless. I'm a walking disgrace because I'm an Indian.* With that belief instilled in George, the school's curriculum was successful. The clay of his impressionable mind had been fired in the kiln of racist doctrine and had taken on a grotesque, useless shape. They had successfully made him forget who he was. Right then being Nuxalkmc had never weighed more heavily upon George than it had with that stark and bitter insight.

Ultimately he acquiesced, consenting to the exchange of his innate, inestimable value for the mantle of profound shame. From that day forward, instead of delighting in his uniqueness, George became an active participant in his own destruction.

Even still, George couldn't conceive of enduring another four years in this prison. He had never been so desperate for freedom. His longing was simple. He craved relief from the gnawing hunger, the cold, the abuse, and the anguish of living with himself. He envied Joey. Powerless and without recourse, George lay in the quiet darkness contemplating suicide. He considered his limited options, but he didn't like the idea of hanging himself like others had. So, he accepted the ocean's earlier invitation, settling on being swallowed up by the tides. *Tomorrow I'll find a way to get to the water.* Once he had made his decision, his fantasies shifted to deliverance by his own hand and the liberation it would bring. With his mind made up, George noticed something peculiar, an unnerving calm that began permeating his body. George openly welcomed the ghostly serenity, allowing it to creep into every recess. Accepting death as a real alternative had given George peace at last. And he had no hesitations about killing himself–until he remembered one small detail. Mary, his tenderhearted sister who had Mother's eyes and Father's smile. George saw his whole family on her delicate face. His heart sank. *I can't leave her alone. Not here. I gotta try to protect her.* With loyalty overriding his plans, the peacefulness abated. Mary was the single, tenuous thread keeping him from annihilating himself. So, instead of carrying out his scheme, George withdrew inside himself and hunkered in a cocoon of hurt. The previous cavalcade of ugly ideas resurfaced and continued throughout the night, punctuated by an ephemeral, restless sleep. It was well past midnight, and all he knew was the icy darkness.

Chapter 26
1992
Vancouver, British Columbia

It was well past midnight, and all he knew was the icy darkness. The shadows of his work life had crept out of their lair to dispense another rough night for Trevor. His body felt forever cold, a long-standing, persistent chill in his core that simply would not recede. It didn't matter how long, or how hot, the shower was, Trevor couldn't warm up. This was day three of four days off and his third night on the roller coaster.

Trevor lay in bed staring wide-eyed at the ceiling, drowning in cold sweat, his mind spinning out of control. It was two a.m. Each bad call had chiseled another crack in his psychological dam. Tonight the endless barrage had broken through and was cascading into an unwilling consciousness. And those memories burst forth intact. Trevor could smell the smells and taste the air. Every gory detail was burned into his brain. The song playing on the radio of the drunk's car; the smell of wet leaves mixed with blood; a little white shoe; a simple cotton dress; the sky blue ribbon that had tied her hair back. Childhood innocence perverted and dripping with crimson. The never-ending parade of images trooped through his mind's eye like archival footage, bombarding Trevor in an excruciating, infinite playback loop.

Peeling back the damp covers, Trevor sat bolt upright on the edge of his bed. Anxious droplets streamed off him as he tried coaxing himself back from the brink of overwhelm. He tried pulling himself away from the chasm of horror. He tried carving out some small shelter amidst the deluge of emotions and memories transitioning into his awareness. But Trevor was a poor swimmer drowning in a sea of unacknowledged grief and revulsion.

But before he succumbed to the pounding surf of his emotional turmoil, an improbable four-legged savior named Storm tossed him a life ring. The dog possessed an exceptional ability to sense whenever Trevor began spiraling into his personal abyss. Tonight it was evident to Storm that Trevor's anxiety was rising out of control. With his friend straddling the boundary between past and present, a dutiful Storm got up and laid his head on Trevor's leg. At first, he just stared at his embattled master. Getting no response, he whined and nudged Trevor's thigh. That simple, intuitive gesture broke the unholy spell, snapping Trevor's awareness back to the moment. "Thanks, buddy," he said, reaching down and stroking Storm's head, grateful to be rescued from paramedic purgatory.

Storm was just repaying the favor. You see, a couple of years ago Trevor had rescued him. One sunny June morning, on an impulse, Trevor had decided he wanted a dog. To get a puppy from a pet store or a breeder would have been a violation of Trevor's character. No, he was a rescue worker. So, he went straight to the local animal shelter to find the perfect companion.

That was the day Trevor granted clemency to one rather notable canine whose residency at the shelter was about to come to an abrupt end, adoption or not. This particular dog had become legendary with the shelter's staff, or infamous, depending on whom you asked. His deserved reputation hinged on a suspiciously psychotic demeanor. Imagine, a hefty muscle bound hound who, in his calmer moments, bounced four feet off the ground. One whose play growl unnerved some people and made others cover their jugulars in preemptive self-defense. This coupled with his frenzied behavior made him a good candidate for a doggy straitjacket. There was little doubt the mutt was a handful-and-a-half, resulting in the shelter's staff being convinced he was unadoptable. Though the dog was not the least bit aggressive and never tried to hurt anyone, it was all just a matter of bad PR on his part.

Aside from the dog's overly energetic personality, what most people couldn't get past was the mix of breeds. His official pedigree, as close as anyone could figure, was Rottweiler and Pitt Bull, or as Trevor would christen him, Pittweiler. The dog's heritage was never an issue for Trevor, he was used to advocating for the marginalized. To him, the dog was a mutt plain and simple. And what Trevor came to value most about his adopted friend was that he possessed an unparalleled zest for life. He had no class, no manners and best of all, no worries.

Initially, the shelter's staff had encouraged Trevor to consider a couple of their more recent arrivals, but they hadn't felt right to Trevor. Hoping for an undeniable spark of chemistry to befall him, Trevor wandered around the facility. He had already spent the better part of an hour pacing up and down the shelter's aisles when something caught his eye. Feeling compelled to investigate this oddity, Trevor strode through the pandemonium for a closer look. Amidst the canine chaos, Trevor discovered a black and tan bastion of serenity sitting at the front of his run. The dog never took his eyes off Trevor as he approached. The would-be master knelt in front of the cage. "What're you in for, big fella?"

There was a long pause while the two scrutinized each other.

"I dunno...I work weird hours..."

The dog sat quietly, wagging his long tail whenever Trevor spoke.

"And I don't share my bed."

The mixed-breed monster didn't flinch and continued staring at Trevor. Trevor felt the tug, but he hesitated. So it was left to the furry one to break the stalemate. He signaled Trevor by raising his paw onto the wire enclosure as if to say, *Come on dude. We both know I'm the one.* That moment sealed the deal. In reality, Trevor didn't have a choice. The dog had picked him. And it felt suspiciously predestined.

Arriving home for the first time with the dog Trevor realized this adoption was the equivalent of a doggy bait-n-switch. When Trevor opened the door, he unwittingly unleashed a deranged, four-legged tornado. The dog took off, tearing through the basement suite like a hurricane and narrowly missing Trevor's prized, spindly philodendron. Sprinting at full speed, the rascal made a dozen loops through the modest space before his afterburners flamed out. The way that dog behaved he may as well have been on crack; a delightful mix of rabid squirrel and joy personified. Trevor even wondered if he didn't see tiny horns growing out of the dog's head. But at last, the frenetic homecoming ended with the dog coming to a screeching stop, panting heavily and tongue hanging unceremoniously out of his mouth at the feet of an amused Trevor. All the proud new owner could do was stand there laughing. "Well, I guess I'll call you Storm."

Call it kismet or perhaps karma but the indisputable fact was the fast friends were made for each other. And as months passed, Trevor became heavily dependent on Storm, needing that dog far more than he was comfortable admitting to himself. Except for Wendy, Trevor didn't trust people. And if it weren't for his somewhat demented canine amigo, off the job, Trevor would have lived a hermit's life.

So tonight, as the demons from a myriad mix of bygone calls demanded their piece of psychological flesh, Trevor yielded to his good friend's advice. Laying back down he invited Storm up on the bed with him. The dog didn't need a lot of encouragement. Without delay, seventy-five pounds of hairy hedonist landed on top of Trevor with a great loving thud.

Storm nuzzled his head into the crook of Trevor's arm, closed his eyes, took a deep breath and sighed before his breathing slowed and deepened. Trevor found the rhythm soothing and hypnotic, and it made him feel like he might be able to sleep after all. That night Trevor didn't reach for the vodka bottle perched on his rickety nightstand.

Chapter 27
Meanwhile...
Vancouver's Eastside

That morning Mary reached for the clean rig perched on her rickety nightstand. She was proud of herself. Not only had she turned enough tricks last night to afford the next four or five fixes, but she had made it back home to use in private, though her preference for privacy cut both ways. She had seen countless others perish from the same decision, and knew the risks of using heroin alone. But she had an ongoing arrangement with her dealer. He was candid regarding the current batch's strength and composition, and cautioned Mary if he thought it was cut with something dangerous. And it was all in exchange for regular blowjobs. It was cheap life insurance.

Mary had no illusions about her addiction. Her maxim was pragmatic and straightforward. *If this shit's gonna kill me, then I wanna die on my terms, in my own room, not lying in some filthy back-alley.* And Mary knew eventually it would kill her. It always did. For her, it was never a question of if, only a question of when.

Despite the danger of a solo hit, Mary preferred getting high in her own place instead of some anonymous alleyway. She abhorred watching other junkies nod off in such squalid conditions; mere steps away from where they had bought their fix. It sickened her to see them lying sprawled on the ground between dumpsters or slumped in a darkened doorway, often with the rig still hanging out of their vein. That depressing sight was the neighborhood's singular constant. Regardless of the rain, the snow, or the heat, it was a scene that had played out endlessly for generations.

For Mary, like most addicts, getting high was about coping, about managing the constant emotional pain and anxiety about her past, present, and in all likelihood, her future. Mary never talked about the future. It was a taboo subject. Each of Mary's imagined tomorrows was devoid of her desires, myriad things she knew she would never have; a real home instead of a rathole; meaningful work instead of prostitution; a tranquil mind instead of a litany of anguish; and sobriety. But Mary's longing for a family of her own underscored her most heartbreaking loss, her inability to bring forth life. Not that her current circumstances would have allowed for it. Mary knew the simple notion of having children was a ludicrous, far-fetched delusion. But however out of reach her fantasy was, it lingered as an irrepressible yearning, and remained an abiding source of mourning. So, Mary avoided self-indulgent daydreams that only drove her further into the trap of unrealistic hope. Because escaping hope's snare meant Mary would have to turn her back on the life she wanted and return to face the wilderness of her prevailing condition. It was a vicious and unforgiving cycle of deepening despair. So over time, Mary realized it was far better to remain hopeless than to torture herself with impossibilities. And she had come to realize some truths about her emotional pain. That optimism created it, the past was brimming with it, and the present was about managing the two. In the end, it was a simple equation. The junk killed the pain, and made her forget. And through it, Mary gained what she sought, blissful, albeit temporary, amnesia.

That morning Mary had remained true to her convictions by returning to her building before using. It was located six blocks east of Main and Hastings and two blocks south of the loading docks, where longshoremen toiled and container ships were a constant presence. The four-story walk-up housed an eclectic sampling of the working poor and the addicted. Mary had chosen the place intentionally because it was not in the middle of the war zone of Hastings and Main. That decision was a unique, yet effective way of limiting her exposure to the lure of unrestrained drug use, which had seduced throngs into an early grave. Mary just wanted to kill the pain, not herself, at least not yet.

A microcommunity had developed over the years within the crumbling plaster walls that Mary called home. And once the initial shock of city life had lessened, she had gladly assimilated into its fold. Everyone helped each other out as best they could. Random acts of both kindness and generosity lived in tandem with the surrounding environment's unpredictable brutality. With few exceptions, it was a sanctuary where vulnerable, marginalized people banded together for their common welfare.

It was with that common welfare in mind that Mary looked in on Marjorie each evening before heading out to work, ensuring the senior had everything she needed. In turn, Marjorie checked on Mary each morning making sure she was present and accounted for. This morning was no different. Mary answered the gentle rapping on her door. "Hi, Marjorie."

"Oh good morning Mary. I see you're home safe and sound."

"Yup. I'm in the same shape as when I left."

Marjorie opened her arms. "Come on now love, give us a squish."

Mary stepped out of her room and into her friend's embrace. After welcoming Mary home, the elder made her usual remark. "I still can't get over how much you look like Anne Bancroft." Knowing it was a compliment Mary smiled. She just didn't have any idea who the hell Anne Bancroft was.

"I'll look in on you tonight before I go out," Mary said.

"Thank you, dear. Be a good girl now."

"Always. Bye Marjorie."

"Goodbye dear."

The morning's ritual homecoming was accomplished as usual, facilitated by the women's close friendship. The two parted ways in the narrow hallway, one readying herself for a doctor's appointment later that morning, the other off to satisfy the requirements of addiction.

Back in her room and sitting on the edge of her sagging mattress, Mary paused from the task at hand to notice the subtle beauty of the early dawn light breaking over the city. But she couldn't tarry, or the nausea would start. Soon after, as she had done hundreds of times before, she gradually released her life's cares into her left arm. Sighing heavily, Mary laid back and sank into the timeworn mattress while the impressions of yesterday receded into abeyance. It took fewer than ten seconds before she slipped into unconsciousness and embraced the transient comfort she had bartered her dignity for. That particular morning the sound of Marjorie's canary greeting the new day accompanied Mary's descent into oblivion. The bird sang the sweetest song that morning.

Chapter 28
Meanwhile...
Vancouver's Stanley Park

The birds sang the sweetest songs that morning. With their delicate melodies echoing off the last remnants of fog that wafted up from the calm morning ocean, a profound tranquility embodied these surroundings. It was why Wendy chose to run here. She hoped its serenity would rub off.

Wendy had already gotten her legal buzz earlier in this morning's routine. And she had welcomed the sweet endorphins which now pulsed through her body, making her feel almost invincible. Better yet, her favorite part of the route was fast approaching. Spurred on by the runner's high, she zipped across the road opposite the seawall and onto a trail in the adjacent woods. There the forest floor was soft to run on, and the dense canopy of cedar and fir trees muffled the harsh city noise, thus bestowing a near Zen-like atmosphere upon her workout. In that forested cathedral, Wendy found the rhythm of her pace soothing. Soon her footsteps became hypnotic, and with every stride, the tiniest piece of her work's burden melted away; running brought Wendy as close to the moment as she could get, though some days that was harder to achieve than others. Her grim stockpile of memories, coupled with the nauseating potential of the next shift, kept Wendy suspended in one of the countless forms of rescue worker purgatory; one where impressions from the past blended with those of today, to create nothing but anxiety about the future.

But for right now, Wendy fixated on the experience of running. How the cold air caressed each cell as it passed through her lungs; how her muscles shifted and balanced as she moved; how the beads of sweat grew larger, and the way they fell from her brow. It was in this simple, mindful way that Wendy became free. And no matter how short-lived, a glimpse of liberation was all the sustenance she needed.

Though fitness was the pretense of her run, in reality, it was a ritual of pilgrimage, a meditation and cleansing of her mind before she met with her redeemer, the ocean. Wendy was physically spent by the time she reached the shoreline, having nothing left to offer up to the sea's altar except the vestiges of her tortured psyche. She came to rest on an outcrop of gray bedrock, which had been exposed by the low tide. Wendy sat and without thinking matched her breathing to the comforting tempo of the waves.

Slowly, the ugly thoughts and images receded, and with her mind still, her body started to settle. A minute passed. Then another. And another. Finally, Wendy's physical anxiety began to lessen. Her guts unclenched, and she could feel her weight pressing on the bedrock beneath her. The reprieve washing over her felt like it would continue, but a siren off in the distance assaulted that pensive moment. Wendy startled. *Shit,* she thought. And with that, her hard-earned repose vanished instantaneously. Oblivious to the adrenaline sparked by the familiar noise, and having no choice, Wendy obeyed its compulsory decree by jumping upright and beginning her running meditation all over again.

Another hour passed before her routine came to an exhausted conclusion in front of the Stanley Park totem poles. Her workouts rarely took her this deep into the park. Wendy much preferred the isolation of the wooded trails or the seawall. Normally there were hordes of tourists milling about the totems. But being early in the day they had yet to arrive, so Wendy had the place almost to herself. She chose a bench giving her a view of the ocean, the mountains, and the totems and sat down to rest. In that snippet of time Wendy felt as relaxed as an off-duty paramedic could feel which was a state most people would find to be one of intolerable tension. But for Wendy, this was as good as it got. She felt marginally better, and any relief no matter how short-lived was a goal worthy of her effort.

Leaning back on the bench, Wendy stretched and allowed herself to enjoy the faint warmth of the early spring sunshine on her face. Opening her eyes, she looked with awe upon the vertical guardians towering before her and began contemplating their sophisticated designs. Wendy understood the significance of most of the intricate images, and she felt a deep connection to the artwork. As she rested there studying the ancient art forms, a broad smile broke over her countenance. Surfacing in her mind's eye was the wrinkled face of her old friend, the elderly Nuxalkmc man she had come to know simply as Grandfather. A cascade of images flooded into her consciousness and, much to Wendy's surprise, they were pleasant ones. The totems must have worked their magic, having provoked fond memories of Grandfather and his carvings. Those charming effigies he created from nothing more than a piece of cedar and a tiny curved knife.

Wendy welcomed the recollections. Over time, the two had had countless meetings. Yet here she sat, almost two and a half decades later, with one particular encounter replaying in her mind. Wendy remembered having come upon him early one morning at the beach. Grandfather had been sitting on their log. "Good morning Wendy. Come and sit with me."

Wendy complied but not before covertly wiping tears from her face. She assumed her usual perch as he began carving a block of cedar that he had produced from his coat pocket. Grandfather could tell she had been crying and she knew that he knew. But somehow, Wendy didn't feel vulnerable when she was with him. What was more, Grandfather's irresistible presence had the effect of calming her right to her core. Sitting next to her old friend while he carved another magical creature, Wendy momentarily forgot why she had been upset. She watched, mesmerized, as he persuaded bits of wood away from the emerging form underneath. Grandfather taught as he worked. "Did you know that Frog can call the rain that makes everything clean?...And that Frog helps people to cry."

"Why would Frog want people to cry?"

"Because my dear, shedding tears can make you feel brand new."

Tilting his head towards her, he looked into her reddened eyes and smiled. His gaze touched Wendy on a level she could not describe. More than anything else, she remembered his compassionate eyes because when he looked at her, he made her feel like she mattered.

"This is why you should never be afraid to cry."

"Really?"

"Yes, really. Tears are healing...Unshed tears will make you sick. And that is just one way to hurt your spirit."

Wendy wrinkled her face and reflected on his words before asking, "How else can you hurt your spirit?"

"By forgetting who you are."

"You mean you don't remember your name?"

Grandfather laughed. "No. I mean you forget what it's like to be you. You put on a mask and pretend to be someone you're not. And if you don't ever take off the mask, pretty soon you think the mask is you. But the mask made the real you disappear. And that hurts your spirit. It's like you've cut off your hand and your arm no longer has a purpose."

Wendy thought for a few minutes. "How can you tell if your spirit is hurt?"

"Well...your medicine isn't very good."

Wendy knew exactly what Grandfather was implying because he had said it a lot. "Remember, you can tell a lot about people by their medicine."

A year or so ago, when Wendy had first heard Grandfather say this, she thought he was talking about what brand of cough syrup people used. But she was an astute eleven-year-old, and it hadn't taken long for her to understand what he meant. She intuited he was talking about a person's inherent way of being. Basically, it amounted to what a person's natural gifts were and how they used them to make things better in the world. But if you had forgotten who you were, you had bad medicine and often made things worse. At that particular time in her life, in the midst of all the abuse, Wendy was unsure of herself and was beginning to feel worthless. That day, with her voice dripping with anxiety, she had put a courageous question to him. "Grandfather...What is...what is my medicine?"

Grandfather was unreserved. "Oh, it's good!...It's very good."

And he had looked at Wendy with gentle affection before continuing. "You have Frog medicine you know."

After hearing all the stories about the extraordinary creature named Frog, Grandfather's response had delighted the little girl. "Really?"

"Yes, really."

"Wow," she had said, her eyes sparkling and wide.

It had been those few, enchanting, well-timed words that had saved Wendy. You see, her little spark had been in jeopardy of extinguishment from the brutality of her day-to-day life. That day, almost twenty-five years ago, Grandfather had validated her existence in a compelling, meaningful way. And Wendy had resonated with every syllable. Having him affirm her value as a person was akin to throwing gasoline on the withering ember of her spirit. And it had exploded, burning brightly for the first time in her life. From that day forward, whenever Wendy felt coerced to accept her beatings because she was told she deserved them, she refused to wear the mask and clung to her venerable friend's words; those few, enchanting, well-timed words.

Until now, sitting in front of those totem poles, Wendy had never fully appreciated how much she missed his company, but more importantly how much of a difference he had made in her life. Grandfather had imparted wisdom to her that Wendy still relied on today. *He gave me so much and treated me just like a granddaughter. I wonder if he had grandchildren of his own?* she pondered. Quite unaware of the broad smile continuing to reside on her face, Wendy sat reminiscing about her long-lost redeemer, when she remembered the parting gift he had mysteriously left for her so many years before. That tiny carved Frog had been Wendy's constant companion, and she had carried it in her pocket for years.

Chapter 29
Six Months Later - Autumn 1992
Vancouver's Downtown Eastside

That tiny carved Frog had been George's constant companion, and he had carried it in his pocket for years. Frog was special to him. Frog was the first form Grandfather had taught him how to carve. George loved the stories about Frog, the Great Cleanser, and Healer. Somehow having Frog near him was like having Grandfather close. George tried not to think about how much he missed him.

Over the years, George had made regular additions to the varied flock of animals in his carving repertoire. "Enough to fill an ark." He would often say, joking with the tourists to whom he sold his wooden creations. They rarely quibbled about the price of one of Noah's herd; bad enough it was often a pity sale. George never deluded himself about the quality of the works he peddled. He didn't have the luxury of time to properly finish the pieces. His handiworks were simply a means to an end, to prevent the d.t.'s.

By George's own estimation, selling his artwork was a dignified occupation and much preferable to panhandling. He despised panhandling. Resorting to it only when sales were slow, when he needed a bottle to prevent seizures, or when he was too drunk to carve. His scarred and often bloodied hands stated the obvious. Drunken carving was not safe carving. Nonetheless, George had an artistic gift. Despite his alcoholism and given the few tools he owned, there were times when he produced some unusual and intricate pieces.

George knew the best place to ply his wares was at the edge of Gastown, Vancouver's first street and now the center of tourist activities. Though he certainly wasn't welcome near several of the art galleries–who dealt primarily in Indigenous art–that lined the three-block stretch of cobblestones. They had made that abundantly clear by shooing him away, claiming it was unfair competition. But George knew the real issue was his worse-for-wear appearance. Yet there was one gallery owner who had taken an interest in George's talent. She had spoken with him recently when George was sitting on a bench across the street from her store. "Good morning," she said.

"Good morning," George replied.

"I own the gallery across the street. I've been watching you, and–"

George interrupted her. "Okay, okay, I'll move along," he said, reaching down to gather up his tools.

"No, no. Please, it's all right. I've been watching you, and I think you have real potential. I'd like to buy some of your pieces to sell in my gallery."

"Yeah?" said a stunned George.

"Yes. But I have one stipulation. Your work must be properly finished before I can sell it. You understand?"

"Yes...Okay...I'll do my best."

"Come and see me anytime when you've got a few finished pieces."

"I uh...I will...uh...thanks."

She reached out and shook George's hand. "I look forward to seeing your artwork in my store."

With that, she had turned around and left a gobsmacked George sitting with his mouth open. It was a fantastic opportunity, one that had both astounded him and kindled a twinkle of hope. But what was more, it made George think. Forcing him to consider things he had been reluctant to think about before. *Maybe...I could do what I love...Maybe...I could earn a decent living...Maybe...I could have a nice place to live...If I can finish my pieces properly...If I don't have seizures...If...I can get a detox bed...If...I can stay sober...If...The voices and flashbacks would stop without the booze.* If, if, if. And just like that, his aspirations suffocated in a great vacuum of doubt.

So far, the bench George had laid claim to on that fair Sunday morning had produced substantial foot traffic, and he had already made three sales to a passing group of Asian tourists.

By the sun's angle, George suspected it was probably well past noon. He asked a passerby, "Excuse me, ma'am, do you know what time it is?" She pretended George didn't exist. So he asked again; and again; and again; eight requests in total. Each time receiving either the cold shoulder or the usual sarcasm, "Time to get a job." Still, George remained polite. On his ninth appeal, he was granted his daring request, although reluctantly. It was one o'clock. Time to meet his sister for coffee.

Chapter 30
Meanwhile...

It was one o'clock. Time to go get coffee. That modest objective at the start of each shift ranked as priority number one for Wendy and Trevor, though it was grounded in a great deal more than a shallow desire for caffeine. The mere act of it represented something much more profound; a predictable, regimented routine. It was a welcome, and all too often necessary counterweight to the inevitable chaos to follow. By its nature, the job was unpredictable, so it cried out for as many dependable patterns as possible. Getting coffee was their ritual. It was their way of bringing order to disorder, control to the uncontrollable, even if it was only briefly. If a call interrupted that simple quest, the two felt unsteady, as if knocked off their centers. And they would both feel that way for the rest of the shift.

Trevor stood at the coffee counter stirring in his fifth sugar packet. "Never underestimate the power of caffeine and sugar."

"Amen," Wendy sang.

They had barely put the lids on the fresh brew when a call came in. "Forty-Eight Charlie, code three for the overdose, fifth floor, one fifty-nine East Hastings, the Balmoral Hotel."

Wendy paid for the coffee, Trevor acknowledged his dispatcher, and the two headed back to the car, cups in hand, ritual fulfilled, grounded and ready to work. Climbing into the front of the ambulance Wendy groaned as she grabbed the crew report. "I'm doomed to drink cold coffee aren't I?"

Trevor lit up the car and accelerated while rolling his eyes at her. "Like you weren't expecting to work today?"

"Maybe I should just switch to iced coffee. Then I wouldn't be constantly disappointed."

Weaving the ambulance through the dense traffic, Trevor didn't miss a beat. "Nah, you'd just bitch that it got warm."

Wendy smirked while lamenting over the siren's blare. "Okay, so why can't they just make coffee that tastes good at room temperature?"

Edging his way through a red light, he countered, "Don't you know the definition of insanity?"

Putting on her gloves, Wendy followed the script. "And that would be?...Oh, wait. I think you've said this before."

Trevor laughed at the irony before answering, "Doing the same thing over and over and expecting different results. Remember?"

Lightly smacking her forehead with her gloved hand, Wendy concluded the ritual. "Oh, now I get it! Like expecting my partner not to spill my room temperature coffee while I'm actually working in the back of the car."

Predictable, regimented routine.

That short conversation was as long as it took to arrive at the Balmoral Hotel, a rather infamous rooming house in the area. If drug addiction were an earthquake, this place was the epicenter.

As the partners had done a thousand times before, grabbing their gear they entered the decrepit lobby and began the strenuous trek up the creaky wooden staircase. Even loaded down with their equipment, they still made it up to the fifth floor in less than three minutes. Making their way down the long, narrow hall that separated the dozen or so cramped rooms lining it, they assumed their patient belonged to the vertical foot they saw protruding from around the corner at the far end of the passageway.

One glance at the foot's owner was all it took to know, with almost one hundred percent certainty, what they were dealing with–heroin–and too much of it. Lying on the floor at their feet was a woman in her mid-thirties who was not breathing. Safe to say, from the sight of her plum-purple face, she had not been breathing for quite some time. Both her arms were brimming with track marks and her pupils were so constricted they were little more than pencil dots. Luckily, her heart hadn't stopped–but that could change at any second.

The two paramedics plunged to the floor. Trevor got to work by establishing an airway and ventilating the woman. With every squeeze of the bag he used to breathe for her, her color improved, the purple transforming into pink. As Trevor took charge of the immediate life threat, Wendy ruled out any obvious trauma, gathered baseline vital signs, tested her blood sugar and began the challenging task of looking for a vein to use for an intravenous medication route. Just as she picked up the patient's left arm, Wendy startled, jumping backward. "Shit!"

Trevor giggled as Wendy stood there cursing a cockroach that had scurried out from underneath their patient. "Fuck me!"

"You know, the sooner you get a line, the sooner we can get outta here," he said.

Wendy was still flinching. "God damn, fucking bugs!"

"I'd love to give ya a hand, but I'm kinda busy right now."

Of course, that kind of drollery deserved "the look." So, she flashed it, returned to the infested floor and continued hunting for a useable intravenous route. "Man, she's got nothing left for veins. How she's managed to fix with is beyond me."

Several more minutes of fruitless searching passed. The only thing standing between this woman and a tray in the morgue was Trevor and an Ambu bag.

"Gettin' kinda tired of bagging her," he teased.

"Gettin' kinda tired of a partner without any stamina," she replied.

As a last resort, Wendy checked the woman's feet, but those veins were just as scarred and useless. "Well, it's the emergency vein or nothing."

Wendy was referring to a tiny vein on the back of the thumb that most people possessed, and most junkies would never use. Less than ninety seconds later, the capable paramedic had established a tiny IV line, and their patient had received her first dose of Naloxone, known on the street as Narcan or the heroin antidote. The next forty-five seconds were critical. The drug needed only a short time to work. If the woman did not respond, this likely was not a narcotic overdose.

Within half a minute, her eyes started to flicker. Her gag reflex would return rapidly, so Trevor removed the tube from his patient's throat just as she began taking breaths on her own. She woke up fast, startled and disoriented. Trevor was ready. "It's all right. It's all right. You overdosed, and we're here to help you. You're okay now. Can you take some nice deep breaths through this oxygen mask for me?"

Mary complied.

"Let's get you off the floor and sitting up," said Trevor, helping his patient to lean against the plaster wall.

"Your name's Mary, right hon?" he asked.

"Yes."

"You remember us? I'm Trevor, that's Wendy."

"Oh yeah, sure."

"We need to ask you some questions, okay? Just keep that oxygen mask on your face for a while yet," he said

A rattled Mary said, "Okay."

Noticing Mary was starting to shiver, Wendy wrapped a blanket around her shoulders. "There you go."

"Thanks."

Squatting beside her patient Wendy continued the assessment. "Do you know where you are?"

Mary looked around the hallway. "The Balmoral, I think."

"That's right. You usually use coke, junk, both?"

"Just junk."

"Okay. Now, Trevor's gonna take your blood pressure, and I'm gonna listen to your lungs. Good with you?"

"Yeah...whatever you need to do, thanks."

From the brink of death to fully functioning in under a minute, these miraculous resurrections would often amaze onlookers. To Wendy and Trevor, it was a reprieve from having to carry an unconscious person down several flights of stairs.

Wendy asked, "Have you ever overdosed before?"

Still recovering from her ordeal, Mary shook her head and whispered. "No."

On hearing the answer, Wendy went into paramedic infomercial mode. "Well, when we found you, you weren't breathing, and you were purple, which meant you hadn't been breathing for quite some time."

Mary gasped. "Jesus!"

"You're okay now because we gave you a drug that made you start breathing again. The problem is this: the drug we gave you doesn't last as long as the heroin, so when the antidote wears off, the heroin can kick back in and you could stop breathing again. You need to go to the hospital so we can watch you in case that happens. It'll only be for a few hours, just to

245

make sure you'll be all right. And no, the cops won't be there."

Mary understood the seriousness of her situation and heeded Wendy's trusted advice.

Reaching down, Wendy took Mary by the arm, helping her to stand up. "Easy now. You let me know if you're not up to walking, okay?"

Mary rose from the floor as if nothing had happened. Tethered to her rescuers by the IV line, she followed them downstairs. On the third flight of stairs, a sudden realization struck her. "Hey, isn't this Sunday?"

Trevor said, "Yup."

Mary became frantic. "Oh my God. What time is it!"

"It's about one thirty in the afternoon," he said.

Tears were welling up in her eyes. "Oh, I'm late, I'm so late!"

Wendy said, "Calm down Mary. What're you late for?"

"I gotta meet my brother at the Ovaltine. He'll get real worried if I'm not there. I have to go see him! I have to! I'll be okay. I can get George to watch me. That's just as good as the hospital, right?" she pleaded, more for George's well-being than her own.

Wendy intervened, placing her hand on her patient's shoulder. "That's really not in your best interest Mary. If something happened again, your brother wouldn't be able to help you. And honestly, you're more good to him alive than dead. Don't you think?"

"I guess...you're right...It's just that he'll be real upset cuz I'm not there."

Trevor was growing impatient and just wanted this call over with. To hurry it along, he blurted out a surprising suggestion. "Maybe we can give your brother a message after we take care of you at the hospital."

Mary was thrilled by the generous offer. "Would you really do that?"

Wendy's face wrinkled in puzzlement before saying, "Look, we'll try. But you know we don't exactly take appointments."

Letting out a big sigh, Mary said, "Oh, if you could just try. My little Georgie'll be worried out of his mind."

"We'll do our best. I promise," said Wendy, turning around and giving Trevor the "what the fuck?" look.

Shortly the trio was in the ambulance and on their way to St. Paul's. Wendy made sure Mary was comfortable and didn't need another dose of antidote.

"So Mary, can you tell me if you're allergic to any medicines? Are there any medicines that make you really sick?"

"Not that I know of."

"Okay. How about medical conditions? You know like diabetes or hepatitis?"

Mary was hesitant. "Does everything I tell you stay between us?"

"Yes, of course, everything's confidential. The only people who will know what you tell me are the doctors and nurses at the hospital."

"Okay. Cuz when you talk to George, I don't want him to know I'm sick...I don't want him knowing I got HIV."

Wendy nodded. "I promise. It's no one else's business."

Mary took a big breath. "Okay, that's good."

"How long have you been HIV?"

"Bout' six months. I was at the clinic for my arm, and they did the test."

"I'm sorry Mary. That really sucks."

Mary wore a half grin. "Yeah, it does...But we all gotta die sometime, right?"

Wendy shrugged. "Yeah. That's true...You mind if I get some paperwork done?"

"Oh, sorry. Go ahead."

Wendy squeezed her patient's hand. "You've got nothin' to be sorry for."

While Wendy scribbled, Mary withdrew into her thoughts, and a tense quiet descended on the ambulance. Several minutes had passed before Mary turned to Wendy and asked, "Did I really...did I really stop breathing?"

Wendy saw her patient was struggling with a somber truth, so she lowered her voice when answering, "Yes, yes you did. You were very purple when we found you."

After thinking for a minute, Mary's droll wit surfaced. "Did the color match my blouse at least?"

Wendy chuckled, and Mary shared the nervous laugh. Mary was scared, and Wendy knew her humor was a coping mechanism. That much at least, the two women had in common.

Studying her patient further, Wendy made a strategic, but tactful inquiry. "Mary, I know you, and I know you're normally very careful when you use. So, what happened today? Is there some new stuff out there? You change your dealer?..."

Feeling like she owed the paramedic something, Mary was straightforward. "I did a trade, you know? I didn't fix it myself. I should've..." Wendy knew exactly what she was referring to, sex for drugs, and didn't push the issue.

Having arrived at St. Paul's, it didn't take long to transfer Mary's care to the hospital staff. Trevor waited until their patient was out of earshot before asking Wendy for a street update. "So do you think we're gonna be doing a bunch of these today or what?"

"Mmmm...dunno...I don't think so. Might be a one-off. But I wouldn't bet on it."

Trevor was irritated. "Lotta good that intel did. Could you be anymore noncommittal?"

Wendy laughed. "Says the guy who hasn't had so much as a date in two years."

The promise they had made to Mary was at the forefront of Wendy's mind. "Are we ready to get back into service? We've got a message to deliver."

Trevor growled at her unexpectedly. "So now we're fucking Western Union?"

His childish attitude caught Wendy off guard, and she snapped back. "Oh for fuck sakes Trevor. It'll take all of two minutes, and we'll be back in our area, so there's no threat of us doing calls in taxpayer land. Besides it was your fucking idea, remember?"

She was right, and Trevor knew it. It wasn't a big deal. It was just sometimes he felt like there was nothing left to give. Today was one of those days. And lately he had had mood swings, which were becoming especially noticeable to his partner. Trevor needed to fight, he just didn't want to do it with Wendy. So he acquiesced. Though he wasn't finished indulging his bitter mood. "Yeah, yeah. Let's just get it over with."

Grabbing their gear, they began walking back to the ambulance via the ER's long hallway.

Wendy asked him, "You know who Mary's brother is?"

"Uh, let's see, some Native guy who lives in the skids. Could you narrow it down a little?"

She nudged his side with her elbow. "We know him. He's a regular."

Trevor's hostility grew. "Yeah? That doesn't fucking help. Who is he?"

"Okay, remember a few years ago, the guy in Oppenheimer Park who freaked out on us yelling 'don't take me away'?"

Annoyed, Trevor shoved the oxygen cylinder at his persistent partner for her to secure in the ambulance.

She paused hoping Trevor would remember. "He pushes a shopping cart around sometimes?" Which only elicited further groaning from Trevor.

Wendy was undeterred. "You gotta remember the guy we whistled out of VGH to St. Paul's because they wouldn't give him a bed?"

As Trevor stuffed the jump kit back into position, he remained indifferent, and mute, to the one-sided conversation. And he found Wendy's tenacity about the subject irritating.

She gave him one last, playful hint. "I'll take 'Calls That Ended in Disciplinary Hearings' for $200, Alex."

Trevor's calm exterior disguised his mounting tension. He was about to lose it over this stupid guessing game. Throwing daggers with his glare, he told her to "fuck off" without moving his lips.

Wendy had been trying to lighten his mood, but it wasn't working. She was losing patience with him and becoming exasperated with his increasingly unpredictable temperament. In her view, his unwarranted dirty look was unacceptable. So she shelved her normally congenial tone and confronted him. "Okay, your Grumpiness. What is the big deal?...And what crawled up your ass today?"

Her unexpected bluntness slapped Trevor upside the head, making him rein in his temper. Lately, it had been all he could do to drag himself into work, let alone go above and beyond. Regretting his passive-aggressive tone, he diverted his gaze, sighing in lieu of an apology. "Nothing. Whatever...Let's just do it."

Climbing into the front of the car, Wendy was terse. "Good."

A subdued Trevor took out his frustrations by throwing the ambulance into drive and making a beeline for their area.

In the back of his mind, Trevor knew once he'd made that promise to Mary they were bound to keep it. To Forty-Eight Charlie, keeping a promise was about much more than personal integrity. Trevor knew better than anyone the vital importance of building trust on the street. In a place many feared to work, Trevor felt reasonably safe. He and Wendy had spent several years treating everyone they encountered with respect and building strong relationships along the way. Of course, some occasions demanded the crew set firm boundaries, but it was always for their patients' own protection. The pair made it a priority to develop a solid rapport with the denizens of the community they served. In turn, they were repaid with the best, and cheapest, life insurance available. "Their people" trusted them, and more importantly, respected them. Unlike others, who felt entitled to demand respect simply by donning a uniform, Trevor and Wendy strived to earn it every single shift. By routinely engaging in small acts of kindness, over time their efforts coalesced into a fabric of mutual esteem.

All their intentional goodwill was validated one day when Forty-Eight Charlie attended to a "man down" call at Main and Hastings. A crowd of several dozen onlookers had formed around the two paramedics as they worked and Wendy and Trevor could overhear their comments. "Oh good. It's them. They're okay. They'll treat 'im good." That was the day the partners knew they had become a valued part of the neighborhood. So, to Forty-Eight Charlie, keeping their promise to a community member was vital.

Within ten minutes, Forty-Eight Charlie had made it back to the skids and pulled up in front of the Ovaltine Cafe. Wendy spotted George's shopping cart in the alley around the side of the building and knew George wouldn't be far away.

"I'll be back," she said.

Trevor replied, "Don't threaten me."

Wendy jumped out of the car and strode into the landmark eatery. The place had displayed the same neon sign for more than fifty years and, in fact, still served Ovaltine.

Wendy scanned the restaurant and found her man seated in a booth halfway down the aisle. He sat facing the diner's doorway and was nursing a cup of black coffee, his stare fixed on the now tepid liquid. Not wanting to alarm George, Wendy approached him calmly. She noticed his hygiene was better than it had been at times and he appeared sober and oriented. His salt and pepper hair and deeply furrowed, leathery face belied his relative youth. Right then it struck Wendy how fast George seemed to be aging.

Time and again, positions of power were misused in this neighborhood. Sensitive to this reality, Wendy tried to be as non-threatening as possible. She crouched down, greeting him in a light and welcoming tone. "Hi, George."

He gazed to his left and upon recognizing Wendy, chuckled. "Hello, my angel. Hey, the food isn't that bad here."

Sharing his laugh, she reached out her hand to shake his. "How you doin'?"

"I'm okay. I'm waitin' for my sister."

"Well, that's why I'm here George. I just saw Mary. She's okay, so don't worry. But she's not gonna be able to come today because she's at the hospital for a checkup."

Regardless of Wendy's assurances, George appeared stunned by the news. He whispered, "What's wrong?"

Tenderly, Wendy placed her hand on his. "Mary's just up at the hospital for a checkup. No big deal. She'll be back home in a couple of hours."

George wore a pained expression. Locking his eyes onto Wendy's, he was candid. "She o.d.'d, didn't she?"

Wendy squeezed his hand, remaining silent in the face of his intuition.

George stared back down at his cup of coffee, his eyes welling up with tears. Wendy scrambled to lighten the mood. "You know how I know she's okay George?"

George raised his head and looked at Wendy.

"Cause' when I asked her how old she was, she said, 'Old enough to know better, but young enough to do it again.'"

A wispy grin crept across George's face. "Yeah, that's my Mary."

"Honestly George, Mary's fine, and she'll be back home in a couple of hours. She really wanted us to come find you and let you know so you wouldn't worry about her not showing up."

"O...okay...th...thanks...th...thanks for that."

The news had blindsided George, and it was all too much for him to bear. To say he seemed stunned would have been a gross understatement. George was panic-stricken. Their predictable Sunday routine kept him sane. It was a way of bringing order to disorder, control to the uncontrollable, even if it was only a brief illusion.

It went without saying Mary was George's indisputable reason for living. If something were to happen to her, George would have been left emotionally destitute. He craved the experience of her kissing his forehead and calling him her "little Georgie." With this meager exception, his life was otherwise devoid of compassionate human contact. That whiff of affection from his sister was his only social interaction that was not based on humiliation. And George needed that as much as he needed oxygen. From Monday to Saturday, he just went through the motions, a halfhearted existence. But on Sunday, he came alive. George lived for Sundays.

Now all that was in jeopardy. The fact was, Mary had overdosed. Bubbling up from his core was the sweeping despair of helplessness. George could not stop Mary's addiction to heroin anymore than he could stop his alcoholism. At the very least, those precious few moments they met for coffee on Sundays allowed him to pretend he could protect her, even if the idea were bogus. The reality was, Mary had overdosed, and there was nothing George could do to stop it from happening again. He was powerless to protect her. Just like when they were kids.

Speechless, George struggled to process the disconcerting message as Wendy listened to an incoming call over the radio. "Forty-Eight Charlie, code three for an assault..."

"Take care of yourself. Okay, George? I gotta go now."

"Yeah...Okay...Thanks..."

"You're very welcome."

George was anything but grateful for the paramedic's message. That disagreeable piece of news had unleashed the past, unlocking floodgates of emotion and allowing a tidal wave of rage to seek an outlet. At that moment, all George could envision was that craven, black-robed degenerate, and the slimy look he used to give his sister.

Sitting there immobilized, he watched as Wendy left the diner and the paramedics drove away, lights flashing and siren blaring. Five minutes later, he stood up, left enough change on the table for his coffee, and fled out of the cafe. He had a single compelling mission. He was off to find a bottle–a full bottle. It was days like this he needed a full bottle. He would need a full bottle to numb the impulses that had broken loose inside him, commanding him to destroy the people who had destroyed his family. Mission in hand, he shuffled up the alley behind his cart, disappearing into an aura of hopelessness as the skies came forth with vast, seemingly endless, raindrops.

Chapter 31
Five minutes later...

Mission in hand, the crew sped to the scene of the assault, about to be swallowed up by an aura of hopelessness as the skies came forth with vast, seemingly endless, raindrops. The ferocious downpour pelted Forty-Eight Charlie, soaking them to the skin as they pulled their gear from the back of the car and single-mindedly made their way to the basement suite's entrance.

Nothing could have prepared them for the scene that was about to greet them. All Wendy and Trevor knew was they were backing up another crew for an assault. They had been told nothing else. It was an assault all right, an assault taken to its extreme. It was a murder. And not just your run of the mill, everyday kind of interpersonal nonsense where one idiot was talking instead of listening, and another idiot helps him shut his mouth. No, this was the kind of regrettable experience that kills a piece of your spirit. Murdered children have a way of doing that to you.

The ensuing minutes would be forever tattooed on their souls. All thanks to an intense plethora of images, smells, sounds, textures and emotions few people could hope to remain unscathed by.

He was six, or maybe seven, lying in a lake of blood and in cardiac arrest, slaughtered with a butcher knife by way of a relative's calculated, despicable act.

The first crew on scene was frantic and doing their best to bring color back into the little one's face. Wendy and Trevor entered the call, and their feet turned to concrete, disconcerted by the surrealism permeating the room. Either by training or by nature, they shoved aside their immediate reactions and flipped into autopilot. Within minutes, the child was off to Children's Hospital. He was declared dead less than half an hour later.

Trevor and Wendy retreated from Children's Hospital in a zombie-like state, girded by an oppressive silence in which they swam, hopelessly engulfed. And they neither fought its ebb nor its flow, fearing to tease apart the numbness, the rage, and the grief. Without mercy, the two replayed every detail with a hushed reverence. Forcing themselves to relive the call from Hell over and over again. Making every attempt, however futile, to reconcile a dead child; a dead, murdered, child. But tears could never erode the call that was already chiseled into the granite of their psyche.

The drive back to their area was fraught with a nauseating atmosphere. Staring glassy-eyed out the passenger window, Wendy broke the awkward calm by mumbling under her breath. "Evil."

Trevor wore a similar expression as he drove. Nudged to the present by her remark, he glanced at his partner. "Evil, Gracie?"

Wendy's voice bore an eerie chill coupled with a sigh of resignation and a profound sense there was currently less of her present to answer. "Some things...are just plain...fucking...evil..."

Her throat tightened, cinching her words, and her eyes stung from tears whose exodus was denied. That was the last they ever spoke of it.

And as if heaven was trying to make a point, the somber gray skies mourned heavily for the rest of their shift. The darkness of that day was unusual, as was the force with which the rain fell.

Chapter 32
Two years later - Autumn 1994
Vancouver's Downtown Eastside

The darkness of the day was unusual, as was the force with which the rain fell. Inclement weather notwithstanding, Trevor climbed into the driver's seat of the ambulance, sank into the worn upholstery and set his coffee cup into its holder. It was their first shift of four and his day to drive. Wendy joined him, climbing in on the opposite side of the cab. She was unenthusiastic, and her mood was an excellent match with the dismal weather that day.

"Main and Hastings?" he asked.

"Yeah...sure."

The knot in her stomach, which had been growing since the previous night, loosened when she saw Trevor actually come to work today. Lately, he had been missing work, a lot of work. His excuses varied, but Wendy wasn't fooled. She knew exactly what was going on. Trevor was getting fucked up on a way-too-regular basis. And his drinking was putting their partnership at risk. A paramedic's sanity is anchored to a regular, dependable partner who they can trust. Trust to have your back when you're on a call, trust to not take unnecessary risks, trust not to treat people like shit and trust to have competent medical skills. Trevor hadn't worked six of the last eight shifts, and there was no mistaking Wendy was pissed with him for it.

But at that moment, Wendy gladly overlooked the undeniable smell of ketones on Trevor's breath in exchange for the fact he was sober and present. At least for this one shift, she could feel safe. For right now, it was all that mattered.

The tension in the cab between the two of them was only surpassed by Wendy's refusal to focus on the two-thousand-pound elephant in the room. She chose a specific subject of conversation in the dim hope of keeping the communication light and open. She had also assumed, correctly, Trevor's dog was the only thing keeping Trevor relatively functional.

"How's Storm?"

"Umm...He's okay...Seems to have slowed down a little."

"He's how old now? Must be seven or eight?"

A contrite Trevor answered between sips of his strong dark brew. "Mmm, probably at least that. I've had him four years, and I don't know how old he was when I got him."

Wendy knew Trevor well enough to know he was hiding something. You can't spend twelve hours a day in close, often intense, quarters without developing an intimate knowledge of someone, let alone a tight bond. Their relationship was more like a marriage than either of them would admit. But even that description failed to accurately define a good working partnership, especially theirs. Married couples generally didn't have to trust their spouse with their life on a daily basis. Wendy and Trevor did. And they had put it to the test on more than one occasion, like the call they did a year or so ago.

They had been dispatched on a routine call for "a man with a headache." When they first arrived, Wendy had noticed the knife–Trevor hadn't. The patient had palmed it, with the blade hidden up his long-sleeved shirt. While Trevor was unaware of it, Wendy needed to think fast. She did. Overriding her racing heart, she summoned her calm, steadied her voice and was as nonchalant as possible. "Hey partner, you know I think I just heard Forty-Eight Charlie call a patient code thirty."

That seized Trevor's attention. Wendy had tipped him to a life-threatening situation to which he had been oblivious. With his heart pounding from the surge of adrenaline, he gave their alleged patient a much wider berth and began scanning the entire room for the danger Wendy had just alluded to. But worse, he had broken safety rule number one and had not kept a clear exit open for himself; in that cramped eight by ten-foot room, Trevor found himself trapped between a potential assailant and the door.

Wendy prayed for a break in the radio chatter so she could call for police backup. That opportunity did not present itself. And it was becoming clear Trevor was the intended target. In the room, a cold, calculating energy was approaching its crescendo. There was something seriously wrong with this call. Wendy circled to the rear of their patient while continuing her relaxed commentary about the "other crew." "Yeah. I guess they were going 10-8 in a hurry."

Translation: We gotta get the fuck outta here, *now*!

Unlike the police, paramedics were given no tools or training to defend themselves. Yet they worked in a knife culture, and attacks could be carried out with lightning speed, producing silent, lethal effects in milliseconds. And running away would not guarantee your safety. On the contrary, having your back to an assailant with a blade made you more vulnerable. Understanding this, the two had worked diligently at recognizing and avoiding situations that put them at that kind of risk. However, no safety plan is foolproof.

By design, Wendy stood behind the pseudo-patient, while Trevor faced him head-on. Trevor knew the drill. They had had one other occasion to position themselves like this. Only this time, their roles were reversed. Wendy would need to time her maneuver precisely. Trevor's life depended on it.

With precious seconds ticking by, the uneasiness in the room intensified. Pretending to be calm, Trevor continued his assessment. "So how long have you had this headache for?"

Wearing a look of malice the "patient" refused to answer, instead, he chuckled quietly. And the more questions Trevor asked about the guy's headache, the more apparent it became this call was a setup. Time slowed to a standstill and what followed unfolded in slow motion.

The man exuded a sinister tranquillity when he made the seamless transition from patient to perpetrator. He locked his fiendish expression onto Trevor's eyes before making his invitation. "Are you ready to die, motherfucker?"

Reaching up his opposite sleeve, he sprung the butcher knife out of concealment and laughed while making slashing gestures six inches in front of Trevor's face. "I'm gonna enjoy this." Trevor froze, his gaze transfixed on the gleaming, sadistic blade he believed was about to be thrust into his body.

As soon as the would-be killer stood still, Wendy surged into action doing exactly as she had planned. Grabbing the bottom cuffs of his pant legs, she yanked backward with all her strength, pulling his feet out from underneath him. He fell like the two-hundred-pound sack of shit he was, doing a perfect face-plant on the dirty linoleum floor. He was momentarily dazed, and in haste, Wendy lunged on top of him, driving one knee into the back of his neck and the other knee on the arm still clenching the knife.

Trevor watched as the guy fell face first, hitting the floor with an unmerciful thud. Still frozen and in shock, Trevor stood there in a statuesque repose from the trauma as his partner subdued the threat. He broke free of inertia's grip when Wendy looked up at him demanding, "Little help?"

Trevor's first impulse had been to kick this asshole in the head. He didn't. But he did do the next best thing. He stood his full weight—via his leather work boots—on the guy's hand till he released the knife. Once he loosened his grip on the blade, Trevor kicked it out of reach.

Wendy repositioned the assailant by rolling the guy onto his side, maintaining her left knee on his neck, and her right knee below his rib cage. Taking his top arm, she extended it across her right thigh thereby making a solid, levered arm bar. Ever aware the walls had ears and raging inside with the thought this fucker had just tried to kill her partner, Wendy leaned over and delivered a seething whisper into his ear, "If you so much as twitch I'll break your fucking arm." As she uttered her none-too-subtle warning, she applied just the slightest amount of downward pressure on his levered arm to drive home her point, releasing it as soon as he started to writhe in pain. She concluded with a self-evident declaration, though Wendy considered it a hushed promise, "*Don't* fuck with me."

With that, he cried out like a little girl, "Okay, okay, okay! Don't hurt me!"

By this time Trevor had sliced through the radio traffic, contacted their dispatcher and summoned help. His voice was tremulous. "VPD's on the way."

As Trevor spoke they could hear the police sirens in the near distance. Little brought a faster police response than a paramedic crew in trouble. Within three minutes there were six concerned and mightily pissed off cops on the scene all vying for a piece of the guy with the broken nose. Once the attacker was handcuffed, and on his way downstairs to a waiting wagon, the officer in charge began investigating what had happened to the crew.

Forty-Eight Charlie was out of service for about an hour as they wrote out their statements and got their feet back on the ground. There was the usual friendly banter with the cops from their shift. "Just about got to be a paramedic-kebab, huh Trevor? Good thing you've got a rabid dog for a partner." The joking around helped the adrenaline to subside and lightened their mood–until Phelps arrived.

Phelps's first utterance was typical and ever so heartwarming. "What the hell did you two do to make VPD waste all this manpower!" Had he said it with a grin and a sarcastic tone, Trevor and Wendy would have felt supported. But it was Phelps. He meant every fucking word. He even went so far as to get into a shouting match with the lead investigating officer. "What do you mean you're not charging them with assault! They broke the guy's nose! What kind of cop are you!" The facts didn't matter to Phelps. To him, this was opportunity. There was blood in the water. So, he suspended Forty-Eight Charlie on the spot for assaulting a patient.

The next day Wendy and Trevor attended their disciplinary interviews separately from each other. They each told it like it was and held fast to the facts. Though dumb as he was, Phelps was a master manipulator. And he pulled out all the stops on this one. As far as Phelps was concerned, this time, the bitch was toast.

Phelps sauntered into Wendy's meeting room in first-rate, caustic form. "Do you think the area you work in is the Wild West? We get reports all the time about you roughing up patients. But your days of being a cowboy are over because your loyal partner just flipped on you. He said you went off like a powder keg and hit the patient with your radio. He said he's tired of your unpredictable aggression and doesn't want to lose his job over this."

Wendy sat listening to the casual lies. She didn't reply. Pitting crewmembers against each other and insinuating their partner had changed their story was a typical tactic for Phelps. But it hadn't worked on either Trevor or Wendy today. And that just pissed him off more.

Sitting across the boardroom table from Wendy, Phelps's face grew red while he calculated his next move. "It is not BCAS policy to assault patients!"

"We were the ones being attacked, John. As I've said before, the guy pulled a knife on us–"

Phelps cut her off. "I took the patient's statement, and it's not the way he tells it. He says you just walked up and sucker punched him with your radio. And given your track record Missy, I believe him. You might have fooled the police, but you don't fool me."

Wendy was outraged. But that didn't loosen her stomach or assuage her nausea. "John, are you aware of the fact he's a career criminal with a long history of violence? Did you know that when we encountered him, he was wanted on a Canada wide arrest warrant for murder? Don't you care that he's currently under arrest for attempting to *kill* us? For God's sake John, he specifically called 911 to lure us there to kill us!"

Phelps would have none of it, rejecting her testimony and screaming at her. "Don't be such a drama queen! Neither of you were injured, and the patient has a broken nose! *You* assaulted *him*!"

Wendy couldn't believe her ears. She was being railroaded, although she wasn't surprised. She always figured her career would be ended one day by the BC Ambulance Service's classic kangaroo court system of employee management. At this point, she couldn't help but indulge a private thought. *I guess the only way I'm going to get justice is with a barnacle-encrusted rock and thirty-seconds alone with this asshole.* That made her smile.

"So you're proud of breaking a patient's nose? You think this is funny?"

But before she could answer him, Phelps concluded with one of his quintessential intimidation tactics. Sliding a blank Incident Report across the table towards Wendy he said, "If you don't change your story, I'll see to it you both go down." Implying he would spare Trevor if she confessed and changed her statement. The idea Trevor would be punished because Phelps hated her, sickened Wendy. But she also knew she hadn't done anything wrong.

While her union representative sat there as mute as the furniture, Wendy flashed Phelps her famous "fuck you" look before pushing the blank form back towards him. "You already have my statement."

What followed next was eight weeks of further "investigation" into the incident. When all was said and done, Wendy and Trevor were suspended without pay, pending official termination, courtesy of Phelps.

Meanwhile, the police had recommended charges be brought, and the government lawyer agreed. The prosecutor was currently putting together a case regarding the attempted murder of the crew and he needed one last interview with them. The two soon-to-be ex-paramedics were sitting outside the lawyer's office waiting for their respective turns and killing time by considering new career paths.

"Dog groomer," said Wendy.

"No...Flag person," said Trevor

"Boring!...How 'bout lion tamer?" she said.

"Nah...I know! Cod boat captain," he said.

"Ooooh, I like that one."

Before coming out to greet them, the lawyer couldn't help but overhear their conversation. "Hello again, how are you two?"

Wendy answered, "Good. We're just trying to figure out our new careers before next month's rent's due."

"Getting out of the paramedic game?"

Trevor added, "Not voluntarily. We've both been suspended pending termination because of this call."

"That's ridiculous. You're joking?"

Trevor shrugged his shoulders. "Nope, dead serious. As far as the BC Ambulance Service concerned, *we* assaulted a patient. Therefore *we* are being fired."

Wendy chimed in. "So as a parting gift, we'd really enjoy a conviction."

Knowing he had evidence supporting the crew's account of what happened, confusion overtook the lawyer's face. Of course, he couldn't disclose those facts before trial as it would prejudice the case. But the police had collected a sworn statement from the accused's next door neighbor stating, in part, what the guy had bragged he was going to do. It including him saying he was "bored" and was intending to call 911 to "off a paramedic for the fun of it." The statement went on to say the accused knew paramedics didn't carry weapons, and they were an easy target because they would show up for any bullshit reason he gave, like a headache. It was damning proof of premeditation.

"I really don't like to predict the outcome at trial, but, having said that, I'm quite confident given the evidence we've gathered that a conviction is likely. And I'm presuming the paramedics involved aren't lying?"

The pair answered in uncanny unison. "No, we're not."

Shaking his head, the lawyer asked, "You're serious about being fired over this?"

Wendy continued to minimize the issue. "Yup. But honestly, don't you think my former partner here would make a great cod boat captain?"

The lawyer allowed a puzzled grin to creep across his face, suspecting they were just trying to diffuse their stress.

271

Within a month, the assailant was found guilty of attempted murder. It took the lawyer writing an official letter directly to the head of the BC Ambulance Service to get the heat off Wendy and Trevor. They were reinstated immediately, but ever since then, Phelps had made Forty-Eight Charlie his pet project. He fancied his prey dead.

To commemorate being overruled by his superiors, Phelps ramped up the pressure on his favorite crew. He began shadowing them on calls, appearing unexpectedly at all hours, baiting onlookers and even the patients themselves, all in a relentless quest to fabricate enough complaints to get Trevor and Wendy fired. But what Phelps never realized was the community Forty-Eight Charlie safeguarded could smell a predator a mile away. And they were not about to betray Wendy or Trevor. The two paramedics never gave them any reason to. But that did not mean Phelps gave up on his sworn vendetta. That went on interminably.

Yet through all the bullshit, the unrelenting intimidation, the attempts at railroading and the undermining of their characters, all it accomplished was to cement the two's rapport. Wendy and Trevor had built an enduring partnership; bonded, tested, tried and true. Regardless of the tactics Phelps tried, he could not drive a wedge between them. It was their unwitting revenge. And it drove Phelps fucking nuts.

That morning when Trevor had finally come to work after being absent for six shifts, they were parked, tucked away in an alley beside Main and

Hastings, united in comfortable silence, drinking coffee and watching over their people; sentinels to the marginalized.

Nothing permeated their collective meditation that day. Not the radio traffic, not the clatter of violent rain beating down on the car's roof, not even the smell of ketones.

That morning there was little pedestrian activity on the street. The miserable weather kept the area's residents under what shelter they could find or forge. Four cracked plaster walls or fresh cardboard propped up against a dumpster. If it kept you dry, that was enough. The cold was one thing, but cold and wet could be deadly.

Chapter 33
That Same Day

The cold was one thing, but cold and wet could be deadly. With that in mind, brother and sister dodged the battering rain as they each made their separate way to the Ovaltine. For a Sunday afternoon, the cafe was relatively empty when George first arrived. He found a booth near the back of the humble coffee shop and squeezed himself to the farthest end of the bench, next to the wall. Within a minute, Mary had joined him, and George's face lit up. "Hello, my Mary."

Sliding next to him, Mary wrapped her arms around George and leaned over to kiss her brother gently on the forehead. "How are you my little Georgie?"

Nestling his head on her shoulder, George closed his eyes and surrendered to that tender moment, feeling as if he were in the very presence of Mother herself. It was times like this when Mother's likeness and compassion were so mirrored in Mary that George found it almost unnerving. Once he had soaked up his dose of affection for the week, George opened his eyes and became struck by Mary's thin, frail appearance. "You're skinny. You eatin' regular?"

Mary was tentative. "Oh yeah."

"Cause...Cause you look way too skinny. Like...you're sick or somethin'."

The waitress interrupted. "Here's your coffee."

"Thanks," Mary said as the server walked away.

Mary tensed. "You think this rain is ever gonna stop?"

George could feel his sister was holding something back. So he was blunt. "You...You ain't sick, are ya?"

Bowing her head, Mary fell silent, her eyes riveted on her coffee cup. George became panicked by her body language. In a timorous whisper, he asked, "What's wrong Mary?"

Mary no longer had the strength to keep her secret. "Oh, my little Georgie. I've wanted to tell you somethin' for a long time now, but I was never brave enough."

The space around them grew taut. Scowling at her cup and wringing her fingers around its rim, Mary's trepidation became unbearable.

"What?...What is it, Mary?"

She was agonizing over her impending confession, but it was too late to renege. And George wasn't a fool. "I don't want you to be upset...Okay?...I'm...I uh...a while ago...I found out...I caught HIV."

An earsplitting hush collapsed upon them.

George was in disbelief, his face blank and pale. "What do you mean?"

"It means...I'm sick."

"You mean...AIDS?"

Mary didn't answer. George's jaw dropped. Both sat staring at their mugs.

Divulging her ominous secret had lessened Mary's burden, but by doing so, George's had become too much to shoulder; springing forth from that startling decree came a blast of images rushing through George's mind like a wildfire whose smoldering embers had waited patiently for the perfect gust of wind to usher them back to life. Priests...nuns...black robes...the look in their eyes...their unflinching cruelty...heaps of little dead bodies...and that which Mary had to do to feed her habit. The tenuous dike holding back George's past traumas had shattered, letting loose a tidal wave that bombarded his mind with the all-too-fresh horrors of yesterday. And now, with the disclosure of an all but certain death sentence for Mary, the only person he had left to love, the only person who showed him any compassion, his soul became swamped with raw emotion stemming from profound despair and unimaginable loss. From this, George felt the beast inside him awaken and unfetter its rage.

Mary clasped his hand and whispered, "Georgie?...Georgie."

George became glassy-eyed, his breath quickened and his fists clenched. Hatred's creature had begun its assimilation of him, transforming him and commanding him. Its hunger for vengeance would no longer be denied, and it would only be sated by retribution meted out on an appropriate target. But who would be the scapegoat? Seething with contempt and shrouded by an unnerving calm, George turned to Mary and made a forthright accusation to her face. "It's your dealer's fault. It's *his* fault you're sick."

Mary had never seen George like this before. He was vibrating with rage. She was trembling with fear.

I have to do something to calm him down. Fighting against her own adrenaline, she composed herself, bringing a veneer of calm to her voice. "George, it's my own fault. He didn't give me HIV. It's my fault. I just wasn't careful enough."

It didn't matter what Mary said George was irrational. But even more concerning, he was uncontrollable. He had since been swallowed up, overtaken by his wrath. One glance in his eyes and Mary knew what his plan was. She grabbed his hand with both of hers. "If you love me you won't do that."

George's jaw clenched and his face flushed as he snarled, "He's the one that made you take the heroin. He's the one that got you sick. He's just like the priests! He...deserves...to die!"

"No! George! No! You'll be just like the priests if you do that!"

George was oblivious to her. The beast and its unshackled hatred were now in charge. Brother looked sister squarely in the eye and hissed. "I'm not like them. I'm protecting you. All they ever did was hurt us. Don't you remember?"

With that denunciation, George pushed his way past Mary and stormed out of the diner leaving her alone with nothing but her tears and a cold cup of coffee.

George was on the hunt and soon found his mark loitering in the south alley at Main and Hastings. King of his feral domain, the dealer stood there holding his perverse court while his smug presence soiled the granite cobblestones beneath him. The dealer didn't know George, and he never gave the alcoholic Native a second thought. Nor did he have an inkling that decades of pent-up fury and a quest for spiritual catharsis were about to be unleashed upon him.

George's plan was elegant in its design, flawless in its premeditated delivery and chilling in its nonchalance. Feigning drunkenness, he staggered up the alley, each swerving step bringing him closer to the dealer and closer to revenge. George's instrument of retribution was poised, hidden up his soiled sleeve. His timing was precise, his actions simultaneous. Pretending to stumble, George fell into the dealer, plunging a carving knife deep into his victim's belly. As the blade found a vital organ, his prey didn't make more than a muted grunt. Except by his glazed stare, George said nothing and further twisted the knife. The two men's gazes locked as George thrust the weapon again.

Summoning strength beyond his capacity George drove the blade even deeper into the soft flesh of his quarry, the cold steel flexing with each turn until George could see the life recede from the defiler's eyes. Only then, did George step back and withdraw the dagger.

The dealer slumped backwards against the wall, and his contorted frame inched toward the cobblestones, leaving a crimson smear on the weathered brick building.

One slow footstep after another, George backed away from the lifeless form, engulfed by an icy surrealism. He had done it. At last, he had killed

Brother Murphy. George rejoiced, comforted by the image lying sprawled before him; the twisted, blood-soaked body of the dead priest. Shuffling backwards, George melted into the alley's shadows, mumbling to himself. "He can't hurt you no more Joey...He can't hurt you no more..."

Moments later there were screams for someone to call 911.

Chapter 34
Two Months Later
Beginning of December 1994

There were no screams for someone to call 911. Marjorie had done it quickly, but calmly. That morning she had looked in on Mary and knew something was wrong. At first, Mary claimed, "I'm just really tired." But now that it was late in the evening and she hadn't gone to work, Marjorie didn't hesitate to call for help.

The building's anxious matriarch paced the floor of the dilapidated foyer, waiting for the paramedics so she could escort them to Mary's room. She didn't have to wait long. Forty-Eight Charlie arrived in short order. They entered the seedy building laden with equipment and anticipating another long climb to reach their patient. They were right.

Marjorie led the way, easily outpacing the crew during the eight-flight ascent. Along the way, she made some delicate observations about her friend. "She doesn't look at all well. Not at all...And she has a rather worrisome occupation...Self-employed evening work. Do you understand?"

Wendy replied, "Yes ma'am. Do you think she got injured from her job?"

"No, not this time. I think she's got a fever."

The trio had reached the fourth floor when Marjorie turned to the paramedics and waved a cautionary finger at them. "Now, you two make certain you take good care of my Mary."

Trevor answered while holding the hallway door open for Wendy. "Yes, ma'am. Don't worry, we will."

Marjorie unlocked Mary's room and announced herself in a whisper. "It's just me dear. I've brought some nice people to help you out."

Walking into the room, Forty-Eight Charlie was met by the sight of a shivering, dehydrated woman who was laboring to breathe. The signs were unmistakable. She was cooking up a nice batch of pneumonia.

Wendy bent over and began assessing her patient when she recognized the emaciated figure gasping in front of her. "Hello, Mary. We haven't seen you for a while. You're George's sister, right?"

Through her delirium, Mary glanced up at the paramedic and wheezed. "Do I...know you?"

"We met a while back. It's not important. I see you're having a tough time catching your breath. Let's see what we can do about that."

Wendy and Trevor were seasoned enough to recognize a case of HIV pneumonia when one was staring them in the face. They were on full autopilot mode as they initiated treatment and carried her downstairs in rapid fashion.

"How long do you think she'll be in the hospital?" Marjorie asked.

"That's really hard to say, ma'am. It all depends on how well she responds to treatment," Trevor said.

"Please tell her that I'm coming to visit her."

"I will ma'am," he said on the way out the front door.

Before climbing into the back of the ambulance with her patient, Wendy paused and deliberately took a long, deep breath of the crisp night air. The cold air had a dual effect. It made her feel clean–and awake. She was exhausted.

Trevor motioned to his partner to get in the back. "It's my night to drive, soooo..."

"Yeah, yeah. Geez, what's the hurry?"

"Coffee's gettin' cold," he said smirking.

"Sure, rub it in."

Stooping over, Wendy climbed into the ambulance and walked to the stretcher's head where she plunked herself down in the attendant's chair more forcefully than usual. She was in a pissy mood tonight because she had spent the better part of it ruminating about Phelps's bullshit. To top it off, everywhere in the city the calls were nonstop; stabbings, overdoses, a bridge jumper, even a "car vs. train" incident. *Fuck! I can't even buy a decent call tonight. All Hell's breaking loose and here I am stuck doing a routine medical call. Jesus!* Wendy felt like a starving woman being offered table scraps. She couldn't get her adrenaline fix, so by default self-pity became Wendy's narcotic of choice.

The crew had done everything they could for Mary in the field: oxygen, warmth and IV fluids to rehydrate her and lessen her shocky condition. In that short treatment window, Mary's color had vastly improved, her breathing had eased allowing her to speak in fuller sentences, and her level of conscious awareness was back to normal. Wendy was pleased to see her patient respond so quickly to treatment. The improvement also gave Wendy the opportunity to complete her paperwork. "Mary, please remind me what your last name is?"

"It's Brown...You know...like poop."

Wendy chuckled. "Very funny. Is that your street name?"

"Does it matter?"

"No...Not really...Do you know of any medicines that make you sick?"

"Nope"

"And the building where we found you is where you live?"

"Yeah, for a long time."

"Good. It's important you have a place inside. And it seems like you have a very good friend there too."

"Oh, yeah...Marjorie...she's...the best." Mary started wheezing again.

"Okay, that's enough chitchat for now." That was as much as Wendy wanted to play twenty questions with a tenuous pneumonia patient. "We can talk more if you want, once you get your breath back, all right?"

She double checked the IV's drip rate and sat back to scribble her report, filling in the dry details with plenty of time to spare.

Wendy's mood had yet to lighten up as it usually did when she was looking after "her people." Mary never knew it, but Wendy remained resentful she wasn't on what she considered "a good call." Wendy's pity party was in full swing as she sat there stewing about everything wrong with her life. Trevor's drinking, the steady diet of asshole-induced stress she was shouldering courtesy of Phelps, and tonight's unceasing parade of crappy calls. Oh, she still did her job. She just wasn't happy about it.

"You still look cold hon. Let me fix that," Wendy said tucking another blanket snugly around Mary's skeleton-like physique and turning up the heater.

"Thanks," Mary said. Whose own exhaustion was starting to show its full effect.

It was a gross understatement to say Mary was skinny. She was wasting away. Mary must have sensed the paramedic's concern about her weight. "Yeah...Jenny Craig ain't got nothin' on me...between the AIDS...and the junk."

"Mmmm, not a great combo. Have you eaten anything lately?"

Mary answered wearing a tired grin. "Nah...I don't wanna ruin...my girlish figure."

Wendy managed a genuine smile back at her. "Your breathing seems better. You keep that oxygen mask on," she said while taking Mary's blood pressure.

"Are you still dizzy?"

"Nope."

Wendy readjusted the IV drip rate. "That's good. You rest now."

A contemplative silence ensued, each woman alone with her thoughts. Both were oblivious to the bumps in the road, the lights of the traffic and the chattering on the radio. Mary had donned a solemn expression and was watching Wendy closely. Wendy was too busy feeding from the trough of self-indulgence and secretly bemoaning her life's problems, to notice her patient was studying her.

They were two blocks away from the hospital when Wendy leaned over Mary and switched the oxygen supply over to the portable tank on the stretcher. In doing so, her eyes locked onto her patient's. Mary spoke in an almost imperceptible whisper, full of heartache and longing, and proceeded to drop a bombshell into Wendy's lap. "God, I wish I had your life."

With that little dose of objectivity, Wendy's gut plummeted into her feet. She stood there blank, altogether bereft of a response. What do you say to that? All Wendy managed in return was a dumbfounded stare. Her first impulse had been to break into tears. She felt like a complete and total shit. In that instant, Wendy realized that in comparison, her life was a veritable heaven. She had been blindsided by reality and perspective, the one-two punch of a karmic two-by-four. Wendy was still reeling from the surprise attitude adjustment when they pulled into St. Paul's. She felt sick to her stomach and thoroughly ashamed.

Wendy was desperate for a few moments alone to regain her composure. Once they were inside the hospital, "I gotta use the washroom" was her excuse to flee deeper into the emergency department, leaving Trevor to manage patient care while they waited for a bed.

Relieved to find the staff toilet vacant, Wendy closed and locked the door behind her. She felt the pressure in her eyes and didn't dare look in the mirror. Instead, she sat on the edge of the porcelain to fight the familiar pangs that were demanding recognition. She wasn't physically sick she just needed to cry. Mary's words had pierced a convoluted matrix of psychic defenses that, except in extreme situations, were all but impenetrable. In short, Wendy was a little messed up. But after years on the job, she knew she couldn't allow herself the luxury of her feelings and certainly not her tears. Besides, it felt like if she allowed one tear to flow, the dam would burst leading to an overwhelming deluge. And Wendy also knew if word got out she had been crying, it would all but toast her career. All the credibility she had earned would vanish. This was the female paramedic's mantra of survival: show no weakness. Be strong, or be eaten alive. Be like stone. That was Wendy, a rough, tough, cream puff. No one would have ever guessed it.

Wary of being away from her patient for too long, Wendy stood up, splashed some cold water on her face and mentally sucked it up. Walking down the long hallway, back to where she had left Trevor, Wendy wondered how long it would take before she could make it back to the Downtown Eastside.

Chapter 35
Two Weeks Later
Mid-December 1994

George wondered how long it would take before he could make it back to the Downtown Eastside. Detox was only a mile from Main and Hastings, but depending on the weather's whims, it could be a cold, miserable trek at this time of year, though today there was a welcome reprieve from the typically wet, coastal winter days.

The detox facility was what you would expect of an overused, underfunded social service, with the need for resources perennially outstripping supply. To the public eye, the building was innocuous enough. Its existence was cloaked intentionally, hidden by design in one of the city's industrial areas. The few windows the building possessed gave the drab concrete structure an aura reminiscent of a small prison, with its gray exterior all but disappearing in the winter rain. As a clearinghouse of basic human requirements, it provided desperately needed short-term shelter and other essentials such as laundry and shower facilities. The staff could even muster up the occasional sandwich for their clients; the famous, or infamous depending on your perspective–egg salad.

The dreary edifice consisted of two sides, the long-term treatment wing and the short-term unit where a perpetual game of so-called "catch and release" played out around the clock. George was a frequent visitor of the latter. These short-term clients were usually found on the street and assessed by paramedic crews before coming here. Individuals hovered somewhere between "not drunk enough to warrant medical intervention" and "too drunk to take care of oneself." The endless stream of men and women arriving here via police wagon epitomized this inevitable result of demoralizing poverty. Once helped inside, the inebriated were afforded a blanket and a thin mat on the concrete floor where they slept it off. Staff watched diligently over the piteous souls so they didn't drown in their vomit, ensuring they remained safe until they could take care of themselves once again.

This was the usual point when George would put himself through the pointless formality of asking, sometimes begging, for a long-term medical detox bed. "I'm an alcoholic and I need help. Please. I have withdrawal seizures when I detox. I can't do it by myself. Please."

His one fervent desire was to get sober and stay that way. But with a meager allotment of just thirty beds for a city of one-and-a-half million people, George had a better chance of winning the lottery than receiving meaningful help for his addiction; willingness, sincerity, humility–and desperation–notwithstanding. Even with the unending demand for those precious few spots, George was still grateful to have a place to shower and wash his clothes. And if the price of admission for those sparse luxuries was his dignity, then to him it was a small price to pay.

Although on most days George felt grossly overdrawn on that account.

And today, to add further insult to injury, George's only meaningful possession had become lost on the way here. His carving tools were gone. "Are you *sure* you didn't see my carving kit?" George asked them repeatedly.

"I'm sorry, but it wasn't with you when you got here," said a female staff member. She was right. George had arrived with nothing more than the shabby clothing on his back. His stomach sank at the news, and his face mirrored his devastation.

Another staff member, who had taken a shine to the quiet Indigenous man, sensed how deeply George felt the loss of his valued belonging. So taking it upon herself, she searched through their supply of donated clothing and found George a relatively nice replacement coat. "Here George. I know it's not your carving kit, but it should keep you warmer than your old jacket," she said.

Although appreciative of the gesture, George found it to be a hollow consolation. "Thanks," he said flatly.

His fruitless rituals complete, with a solemn heart and sober brain but without fanfare or his carving tools, George left Detox. Stepping outside he was greeted by brilliant winter sunshine. Though the brightness made him squint, George was relieved he would not have to put his new jacket through any sort of weather testing just yet. He took a deep breath, pointed himself in the right direction and began walking towards Main and Hastings. George made it back home in under an hour, attributing his speed to the egg salad sandwich he had devoured not long before. In reality, his fast pace was due more to the scornful looks he received along his route than the sandwich he had eaten.

George was uncomfortable outside the confines of the Main and Hastings neighborhood where he and "his kind" were granted begrudging social approval to exist. Openly nasty stares dogged him everywhere outside of that arbitrary perimeter. Ironically, the only time he didn't feel invisible was when he dared to wander outside his sanctioned neighborhood.

Arriving back home, George stood at the busy corner as if he were a statue, its bustling activity only a distant buzz in the background of his mind. Expecting his bottle seeking autopilot to kick in at any moment, he allowed himself to merge with the familiar surroundings. Just as he was about to lose himself in that place, George caught sight of the North Shore Mountains through the narrow corridor of buildings lining Main Street. Unexpectedly, an urge compelled him to walk towards the vista. It was as though his feet had suddenly acquired a mind of their own and his body was tagging along for the trip. But more astonishing was that his pervasive impulse to find a bottle was gone. A short walk and ten minutes later he found himself standing at the edge of Portside Park.

George stood atop the rocky embankment admiring the view of the north shore when he felt an inexplicable pull towards a small cove nearby. The strange impulse that had brought him this far continued urging him on. George obeyed by finding his way down to the water's edge and sitting in front of a venerable-looking log, which faced the ocean out of sight of passersby. He sank into the beach. Each tiny pebble, worn smooth by the tides, easily gave way cradling his form with an almost human tenderness. Soon afterward, he surrendered to the heartbeats of Mother Earth, allowing the gentle rhythmic sound of the light ocean waves to move through his body. George had showered at Detox, but somehow lying there made him feel clean in a different, more profound way. It was still daylight and for this time of year, much warmer than usual. The park was deserted, and he was as safe as he could be. So, George dozed and permitted himself the luxury of a nap.

He drifted off peacefully and *found his awareness brought to a stunning ocean inlet at the edge of an ancient grove of spruce trees. He noticed Mary emerge from the forest at the far end of the beach. Her steps seemed to glide over the earth as she approached him. Their eyes met, and she put her arms softly around him. During their embrace, a perfect feeling of peace fell over George. Smiling, Mary withdrew from his arms, and he watched her step towards the shoreline and a small, waiting boat. George could see three figures on the craft with arms outstretched towards the approaching Mary. It was Mother, Father, and Grandfather. Mary alighted the boat. George sprinted after her and jumped onto the ethereal craft. He seized upon his precious family, devouring their loving essence. Not long after, Mother cradled George's head in her hands, "My dear son, you cannot come with us. You must go back to the shore."*

George was heartbroken at the news. "But why can't I come too?"

"Because it's not yet time sweetheart."

With his first step back ashore he awoke with a start.

George found himself unnerved by the intensity of his dream. Startled and breathless, he struggled to keep his composure. He remained on the beach, grappling with the torrent of mixed emotions the experience had brought forth; love, hope, and joy, coupled with grief and loneliness. And it would take quite a while for George to accept the meaning of what he had witnessed. Though if the truth were to be told, there was a hidden part of him that knew exactly what it meant. George just did not want to believe it.

He was readying himself to leave when spied something odd. George wondered if he wasn't still sleeping when he caught sight of what he thought was an apparition; a humble, worn leather case, lying right next to him. He recognized it instantly. It was his carving knives. George never sought or required an explanation. Solemnly, he picked up the small gift, and uttered a heartfelt, "Thank you."

As George stood to leave, clouds gathered, the temperature dropped, and it started raining.

Chapter 36
The evening before...

As Mary stepped outside St. Paul's Hospital clouds gathered, the temperature dropped, and it started raining. She never made it past the parking lot before her little secondhand umbrella was rendered useless by a gust of icy December wind. Wearing just a thin T-shirt and cotton pants, Mary was left with no effective shelter and soon became soaked through to her skin. Though the bus ticket she had received upon discharge gave her some welcome relief from the weather, at least until she went back to work, which was, by necessity, where she was headed now.

Mary had stayed in the hospital only for as long as it took to receive enough medical treatment so she wouldn't pass out when she stood up; intravenous fluids for dehydration and malnutrition with a side order of antibiotics for pneumonia. She had pled with the nursing staff. "Honest, I'm feeling much better. I promise I'll take care of myself at home."

In reality, she felt like shit. More accurately, she wished she felt that good. But the hospital was not going to give her what she needed, what her body was screaming for. Mary was left little choice but to discharge herself from the hospital against medical advice.

So it was that she too made it back to where she was invisible, returning to that familiar, necessary stretch of sidewalk. There Mary strolled up and down the dingy concrete catwalk, which offered her her only hope for relief. The stiff December wind blasted in random bursts, biting at Mary's skin and pilfering her last remnants of warmth. She made every pathetic attempt to keep warm, but she still shivered violently. And her limbs were beginning to ache and cramp for a different reason, as withdrawal trumpeted its arrival. Thus, an orchestra of foreboding symptoms began assembling within her shrunken frame. Mary started yawning liberally, setting the tempo to which the tremors emanating from her core kept time. It was an ominous, silent melody, whose abrasive tune filled Mary with dread. As agonizing as the elements were, they were no match for the symphony now being performed in her body by the dragons of withdrawal. They were now in control, ruling over Mary like a fascist dictator drunk with power. It was during times such as this they possessed her, demanding absolute fealty. She was junk sick. She would now say, or do, anything to overthrow the beasts. And just like that, the stage was set for exceedingly bad judgment.

The pain on Mary's face was evident from a mile away, though she knew it wouldn't deter customers. Her face was the one part of her body that no one paid much attention to. And so, she did her best to appear alluring, forcing an uncomfortable, frigid smile towards the oncoming traffic. She prayed. *Please God please send me a regular, and do it fast.* Mary needed a quickie, for just enough heroin to sate the demons.

An hour passed and the pangs of withdrawal gradually built to their crescendo. But just as Mary's suffering was becoming unbearable, a vehicle coming towards her slowed. Her hopes buoyed, thinking her prayers had been answered. The minivan drove closer, and Mary stopped walking to make eye contact with the driver. *Please stop, please.* Abruptly, the vehicle accelerated, aiming deliberately for a large puddle beside the whore. They timed the stunt perfectly, drenching Mary with a humiliating wave of icy filth. Mary shuddered, spitting the muddy water from her mouth and wiping away what she could from her face. "Jesus Christ!" she cried, her face contorted from anguish. Mary turned away from the steady stream of traffic and began sobbing, her tears mixing with the remnants of dirty water. But without alternatives, Mary turned, put on her plastic smile, and faced the traffic again.

Twenty minutes later, at her wits end and succumbing to increasing desperation, Mary fixed her stare on a decrepit pickup truck slowing to inspect her. She recognized the driver. His looks were unremarkable, but he gave Mary the creeps. She had heard the other girls talking about this guy.

"Yeah, the john's a pig farmer."

"I know who you're talkin' about. That's creepy Willie."

"He's a regular. I seen Tanis go with him."

"Tanis? I ain't seen Tanis in a couple a months."

"Me neither."

"Is he a bad date? Cuz he makes the hair on my neck stand up."

"Yeah, me too...He freaks me out...But he always pays."

"Yup. He does."

"Yeah, that's right."

Mary was cold, wet and in agony. Shivering, she opened the truck's door and crept into the front seat. The vehicle's heater was on full blast, yet Mary was surprised by the intensity of the chill hanging in the air. The man turned down the volume on the radio leaving Christmas carols playing faintly in the background. He glanced sideways at Mary, conferring upon her a most unnatural grin. She forced a smile back while thinking, *It's strange there's no light in his eyes.* Putting the vehicle into drive, he softly wished his new plaything, "Merry Christmas."

Chapter 37
Two Weeks Later - Christmas Day 1994
Vancouver's Downtown Eastside

"Merry Christmas!" yelled the scraggly woman, wincing in pain.

She squirmed while Trevor cleaned the open abscess on her arm as gently as he could manage. "Fuck!...Sorry!...Ow!...Fuck!...Sorry!...Jesus!...Sorry about my language...Ow!...I really do appreciate this."

"No problem. It looks pretty damn sore. Besides, you should hear my partner talk," Trevor said.

"Fuckin' eh," Wendy said from the front of the car.

The woman smiled, took a deep breath and groaned in pain. "You're almost done, right? Cuz, you know, I got someone holdin' my spot in line."

"Yep, we're almost there, but I have to be brutally honest. You really need to go to the hospital and get this abscess taken care of before it bursts and makes you really, really sick. This has the potential to kill you, you know."

Whining and fidgeting like a child she said, "Yeah, I know, I know. But I don't wanna miss Christmas dinner, okay?"

Getting your abscess treated by Forty-Eight Charlie was akin to receiving a meal from the Salvation Army. The bandage was free, but it came with an obligatory side of sermon. Trevor understood he was fighting a lost cause, yet he continued in vain, urging her to take care of herself. "Okay, I get it. But this really is serious. Will you at least promise me you'll take care of this afterward?"

"Mmmm...Well...I dunno."

The exasperated bargaining continued, characterizing the act of dressing the neglected wound as an effort in futility. Predictably, as soon as Trevor had placed the last piece of tape on her bandage, she vaulted out of the ambulance and scampered back to her place in the church food line chirping a hollow pledge. "Okay, I'll go later. I promise."

Trevor wasn't naïve. He knew her assurances were total bullshit, but he understood better than anyone what was actually at play. She was manacled to the carousel of addiction and voluntarily seeking out necessary medical care was not included in the price of her ticket. Unless she was unconscious or knocking on death's door, there was nothing Trevor could have said or done that was going to change her mind.

It was raining heavily that Christmas morning, so rather than getting wet, Trevor exited the back of his mobile workspace by crawling forward through the narrow passageway up to the front of the ambulance. He plunked himself down to finish off his report.

"I assume we'll be seeing her again in the next couple of days? Once she's gone nicely septic?" Wendy asked.

"No doubt," he replied.

"I suppose there's some sanity in her logic. You can't have much of a functioning immune system if you don't eat," she said.

"Yeah...I suppose."

Trevor's face contorted into a devilish smirk. "Yup, she'll be a walking, pus-filled doughnut soon enough. You know, like those squishy Boston cream filled ones you like so much. But instead of custard, it'll be a nice shade of milky green."

His deliberate attempt to nauseate Wendy worked. She cringed. "Geez Trevor! Thanks for the mental picture! Why do you do that? And why are you trying to ruin doughnuts for me? What did I ever do to you!" She was even too repulsed to flash him "the look."

Trevor was rather pleased with himself. But the smug look on his face, in conjunction with the chuckle in his voice did nothing to get him back into Wendy's good graces. "I'm sorry. I just couldn't help myself," he laughed. "Come on, I'll buy you a doughnut for Christmas."

"Thanks, but no thanks. You asshole...This is exactly why you're single. Truly beyond any hope of becoming civilized," she said, smiling. Contrary to her protests, Wendy enjoyed the morbid repartee.

Their droll exchange subsided, and they were readying themselves to find the closest open doughnut shop when a familiar figure emerged from the deluge, approached the ambulance and gently tapped on the side window. It was Jim.

Trevor and Wendy had known Jim for as long as they had been working in the area. A fixture on the Downtown Eastside, he was a middle-aged Indigenous man who not only possessed an imposing physical presence but also a palpable gentleness and soft-spoken manner. Of Haida descent, Jim bore handsomely distinctive features; high cheekbones, deeply set dark brown eyes, a slender nose, broad shoulders and a single braid of jet black hair that hung to the small of his back. Over the years he had displayed an uncanny knack for showing up on a street call at just the right moment, often stepping into harm's way to diffuse a tense situation. For his efforts, he had earned himself the street name of "Peacekeeper." And he was one of Forty-Eight Charlie's biggest assets.

Trevor recognized their ally straightaway and rolled down his window. "Hey, Jim! How's it goin' my friend?"

Jim was subdued but forthright. "Shitty. It's Christmas."

"Mmm...Yeah, I think I know what you mean. It's a crappy time of year for us too, suicides and all. What can we do for ya?"

Jim raised his right hand, which was wrapped in a blood-soaked rag. "Could you look at this for me?"

"Ooh, yes, of course. Let's go into my office back here."

Trevor slid out of the ambulance, motioning for Jim to follow.

"You need a hand?" Wendy asked.

Trevor smiled. "Nah, I got this. Drink your coffee before it gets cold and puts you in a mood."

Wendy smiled back while covertly giving him the finger.

Trevor opened the side doors and invited Jim to have a seat on the bench. "Let's get outta this rain."

The two men assumed their respective roles in the back of the ambulance and Trevor went right to work. Close examination wasn't necessary to see Jim's hand sported a deep gash to the palm and was a pretty significant injury. Trevor recognized it at once as a defensive wound, but he respected the code of the streets enough not to bother asking questions about how his patient came to harm. And Jim tacitly appreciated his discretion.

"Can you move all your fingers for me? Wiggle them? Good. Okay, now make a fist...Excellent."

Having ruled out major tendon damage, Trevor cleaned the gash and began applying wound closures. "I know the answer to this next question, but I'm gonna ask it anyway. Do you want to go to the hospital to get this properly stitched up?"

Jim was polite and predictable. He chuckled. "No thanks, my friend."

Nevertheless, Trevor didn't waste any time mitigating the damage inflicted by the reality of street life. "All right, but at the first sign of infection, you need to get your ass up there. Okay?"

Jim smiled, nodding in agreement, as Trevor continued repairing the wound.

"Are you looking forward to the church's Christmas meal today?"

Jim hesitated before answering. "I may be hungry, but I won't eat that food."

Trevor's face wrinkled in puzzlement at the remark. And the paramedic's reaction did not go unnoticed. Jim thought for a moment, and with a conspicuous lack of enmity, went on to explain. "Look, my brother, in my experience the churches aren't about God. They're about power and control and fear...Especially fear...For years they told me that I was worthless, no good, no better than dirt...because I was Indian...but the Bible doesn't say anything like that...For years the church literally tried to beat me into a being a white man. But Jesus never said to assault your fellow brother...For years they told me my people's ways were those of the Devil. But my friend, I've seen the Devil up close and personal...And I'm here to tell you that he lives in the churches...Today they're feeding all of us "less fortunates" so they can pretend to be saviors, when in fact, they're perpetrators...The truth of the matter is, the churches are the ones responsible for the way my Native brothers and sisters suffer...with their addictions and all...That's why I won't eat their food...I know I wouldn't like the taste of food polluted by so much hypocrisy...And I'd rather go hungry than be a hypo-Christian, like them."

Before his erudite friend had finished speaking, Trevor had completed bandaging the bloody hand. Left with nothing else to do, Trevor sat there struggling to digest the disturbing words. Somehow, Trevor felt like he should be ashamed, like he should apologize for something. Yet, he had no idea what to atone for. So, without an apparent offense, Trevor chose to maintain a respectful silence instead.

Jim was wise enough to surmise Trevor didn't have any context for his explanation. To verify, he asked one critical question. "You ever hear about residential schools?"

Trevor sat there racking his mind but came up empty. He answered wearing a blank look and a shrug. "No, I've never heard the term."

Jim shook his bowed head. "Hmm...Not surprising. It's Canada's dirty little secret you know." Straight away Jim changed the subject by inspecting Trevor's work and readying himself to leave. "Nice job. Thank you for fixing me up Trevor."

"Anytime...Take care of yourself, Jim."

The timing was ideal. Just as Jim slipped back into the rain, a call came in over the radio. They were being dispatched to the neighborhood police station's public information counter. "Forty-Eight Charlie, routine for a distraught man..."

"Routine at the PIC," she called to Trevor as he braved the elements to wave goodbye to Jim. Trevor acknowledged his partner but was preoccupied with the intriguing, one-sided discourse. He climbed back in the front seat and was scrawling the latest call's information on the report when his bewilderment got the better of him. "Have you ever heard of residential schools?"

"You mean like boarding schools?"

"I'm not sure. Jim just asked me if I've ever heard of them..." Trevor's voice trailed off as he wrangled to solve the puzzle his enigmatic friend had given him.

"Well, I've heard of boarding schools before. I suppose you could call them residential schools. That's what they are, aren't they?"

"Yeah...No...No that doesn't make sense from the conversation. There's some big connection to churches..."

"Can't help you, Trevor."

"After this call let's swing by here again and see if we can catch up with Jim. I need to ask him what he meant."

"Sure. Assuming we can get back here."

"You excel at stating the obvious, don't you?"

"Took it up as a hobby since I realized how much it pisses you off. Oh, and by the way, you still owe me a doughnut."

"Don't worry, you'll get your milky-green pus-pastry."

"Jesus! I'm sorry I brought it up."

Moments later Forty-Eight Charlie arrived at the police station. After hauling their gear to the front counter, they found a cop on the opposite side who was deeply engrossed in a crossword puzzle.

"You called?" asked Trevor

Without looking up, the cop pointed impatiently to a bench in the far corner of the reception area. "Over there," he said dryly.

Forty-Eight Charlie saw a lump of dirty, worn clothing sitting hunched over with his head in his hands. Even at a distance, the crew recognized their ongoing regular, George.

As they drew nearer, the unmistakable odor of alcohol filled the air.

Trevor began. "Hey George, what's going on?"

George hoisted up his tear-stained face. He was sullen–and drunk. He recognized the crew and without hesitation launched into a drunken tirade, sputtering details in an increasingly agitated manner. "She's dead. She's gone. Nobody's seen her. Marjorie don't know. They won't help. She's dead! Oh my God, oh my God!"

"Okay George, okay. Try to slow down. Take a deep breath...Come on now. Take a deep breath...Good, very good," Trevor said. "Now, let's try this again. What's wrong?"

"She's dead!"

For Trevor, this was an exercise in futility. "Calmly George, please tell me calmly what's happened, okay?"

"My sister's dead! And they won't do nothin' about it!" George screamed, pointing at the disinterested cop behind the counter.

Wendy interjected. "Okay, okay George. Easy now. How do you know she's dead?"

George looked up at her with bloodshot, glassy eyes and slurred, "I...I had a dream...I had a dream..."

Trevor said, "Okay, George, all right...But you know the police need more than that, right?"

George carried on, his voice cracking with grief. "Mary ain't met me at the Ovaltine now for two

Sundays in a row. Don't you understand? She didn't show up! She *never* misses our coffee time!"

"Maybe she's in the hospital. Why don't we go up and see?" nudged Wendy, hoping a social worker might be useful.

But alcohol was obscuring reason. Exasperated by the fruitless conversation George snapped and began screaming at the paramedics. "The cops won't do nothin!...We're just worthless Indians to them! I'm just a drunk, and Mary's just a whore!...They don't care!...I been to her place and Marjorie ain't seen her for two whole weeks! They even gave her room away!"

Trevor couldn't pry a word in edgewise. George was almost at his wit's end when he unexpectedly changed tack. Misty-eyed, he grabbed Trevor's forearm and began pleading with the crew instead. "The cops, they listen to you guys. They don't listen to me or Marjorie. Can you talk to them? Please? Please?" All at once George's outrage fell away, transmuting itself into raw grief. He broke down sobbing, the tears flooding his face. "Somethin' bad's happened to her I know it. Somethin's happ– "

Trevor had to intercede before George spiraled any further into despair. "Listen, George. I know you're worried about your sister, but the cops will only take your report if you're *sober*. You gotta sober up first, then come back and talk to them, understand? In the meantime, we can get you a ride to Detox if you want."

George was well past grief-stricken and in no condition to heed Trevor's counsel. Despondent and overwhelmed, he lurched to his feet, teetering a moment before staggering towards the front doors, shrieking, "Just leave me alone!" He stumbled out of the building and melted into the gloom of the rainy streets.

Wendy said, "Way to piss him off Trevor." It was a facetious remark. She knew the alcohol was getting in the way of any rational discourse with George.

Trevor sighed. "I think I'm losing my touch."

Without a patient to treat, the crew exited the police station, climbed back into their ambulance and cleared the call just in time to be dispatched for another. They were the closest unit to a stabbing. Ironically, Forty-Eight Charlie was returning to the spot they had just come from, back to the church food line. Within sixty seconds, the crew arrived to find the light had all but vanished from Jim's eyes.

Chapter 38
One Month Later - January 1995
Vancouver, British Columbia

The light had all but vanished from Storm's eyes. The sheer aggressiveness of the cancer was unusual. His playful, devil-may-care attitude had long since been dissolved by the acrid reality of constant pain. Even the Fentanyl patch wasn't helping. Trevor sat in the exam room cradling Storm's head in his hands and wondering if the only reason his friend was still alive was out of loyalty to him. Giving a reluctant nod to the vet, Trevor consummated this final act of love for his friend.

Afterwards, Trevor left the vet's office accompanied by what felt like a massive hole in his chest and a pervasive sense of isolation. He located his car more by chance than design and mindlessly opened the door and sat inside. Swallowed up by the anesthetized state, Trevor could do nothing but sit there for what felt like an hour. He stared straight out the windshield waiting and praying for the tears of grief to flow. There were several times when he felt faint pangs of emotion coalesce and begin to seek a way out of his body. But whenever the sorrow welled up to the point of spilling over, his core tightened further placing an ironclad grip on his impulse to mourn.

In the end, Trevor overcame the inertia of his stagnated grief by defaulting to his most characteristic and reliable coping mechanism. He started the engine and without remembering the drive, found himself in front of a liquor store. He called in sick the next day; and the shift after that; and the shift after that.

Eventually, Trevor showed up at work, skulking into the station on what should have been his last shift of four. Naturally, he hadn't told Wendy about Storm. Instead, he had just disappeared off the radar. As soon as Wendy set eyes on him, she didn't know whether to kiss him or kick his ass. But she wasted no time welcoming him back by firing off some well-ripened, scornful derision squarely in his direction. "Finally decide to grace me with your presence, your Highness?"

Trevor expected his partner's sarcasm, though he was unapologetic. "Absence makes the heart grow fonder." Avoiding eye contact with Wendy he slunk by her into the locker room, accompanied by the all too familiar, pungent aroma of ketones wafting through the air.

Dismayed by the telltale odor of binge drinking and watching Trevor's progressively thin frame creep past her, Wendy's gut seized up. He was wallowing in a chasm of denial. Wendy, however, was not. Was she concerned about Trevor's wellbeing? Of course, but she was also a prime stakeholder in this game. Her pragmatic needs included having a partner who was fully on the ball, not one on the verge of the d.t.'s. That afternoon Wendy found herself thrown into the middle of a double-barreled, fully loaded, hair-triggered catch-22. If she didn't speak up, she would be working with a ticking time bomb, putting both their safety at risk. If she forced the issue of rehab, it would either blow up their relationship, or he would listen and go get help. Either way, Wendy doomed herself to paramedic hell; working every shift for months to come with a different, untested partner. *Fuck! I hate this!* But the responsibility fell to her to do something about Trevor's precarious off-duty habit. And she had to do it for both their sakes. Her choices were clear. Shitty option A: To live with the no longer viable status quo. Or shittier option B: Intercede and lose her partner. In either case, it was axiomatic that Wendy was royally fucked.

As fate would have it, a call came in before Wendy had the chance to confront him. She drove as Trevor sat huddled across from her, trying to shield his eyes from the diffuse light of the overcast day. His head was splitting. *Thank God, this isn't a code three,* he thought. The traffic was light, and the crew arrived at the call within a couple of minutes. They both exited the ambulance and wasted no time in making their way towards their "man down" who was lying on the sidewalk in a sheltered doorway.

Wendy took the lead, hoping the man was just sleeping. "Good afternoon, Sir."

A muted, "Fuck off!" reverberated from underneath the heap of dirty clothing.

"Someone called us to make sure you're okay," Trevor explained. "If you could just answer a couple of questions for us, we'll leave you alone."

"I said fuck off!" screamed the lump.

"All righty then," Wendy said, turning around. Just as she did so, the man rolled over and made a lame attempt at punching her. Catching the movement out of the corner of her eye, Wendy avoided the blow without missing a stride, and unperturbed, continued walking back to the ambulance. This was par for the course, just another swing and a miss. Normally Trevor would have said, "Have a nice day," and cleared the call. But today, he took grave exception to the gesture.

Trevor snapped. He lunged at the man, kicking him and screaming, "How dare you take a swing at my partner!" Wendy was dumbfounded for a couple of seconds before leaping on top of Trevor, pulling him off the man who, in addition to trying to get to his feet, was struggling to reach for something in his coat pocket. "Stop it, Trevor! That's enough!" Seizing Trevor by his belt and his ear, she yanked him back behind the ambulance and out of the immediate danger zone.

The once slumbering lump now stood six feet tall and was brandishing a homemade knife, his actions fueled by rage and Trevor's foolhardy judgment. He stumbled forward, the blade pointing the way towards his quarry when a fellow street person materialized, grabbed the arm holding the knife and urged his comrade, "Come on man, let's get outta here! The cops 'ill be comin'!" Before vanishing into the nearest alley, he bade Trevor farewell. "I'm gonna get you! You motherfucker!"

Shoving Trevor into the back of their ambulance, Wendy jumped in herself and locked the doors behind them. Out of the side window, she saw the knife and its owner retreat. She took a deep breath, making every attempt to calm herself when Trevor made another misstep. "What the fuck was his problem?"

It was the wrong thing to say. Wendy   erupted. "What the fuck is *his* problem? What the fuck is *his* problem? What the fuck is *your* problem, Trevor! You almost got us killed you dumb fuck! And now you've got a fucking target on your back! What is wrong with you! Never mind, I'll fucking tell you! It's your fucking drinking! Every fucking shift that you *bother* to show up, I smell the fucking ketones! Jesus Christ! You don't shit where you eat Trevor! And if I had any fucking doubt about whether you've got my back, you just fucking proved that you don't!"

"But I–"

"No! No fucking excuses! God damn it!" Wendy shouted, kicking open the side door and going outside to try to calm down.

Trevor sat in silence, listening to his partner continue to curse him from outside. She was the one person he cared about, the one person he could trust, and he had betrayed her. Wendy had every right to be furious with him. Trevor also knew there was no way in hell she was going to buy any lame-ass excuse for his dangerous behavior. He hung his head in his hands. *What the fuck have I done?* His denial's arrogance evaporated, and he sat there bereft of excuses and swallowed up by a sea of shame.

Wendy continued pacing the sidewalk, in a state of anger so intense she was shaking. It took about fifteen minutes before she was composed enough to be able to drive safely. Then she called dispatch. "Hi. My partner's come back to work too soon. Yeah, he's still got the flu. He's going home now."

She turned to Trevor. "I just lied for you. I won't *ever* be doing that again. Get your shit together."

The short drive back to the station was done in a tension-filled silence. Once they arrived there, Wendy whispered calmly, "You know, they can't fire you *before* they've dried you out...So you've got a call to make." Trevor could not look her in the eye. Staring straight ahead, he just nodded. He longed to tell Wendy how sorry he was for putting her life in jeopardy, for letting her down–for being a drunk. But somehow, the words felt hollow, so his lips remained motionless.

Trevor left the station and drove directly home. The first thing he saw as he entered the lifeless apartment was Storm's leash and collar hanging on a coat hook in the hallway. But Trevor was already so numbed by the events at work that even that bitter reminder didn't faze him. He wandered past the poignant mementos and fell into his chair, despondent. Trevor was relieved to be alone. But at the same time, he was aching for connection. Unable to bridge the two he tried sleeping. But he couldn't.

As he lay in bed, something other than the ceiling was staring him in the face; the fact that he needed to take responsibility and own up to his shit. Those notions thoroughly sickened him. The intensity of the shame he felt about conceding to the label of "alcoholic" was immeasurable and, as it would turn out, insurmountable.

So, that night Trevor found himself at the crossroads of sobriety and addiction. The first and healthiest path before him lay in uncharted territory, laden with emotional landmines. The second was familiar, comfortable and easily tread upon. Trevor believed that pathway had served him well, until now. But the ogres of addiction were not about to allow their existence to be jeopardized by a road to redemption. Besides, they were fully aware Trevor had to pass through the tollbooth of humiliation to get there. And that was a price most people weren't willing to pay.

So, to keep himself safely insulated from experiencing his shame, or admitting his problem, Trevor started rationalizing. And he spun some pretty convincing propaganda. *It's not my fault I drink. It's the damn job's fault.* Half-truths made whole.

Was it true Trevor needed help erasing the memories–murdered children and mutilated bodies, the screams and the smells–which had been seared into his mind? Yes, absolutely. And if he were given enough time he would always start feeling better; until, wham, another bad call. If sobriety was a rowboat, Trevor had been trying to sail his through a perennial gale with the storm's waves swamping his craft relentlessly. And Trevor couldn't bail fast enough. He was drowning and without a rescuer.

Pretty soon, personal responsibility meant using every means necessary to keep his dinghy afloat. Alcohol was his bilge pump.

Which was why so many years ago, after making a pact with the devil in exchange for quiet in his head, he had taken that first sip of vodka. And tonight, without reading the fine print, he obliged his master and renewed the contract.

But Trevor's plummet to self-destruction wasn't quite fast enough. So, he summoned a tailwind by allowing the granddaddy of malignant alcoholic reasoning to rule his thoughts: sanctimonious justification. *It's not like I'm homeless, living on the street, or unemployed. I'm a paramedic, not an alcoholic.* That was a pivotal moment. It was the point at which Trevor *became* the delusions of alcoholism. Delusions, which continued, unabated and unrestrained, making any and all attempts to regain the ground they had lost earlier that day to Trevor's brief flash of humility. And it didn't take long for him to fall prey to his insane logic. In an instant, he was sucked under by the vortex of crazy making. *I don't drink that much. I can stop anytime I want to.* With all the necessary mental defenses now in place, Trevor pushed aside his coffee mug, cracked open a fresh bottle and took a deep swallow from its long neck. Not a single shot had been fired in the battle for his sobriety as he surrendered unconditionally to the relentless madness in his head. It was also the precise moment when Trevor relinquished control of his life. What little enjoyment he had gleaned from living had disappeared along with his dog. Having been replaced by unconscious self-loathing and a bitter resentment of the misery he had not only witnessed but also endured. So it was by design he finished the bottle.

By the end of her shift, Wendy had settled enough to allow her partner a modicum of compassion. She called him to find out how he was doing. *Answer the phone, damn it.* He didn't pick up. *Maybe he's sleeping.* But that idea didn't assuage the growing tension in her belly. Something did not feel right, so she got in her car and drove directly over to his place. Knocking on his door, she became frantic. *Come on Trevor. Answer the fucking door. Where are you?* Now she knew something wasn't right. Sprinting to the rear of his suite, she peered through the window and saw the vague outline of a heaped body lying on the kitchen floor. After kicking in the door, Wendy attended to Trevor before calling 911.

Trevor's blood alcohol level on admission to hospital was hovering in the lethal range, and the head trauma he had suffered from hitting the floor could have also killed him. Though for better or worse, he was alive. But more significantly, all his secrets were out in plain view. Reckless living and ambivalence about life had led him here. Those were going to have to be things of the past, at least until he was out of rehab. The choice was his. Trevor knew from now on his life was going to be different. And it scared the living shit out of him.

Two days later Wendy tapped on the door of his hospital room before poking her head inside. "I'm looking for a guy with a splitting headache. I brought him some decent coffee instead of this hospital swill."

Glancing over, Trevor found himself feeling excited, and ashamed to see Wendy.

"Man, you look like a raccoon. I hope the other guy looks worse," she said.

"Yeah, well, it was quite the sucker punch," he said, making minimal eye contact.

"I can see that...Are you up for some company?"

"Seeing as how you brought coffee, come on in. May I offer you some vintage Jello-O?"

"No, thanks. I like mine without a rind."

"Too bad. You don't know what you're missing."

Reaching towards him with the double latte/peace offering Wendy said, "Here you go. Seventeen sugars. Just the way you like it."

Their asinine small talk served a dual purpose. It opened up communication between the two for the first time since Trevor had given Wendy a reason to rip him a new one, and it helped assure themselves their relationship was still okay. But what was palpable in their exchange was the tender, apologetic tone they used with one another.

Trevor sputtered. "I'm uh...really...you didn't deserve–"

"Yeah, me too," she said.

Trevor motioned, and Wendy sat down in a chair next to his bed. They didn't need to broker a peace. The two naturally fell back into the comfortable silence borne out of their strong bond.

Eventually, Wendy broke the stillness. "You know, we should just stop fighting the inevitable and go buy a cod boat."

Trevor grunted at her suggestion. He was wrestling with an abundance of anxiety about how to tell her something. Gathering his courage, he forced himself to speak. "You've probably guessed I'll be away from work for a while...They're uh...sending me out to Still Lake Centre...You know...To weave baskets."

Wendy's eyes welled up with tears of relief at the news. Reaching over, she grabbed onto his hand and squeezed. A knot in her throat kept her voice subdued. "That's great news. I know you'll do well...I'm very proud of you."

Trevor's throat tightened. "Really?" he whispered.

At that moment, Trevor didn't know which was more terrifying, the enormous shame he felt by admitting he was alcoholic, or the unexpected and overwhelming redemption he had just received from Wendy.

She didn't hesitate. "Absolutely! It takes really big balls to work on your shit like that...Besides, once you learn basket weaving you'll have a trade to fall back on, right?"

Trevor smirked and sighed, "Sorry about you not having a regular partner till I get back."

There was a lengthy pause before Wendy responded. "Well...You know I've been doing a lot of thinking lately...and I've come to the conclusion that I could do with some rehab too."

Trevor cocked his head, his face quizzical. He knew Wendy didn't drink, and unless she had been hiding the track marks between her toes, he was pretty sure she wasn't an addict.

Wendy was shaking her head. "No, no, not *that* kind of rehab. You know I love working in that area, I love the people, I love the calls...It's like the best chocolate cake ever...But I've come to realize, that if that's *all* you eat, you're *gonna* get sick...It's hard seeing people at their absolute worst all the time... I feel like my soul's being dismantled piece by piece...and it's making me forget who I am...I want to hold on to what's left of me...I want to try to be normal...Whatever the fuck that means."

Trevor was nervous. "So you're quitting?"

There was tenderness in her voice. "No, but I am gonna take that posting in Bella Coola...Get outta the city, go back home...I love my job. But I just can't take the intensity of it here anymore, you know?"

It was right then Trevor realized how much of a toll their work had been taking on her. He would have to grieve losing her, but he knew deep down she was right and her decision would likely keep her from imploding like he had.

Nodding, he irked out a smile. "Well, you know what they say?...You can take the girl out of the Skids, but you can't take the Skids–"

"Yeah, yeah, yeah."

"...out of the girl...Too bad you're giving Phelps exactly what he wants. No doubt he'll be gloating about you leaving."

Wendy grabbed onto his arm. "Oh my God! I just about forgot to tell you!"

"Tell me what?"

Wendy started chuckling. "Okay. There are two parts, the good news, and the bad news. I'll give you...I'll give you the good news first." But that was as far as she got. Wendy broke down roaring in laughter. It was so infectious Trevor couldn't help but laugh too, although he had no idea why.

Catching her breath, and with a sense of joyful relief, Wendy proceeded to enlighten her partner. "Guess who just got suspended pending termination?... Trevor wadded up his face. "Okay, wait. Before you answer, I'll give you the bad news. The reason they're firing him is because he's been arrested for assaulting the sex trade workers in our area. The sicko was buying sex and then beating up the women."

From the gleam in Wendy's eye, Trevor knew only one person could fit that bill. "No fucking way! Really?" he said with both disgust and joy ringing in his voice.

"Yup! That fucking misogynist pig, your friend and mine, the fabulous, dumb-as-a-bag-of-hammer handles, John Phelps."

"Holy shit!"

It was the nuclear bomb of gifts, one Trevor wasn't expecting. And it gave him a mind-boggling sense of relief. Not only was a sexual predator off the streets but also a primary stressor in his life had just vanished. The liberating news gave Trevor a glimpse of hope, as though a lead curtain had lifted and he could envision himself having a real chance at leading a sober life.

"How fucked up is that? Clearly, I wasn't the only woman he hated."

Trevor was laughing. "Oh, absolutely...So, no more constant harassment at work? Honestly, I don't know if I can function without someone gunning for me."

With that, the two partners sat enjoying their coffee and their matured, comfortable silence for the last time.

Her cup empty, Wendy broke their meditation by getting up to leave. "Well, I should get going. Good luck with those baskets."

This was Trevor's last chance. Mustering his courage, he made a wry insinuation. "Soooo, maybe I can dock my cod boat in Bella Coola sometime?"

"Really Trevor?" Wendy smiled. "Sexual innuendo after all this time?...I'll see ya."

Trevor wore a subtle and slightly embarrassed grin. "Yeah, see ya."

Before Wendy turned to leave, their eyes met, and they exchanged what could only be described as a feeling of deep gratitude for each other.

But Wendy didn't get more than ten feet down the hallway when she heard Trevor *finally* get the last word. "You gotta dirty mind girl. I said *dock*!"

She didn't stop, she didn't slow down, she just smiled while glancing out the window to a surprising, yet welcome sight; sunshine.

Chapter 39
Three Months Later - Spring 1995
Bella Coola, British Columbia

The spring sunshine was a surprising, yet welcome sight. It felt glorious and coupled with the sweet spring air it was just the medicine Wendy knew she needed. It had been three months since the move from Vancouver. And although it had logically felt like the right, even necessary thing to do, Wendy's attempts at exorcising the ghosts who plagued her were proving ineffective.

The abrupt change in workload was by itself disconcerting. Wendy had gone from doing twenty calls per shift to doing less than twenty calls per month. Whereas in Vancouver her mind and body had been kept busy with the repeated and intense need for her medical skills, there were few such distractions here. But regardless of the slower pace, Wendy's mainspring remained overwound, always at the ready to fuel whatever requisite action the situation demanded. And her problem was made worse by working in this sleepy, remote little village, which provided no outlet for such hypervigilance. Here there was only quiet, and time. With such previously essential diversions now lacking, Wendy had no choice but to acknowledge the void. That place where the imprint of every bad call dwelt, where they stirred, demanding acknowledgment and seeking deliverance from themselves. And increasingly, flashbacks became their ultimatum and nightmares their blackmail.

It was in this perpetual state of anxious tension that Wendy found herself making a daily pilgrimage to the beach. As a penitent to the shrine of the familiar shoreline, she brought a silent petition. She sought relief from her torment, a cure for the bundled knot of indistinct emotions ravaging her body. She could not have told you what she so urgently needed. Perhaps it was redemption, or maybe absolution. In either case, the remedy remained elusive.

Today the skies were clear, the water unusually calm, the perfect conditions for skipping rocks. One after another, as if casting off each tormenting image, Wendy sent stones slicing through the gentle waves until her arm burned with exhaustion. With nothing else to occupy her time and with this form of penance being ineffective, Wendy wandered up to the furthest end of the pebble-strewn shoreline. It felt like another lifetime since she was last here, at the special place where she and Grandfather had first met those many distant years ago. She stopped and faced the ocean as faded images of him seeped into her mind bringing a wistful smile to her face. It wasn't to last. A moment later, the nostalgia dissolved and the pangs of anxiety and nausea that were her constant companions swooped into Wendy's body once again. In retaliation, she soldiered onwards.

Walking a few more yards, she spied it, a scarred old log who had witnessed countless seasons pass from its permanent place on the beach. Although to her adult eyes it seemed a good deal smaller, she recognized its distinctive curves and knot patterns. It was indeed the same log she had hidden next to as a child.

"Well, hello old friend," she said, louder than she had intended. The ancient, linear fortress seemed to reciprocate her greeting, offering itself up to Wendy to settle herself upon. As she had always done, she sat on the ground and leaned against the driftwood barrier, enjoying the same feeling of protection it had always provided. She rested while drinking in the serenity of the natural beauty encircling her. On an instinctive level, she was courting a connection to the place, petitioning it to help her build an ethereal bridge between the chaos within and the calmness without. Mindful of her every action, she pushed on her feet, burying them slightly in the pebbles and focusing on the sound they made. Taking a deep breath, she closed her eyes and let the gull's call reverberate in her mind. All at once, a delicate, intangible energy embraced her, allowing her anxiety to diminish and her gut to loosen. Surrendering to the experience, Wendy allowed herself to simply become that moment.

Time became inconsequential. Wendy had spent several glorious minutes submerged in the experience when she noticed a distinct gentleness begin permeating the air. She recognized it instantly. *Grandfather? No...That's absurd.* Yet the feeling was palpable. Twisting her head around, Wendy began searching for the elder as if by some miracle he was still alive. But their eyes did not meet. *He can't be alive. It's ridiculous. It's gotta be my memories.* Nonetheless, her awareness of a presence expanded. Growing more attuned to it, she sensed it grow stronger, more alive. When out of nowhere, Wendy swore she heard his distinctive voice whisper, "Thank you." That was it. *What the fuck!* Wendy bolted upright, spun around and searched the shoreline, only to find she was alone.

In Vancouver, she had had plenty of experience dealing with psychotic patients who heard voices. At this point, she was beginning to think she was on the verge of psychosis herself when her eyes were drawn downwards. "What the..." Wendy was awed by what she found. Perched atop a piece of cedar bough sitting next to her on the log, was a little carving. It was Frog. Without a second's hesitation, she scooped up the sculpture and held it next to her heart. In the instant she did so, whatever spell that had prevented her from grieving all the gruesome calls, all the inhumanity, and all the tragedy, had been broken. At last, the tears began to flow. And Wendy gave permission for her burden, the bane of unexpressed sorrow, to leave. Rhythmic waves of inconsolable grief, unfettered from their deep recesses began moving through her body. Cradled in a sublime peacefulness, Wendy continued sobbing. To her, it resembled an eternity.

Once the tears had slowed, glimpses of something altogether unfamiliar arose from within, something that had eluded Wendy since childhood. A feeling so foreign to her she didn't even have a name for it. The black glob of heaviness she had borne for most of her life was gradually being replaced by an intoxicating lightness. Wendy was stunned by the change, grateful for it, yet bereft of a definition. She was puzzling over her transformation when her ear caught an odd noise. Squinting, she looked all around but found nothing. Yet she swore she could hear children laughing, but from where? Motionless, Wendy sat concentrating on the vibrations that seemed to drift in from over the water. Before long, snippets of those hushed voices began echoing in her consciousness allowing Wendy to meld with the place. And as she did, she touched the whispers on the ocean and found her answer. For the first time in her life, Wendy was feeling joy. As proof, she began laughing exactly like her old Nuxalkmc friend, uncontrollably and from deep in her belly. She had become possessed; conquered by happiness.

It was a good thing Wendy was alone because she was quite the sight, sitting on the beach, hearing voices and laughing like a lunatic. At that moment, it had seriously crossed Wendy's mind that she may well have been losing hers. But if crazy felt this good, she thought, *Fuck it. I'm all for it.*

Wendy remained perched on the weathered log watching the sunset over the mountains. Her cheeks, taut from dried tears, tingled in the evening breeze off the water. With daylight waning, she stood up to make her way home with a renewed and optimistic sense of self.

Chapter 40
Meanwhile...
Portside Park
Vancouver's Downtown Eastside

George remained perched on the weathered log watching the sunset over the mountains. His cheeks, taut from dried tears, tingled in the evening breeze off the water. With daylight waning, he stood up to make his way home with a renewed and optimistic sense of self.

Earlier that morning he had journeyed to the fragrant boundary where land met sea after having awoken from yet another unsettling dream. Shaken by the experience, George had felt off-kilter for most of the day until he remembered what Mother always said, "If you don't feel right, take it to the ocean." So, that was exactly what he did. And, he did it sober.

As was his habit, George made himself as inconspicuous as possible. He needed solitude today and wanted to avoid prying eyes, judgmental comments, or worse yet, the pity stares. He had to climb over the shoreline's craggy bedrock to do it, but he had found a place where he could be undisturbed and alone with Grandmother Ocean.

The heady salt air, the sound of waves lapping on the rocks below and the calls of the gulls playing overhead were what soothed George that day, easing him into the contemplative state he sought. There, for the first time in years, he prayed, intensely and sincerely.

He needed help. No matter how hard he tried, George could not shake his dream. You see, Mary had come to him last night in his Dreamtime. It had been three months since he had seen her in waking life, since she had disappeared without a trace. But in last night's dream, she wore a gorgeous smile while gliding towards George with her arms outstretched. He had fallen into her embrace. As he luxuriated in her sweet presence, somehow George knew Mary was all right. But just as suddenly as she had come to him, she was gone, and he was awake.

Since the dream, George had been gripped by a harsh reality, the indisputable truth that he was alone. He missed them all so much. Mother, Father, Grandfather, and now Mary. He hadn't a single human being in his life that cared about him. There was no one to talk with, no one to hug, and no one to love. George was so lonely it physically hurt. It was as if his heart had been ripped out and replaced with a chunk of hot lead.

So, George had brought his woe to Grandmother Ocean. And on this day at the water's edge, it had, at last, started to thaw. The long-held boulder of anxiety, nausea, and hurt that made its home in his belly, but especially his grief, had finally begun to dissolve. But more significantly, this was the day George had allowed it to move.

As the hours passed, tears were shed, emotions cleansed, and his body was unburdened. A gradual apostasy was unfolding before George. He had begun a journey of reconnecting with himself, of starting to remember who he was. *I am Nuxalkmc*. He began to challenge the lies he had been taught to believe about himself and began to truly see beyond the stigma of his race or his circumstances, even toying with the idea he needn't be defined by his addiction. Fantastic thoughts ran through his mind. *Maybe I could get a detox bed...Maybe I can get sober...* What followed next is generally considered tantamount to heresy of the established social order. George began to *believe* these things were possible. He even started to formulate a plan that could deliver him out of the hopelessness and despair. *I'll go there every day until I get a detox bed...I won't take no for an answer!* The lies of self-doubt, of self-loathing, of chronic humiliation, were most certainly still residents inside him. But somehow, George felt better prepared to combat their influence. From that, a spontaneous and bold hope erupted inside him. *I know I can...have a better life.* And with that seemingly outrageous ambition, came proof that a tiny revival of his soul had indeed taken place.

That spring evening George emerged from his rocky enclave transformed, possessing a lightness he had not remembered and a steely resolve to have a better existence. And it beamed on his face. Unfortunately, that would be a problem.

The determined grin George had donned drew the wrong kind of attention that evening. You see, for some people it was incongruent with how that type of person should look. At least, that was the opinion of three young men who had just left one of the local strip clubs. George offended them just by breathing. But smiling? That infuriated them. As George passed by the three on his way home, they began harassing him. "Why are you so happy you fucking chug!" taunted the first young man, running up beside George.

"He must've struck gold at the bottom of a dumpster," chimed the second, directly behind George.

The third sprinted in front of their target, hurling insults while keeping pace with a panicked George.

By now, George's grin had disintegrated. He went into survival mode. And as he had done so many times in the past, he tried becoming invisible. Bowing his head, he avoided making eye contact with his persecutors, ensuring his body language said, "I'm garbage. You're superior to me." The whole time George prayed. *Please, please just leave me alone.* Even though he was surrounded, George's only defense was to keep walking. So he did. And it worked–until they tripped him.

George landed on the pavement with an alarming thud, knocking out two teeth and splitting his lip wide open. His carving kit had fallen out of his coat pocket, and by reflex, George grabbed for it. While clutching the worn leather case, one of the assailants stepped on his hand. George grimaced. "Ow. Please. My tools."

"What're you doin'? That's mine you fucking chug!"

Stepping off George's hand, he kicked the carving tools down the sidewalk.

"Who'd you steal that from, huh?"

Trying to sit upright and spitting the blood from his mouth George replied, "I didn't steal it. It's mine."

"Bullshit! You fucking stole it!"

"Honest, I didn't–"

Before George could beg for leniency, a barrage of boots set upon his body.

"Lying piece of shit!"

"Lazy fucking welfare Indian!"

"Who the fuck do you think you are!"

"You waste of skin!"

All three kicked him mercilessly. Multiple blows to George's head, face, chest, and belly. To those young men, beating up George meant they were finally getting value for the tax dollars. It had taken less than one minute for systemic racism, fueled by hatred and ignorance to pummel George into oblivion. After meting out their brand of social justice, they spat on George before walking nonchalantly to their car. They drove home to the suburbs that evening laughing and exchanging congratulatory high fives. "We just did society a favor, boys."

Meanwhile, George lay motionless on the cold sidewalk, surrounded by a bloody pool growing steadily larger with the passing seconds. The drone of the city grew faint to his ear, while quiet hints of a comfortable, gentle laughter grew louder. Little by little, George's essence lifted away from his broken body, merged with the whispers on the ocean and stepped into the loving embrace of his family once more.

Afterward

We cannot mourn that which we do not value.

Appendix

For further reading about Canadian Indian Residential Schools, see the Truth and Reconciliation Commission's report now archived at The National Centre for Truth and Reconciliation: www.trc.ca

About the Author

Born and raised in Victoria, British Columbia, the author felt the desire to become a paramedic at an early age. After graduating from the Justice Institute of British Columbia's Paramedic Academy, she spent the majority of her fifteen-year medical career working in Vancouver's infamous Downtown Eastside.

A career-ending injury sent her back to university where she focused on psychology and First Nations studies. Following this, she worked as a traumatic stress counselor for several years and was a founding director of the Canadian Foundation for Trauma Research and Education.

Still adjusting to life away from the frontlines of emergency healthcare, this ex-first responder enjoys travel, genealogy, and beekeeping. She currently lives in Surrey, British Columbia with her husband Roger, and dog Marlee.